A SHINE THAT DEFIES THE DARK

RUM RUNNERS, BOOK 1

JODI GALLEGOS

Cover Design by: Marya Heidel
Typography by: Gem Promotion
Editing by: Emily Lawerence

To my family. And to grandpa, who's spirit seemed to feature so heavily in one character.

CHAPTER
ONE

APRIL 14, 1930

I didn't go lookin' for Remy Granger that night. I was tryin' to avoid the man in my momma's bedroom the same as she was tryin' to ignore the fact that I knew he was in there with her.

"The Granger boys have set up their own speakeasy for tonight out on Miller's Point," my life-long best friend, Dixie, squealed with excitement and clapped her hands together like a schoolgirl. In that moment she looked more like a wholesome eighteen-year-old than the enchanting platinum blond she'd fashioned herself into.

We sat on the library steps and shared a Coca-Cola as the sun dropped behind the cypress trees, coloring the bayou sky dark purple.

"*And*," she continued, "I've got it on good authority that they've gotten their hands on the best damn hooch in southern Louisiana." She lifted her right hand to pat the carefully crafted finger waves in her short hair.

I ran my fingers through my own thick mass of dark waves, feeling like a rumpled mess.

"Well, if the Granger boys are involved, the law won't be far behind." I'd only been back in Plaquemines Parish for eight weeks. It seemed a bit soon to risk being pinched in a dry raid.

Dixie's shoulders fell. The corners of her expertly painted red lips pulled down in disappointment. Despite my lengthy absence, I was well aware that her pout was just a ploy. I knew Dixie Bajoliére nearly as well as I knew myself.

"Ophelia Breaux." Her voice was loud and full of determination. She angled toward me and crossed her arms. "I ain't seen you in years and we ain't done a damn thing since you've been back. You and I are goin' to this party, and I ain't takin' no for an answer." She pressed her scarlet lips together, and her arched eyebrows dared me to argue.

The thrill of the forbidden had always bound me and Dixie together. Other little girls had been content in playing with dolls; Dixie and I'd filled our days by stealing pirogues and navigating the channels of the bayous.

I couldn't stand to be the one to shy away from our first adventure in six years. Dixie was right: since Momma and I moved back, I'd done nothing but work. *I'm about due for some fun,* I decided.

"I s'pose I could use a drink," I said and then added with a mischievous smile, "or five."

Dixie squealed and jumped up from the step. She grabbed her pocketbook and my hand, pulling me after her, givin' me no chance to change my mind—or my dress.

"Where are we goin'?" I had no idea how we were going to get to Miller's Point. Neither of us had a car, and I hadn't exactly been out to call on any of my old friends.

"To the park," she said, as though that should have been self-evident. "Simon Carre's waitin' on us."

"What if I hadn't agreed to come with you?"

"What do you mean?" Her pace didn't slow.

"I mean, would Simon Carre have waited all night for you?" I was sure he would, if he was as love struck with her as he'd been in the sixth grade. "Or would you have given up on me and gone anyway?"

"If you hadn't come?" Dixie laughed as though the thought of me not goin' along were the funniest joke she'd ever heard.

Simon Carre had indeed waited for Dixie. He had three friends who were just as happy to see her. Each of them nearly fell over themselves to be the one to open her door or bestow her with their most flattering compliment.

Dixie made sure to pay them for their kindness with excess flirtation. I always guessed she'd been born with that ability. I, however, had never been able to bat my eyes and get a boy to do so much as ask, "Got something in your eye?"

I sat in the back seat and stared out at the dark shadows of the land my family had always called home. The nearly bare branches in the orange groves were like tortuous spindles against the glow of the moon. Ghostly silhouettes of moss hung from the cypress branches, seeming to float just above the surface of the water. In the distance, shrimp boats bobbed on the tide, arms outstretched, waiting to lift their booty from the plentiful waters.

I breathed the familiar smells of the bayou. *Oh, how I've missed this.* It was a mixture of rich, musky overgrowth and the subtle hint of the salty ocean in the distance.

"You all aren't plannin' to use your charms to sully the reputation of the God-fearing girls of Point de Concession, are you?" Dixie's flirtation continued until we turned onto a narrow road and headed into the tangled overgrowth of ash and oak trees.

The lights from a few other cars bounced along the road both ahead and behind us. It wasn't a very subtle parade of lawbreakers. Any revenuer who happened past would be guaranteed a bust.

My breath grew shallow and my nerve endings were alight. I peered over my shoulder and searched the brush for any sign of lawmen or snitches lying in wait. I slid my hands under my thighs to minimize the shaking that had overtaken them—this was far more dangerous than two girls stealing a pirogue. We were taunting the federal authorities now, and they took the laws of Prohibition seriously.

Simon turned off the lights as we rounded another turn, and the cars behind us followed suit. The moon was bright enough in the sky to show the way. It wasn't far before we saw the makeshift parking area.

I caught the shadows of people walking into the thick of the trees. Simon parked and we followed them.

The air was dense with the heat and moisture of late spring in the bayou. Crickets chirped, frogs croaked nearby, and the gentle slush of water slapped against the shore.

The trail was uneven and difficult to traverse in the dark. Dixie and I grasped at each other to keep from falling. The T-strap shoes I'd worn didn't have a terribly high heel, but my ankles threatened to roll with every step nonetheless. I was sure Dixie's higher heels would be the end of her if we didn't find even ground soon.

I lifted the hem of my trumpet skirt, the material thin and ragged. It wouldn't stand many more repairs. I didn't want to risk it being snagged by the loose twigs that swiped at us as we followed the dark trail.

The faint sounds of zydeco music drifted on the air and made its way through the trees. A happy chirping melody from an accordion and fiddle filled the night. The tension I'd been carrying floated away with the buoyant melody. My heart began to beat in time to the scratching tempo of the frottoir, and I might have begun dancing right there had my ankles not threatened to roll yet again.

Just as I was about to declare that no moonshine was worth a forced march through gator-infested swamps, the trees opened up and I saw a barn at the edge of a pond. Yellow light seeped through the open doors and between the weathered slats. There were a few cars parked along the structure, as well as in the clearing behind it, and two horses were tied to the low-hanging branches of a tree near the door.

The Granger boys hadn't so much set up a speakeasy as they'd taken possession of an abandoned barn and opened the doors for anyone willing to take the risk along with them.

"Look, Ophelia, it's perfect!" Dixie laughed. She grabbed my hand and pulled me through the line of people streaming toward the doors.

I stopped short and pointed to the roof of the barn. "That boy has a gun."

Simon Carre ambled past me. "There's two in the trees and one over there, too." He pointed toward the field, but didn't stop walking.

Dixie pulled on my hand. "Claude Moret's gang beat Tully Bishop near to death for settin' up his own business," she said. "The Grangers ain't about to take that chance. Besides, the danger's what makes it fun."

Dixie's enthusiasm was infectious. My reluctance was serving no purpose. As cautious as I'd intended to be during our illegal escapade, apprehension melted away as soon as I passed through the open doors. For the first time in five months, I felt like I was just a girl again. Tonight there was no sadness. My only responsibility was to enjoy life back in the most vibrant place on earth.

The barn was nearly filled with revelers already. Summer humidity and bodies in motion had created a wall of heavy, warm air at the doorway. A thick cloud of smoke hovered just above the crowd. Orange embers from cigarettes and cigars glowed throughout the barn. The smell of tobacco and sweat mingled.

"This way." Dixie pulled me again, this time through the maze of people. She led me deeper into the center of the barn, never to be deterred from the promise of adventure.

Music ricocheted off the old beams. Dirt and straw covered the floor. The few old-timers who'd braved the young crowd for the chance to taunt the Prohibition laws danced, kicking up dust. A group of younger people showed off their skills with the intricate new dance steps they'd no doubt learned in New Orleans.

Dixie led me to a corner where an old, weathered board that spanned two barrels served as a table. "Wait here. I'll get us a drink," Dixie yelled over the music.

"I'll come with you," I hollered back. "I don't want to stand here, lookin' a fool, with everyone starin' at me." In the eight weeks since Momma and I had moved back, Dixie was the only one of my old friends who'd come to see me. I knew that Momma's and my return was perfect fodder for sensational gossip. We'd left Point de Concession as members of one of the most powerful families in town and had returned a tragic pair of paupers.

"Nobody's starin'," Dixie yelled over the noise. "I'll be right back." She turned and was immediately absorbed into the throng of dancing bodies, leaving me no chance to argue any further.

I stood amidst the crowd, surrounded by faces that were vaguely familiar yet still strange. Six years was a long time to be gone; no doubt my old school friends thought me as much a stranger as I did them. Dixie was the only one who'd responded to my letters and we'd kept in contact.

My breath hitched as I caught sight of the one other face that had stayed in my memory as clear as it'd been on the day I left. His dark hair was like a beacon, calling my attention through the mass of bodies that filled the barn. He scanned the crowd, but his eyes didn't stop on me for even a second. I was both saddened and relieved.

I was six when I first *really* noticed him. Even then he was trouble—not to mention being the direct descendant of a long line of trouble. For whatever reason—though I always believed it was the Lord's plan—I couldn't get enough of watchin' him. I made a vow to myself that he would be the one; he'd be the first boy I kissed.

Six years later, on the day I learned that my family was moving, I promptly rode my bike through town until I found him sittin' on a curb. He was tryin' to free one of his daddy's cigarettes from its crumbled wrapper. I walked up to him, pulled his face to mine, and kissed him. I left him sittin' wide-eyed—and gap mouthed—on the curb. I got back on my bike without a word and rode home. We left town late that same night.

That kiss was one of the few reminders I had that not everything in Plaquemines Parish had ended badly.

He looks even better now, I thought. I imagined what it would be like to kiss him now. I smiled at the thought of pickin' up where I left off. I'd wait for him to sit down—there was no way I could reach clear up to his mouth otherwise, as tall as he's gotten—then I'd walk right up, grab his face, and lay one on him. And then walk away, of course.

The crowd shifted and I lost sight of him. *It's for the best*, I reminded myself, *don't draw attention to yourself.*

Dixie reappeared. "Here," she said and thrust a metal cup with clear liquid into my hand. I sniffed and the sharp scent snapped at my senses and made my eyes water.

"What took you so long?" I asked.

"I had to say hello to someone," she said, turning her attention to the crowd.

"Who?"

Dixie tipped her head back and took several long pulls from her own mug. I watched, fascinated, as she swallowed again and again.

Not to be outdone by my lifelong ally, I lifted my mug and took two large gulps of my own. The sharp, warm smell of home-brewed whiskey filled the air and the first drink burned its way into my belly. It only took a moment for the warmth to spread, relaxing my muscles and chasing away the cold, rigid tension that had become a part of my daily life. Before I'd finished half of my first drink, the crystal liquid had loosened my joints so that they moved in time to the music.

My thoughts fell away and the music filled my head until I felt warm and dizzy. The joyous energy in the barn took over.

Dixie and I let the music carry us into the fray of bodies. It was a relief to set aside the worry and grief that had consumed every day of the past few months of my life. I embraced the opportunity to exist without thought, to simply be absorbed by the energy of a moment. I danced with one boy after the next to the lively clatter of the zydeco music, determined to immerse myself in the feeling of bliss, if only for one night.

The more I danced, the thicker my mouth became with thirst. I hooked my arm through Dixie's and pulled her from the dance area in search of another drink. It wasn't difficult for us to find a succession of drinks among the flirtatious fellas who had gathered around.

"You remember Ophelia Breaux." Dixie had become the official Re-Welcome Wagon. She grabbed people as they danced past and made sure they knew I was back in town.

"Of course," they'd say. "How's your mère?" or "I heard you

was back." Worse yet, "I was real sorry to hear 'bout your daddy."

My glass didn't stay empty long. My return had sparked an interest among the boys and a lot of sour looks from their gals. I smiled my sweetest smile at them. I had no interest in their fellas and wasn't about to let them ruin my night. But I wasn't about to pay for my own drinks either.

The music was lively and I lost myself in the carefree spirit that filled the barn. Dixie and I danced to nearly every song. We stopped only long enough to catch our breaths or find a new dance partner. A crowd of old acquaintances joined us and it felt as though we were the center of fun.

"Here's a face you ain't seen in a long time." Dixie reached into a group of boys as they walked past us and yanked one of them to the center of our group.

It was as if he'd magically appeared before me. I saw his dark hair first. It was slicked back, but even the oil he'd smoothed over it couldn't control the natural wave. I remembered how it'd hung in his eyes that day when he'd looked up at me from the curb. His face had grown strong and angular. It was apparent that his nose had been broken—at least once —and there was a jagged scar over his left eye. But, it was *him*, and as much as I knew he was no good, he was also perfect.

"Remy Granger," I said, more breathlessly than I would have hoped. I smiled and tried to ignore the fluttering of my heart and the heat that must have certainly stained my cheeks crimson. *Does he think I'm being flirtatious? Am I being flirtatious?*

Remy's eyes moved down my body and then up again. A smile pulled at the corner of his mouth. "I heard you was back. And I've seen you at the church a time or two." He tried to put on an angelic look, but it couldn't hide the devil that glinted in his eye.

"I've noticed you there too." I couldn't stop the flirtatious drawl in my voice. "But only a time or two. And never inside."

"Well, I suspect there's only so much the good Lord is able to do in one day." Laughter bubbled behind the words. "No sense in me using up all his focus when the good people of Plaquemines Parish are needin' him to intervene on behalf of their citrus crops and whatnot."

He leaned toward me as if to speak into my ear, but said nothing. The surge of heat that radiated from his body stopped my breath. I leaned toward him, unable to resist the energy that reached out and wrapped around me.

While the music thumped around us, and bodies moved in unison, Remy Granger and I stood, each simply feeling the presence of the other. The only movement between us was the rise and fall of our chests and the breath that passed between us.

"Well, looks like you *do* remember each other," Dixie said, then followed with, "I'm just gonna go grab another drink." And then she disappeared into the crowd.

"We should probably dance," Remy finally murmured in my ear. His voice was warm and smooth, like honey on a hot summer's day.

I felt his hand snake between my arm and hip, then the pressure as he rested his palm on my lower back—just above the point at which it would have become indecent. His other hand lifted mine and we swayed together. We weren't quite in tempo with the music as the beat was a lively one and we barely moved.

An unfamiliar energy rippled through me and settled low in my belly. Heat flooded every part of my body that made contact with Remy Granger.

The good sense that Momma'd instilled in me urged me to flee. *No good can come of this*, it warned, *walk away now*.

Remy's fingers pressed into my low back, pulling me tight against him.

Stay, the whisper of my own senses implored.

The sway of his body, as he pulled mine along in time, was sultry and seductive. His hips pressed into mine. Each tilt or shift caused mine to respond in kind.

Remy's breath warmed my temple and then my cheek. I tipped my head slightly away and he moved in closer, his cheek soft as he laid it against the side of my head. As we moved together he shifted and his stubble raked my skin. I leaned further into him. He lifted my arms so that they encircled his shoulders and then wrapped his around my waist.

The liquor doubled my vision and loosened my thoughts. I could no longer focus on the music. There was no beat. No discernible melody. A cacophony of sounds clattered in my brain.

All that grounded me to the room was the presence of Remy Granger. I wanted nothin' more than to fall into him. To be absorbed by him and leave behind everything else in the world that had haunted my past months.

The people dancin' around us seemed to become a mass of undulating bodies and my head spun. And then, my stomach lurched.

"Oh, no," I said and shoved away from Remy. I turned toward the crowd and weaved my way through in a desperate attempt to make my way to the door.

Boys grabbed at me as I passed. I shoved them away and stumbled farther into the crowd, certain that this was the way out. Another boy—one who seemed barely able to stand on his own wavering legs—wrapped his arms around me. He pulled me into him and swayed as he aimed his puckered lips toward my own mouth. I pushed against him, trying to break free.

"Let me go!" I yelled above the music.

11

"Jus' gimme a lil' sugar," he slurred. He pulled me tighter toward him.

I felt a bump and the pressure of the boy's arms relaxed. As he let go I saw a hand reach up over his head and pull the boy's head back and away from me. As soon as he released me, and I stumbled back one step, a blow was delivered to the boy's face.

He fell to the ground, his body covered in dust and straw. Blood trickled from his left eye.

No one seemed to notice the scuffle, nor the boy bleeding on the floor. Everyone kept right on dancin'.

"Are you okay?" Remy shook his hand and reached for my elbow, steadying me as I swayed.

"I need to get out—" A sudden flood of saliva filled my mouth and prevented me from saying anything else.

Remy gathered me securely under one arm and pulled me along with him through the crowd. Nobody stood in Remy Granger's way—in fact, the crowd parted steps ahead of him.

I smelled the change in the air before we stepped through the doors. The temperature had cooled only slightly, but it was a welcome relief from the stifling barn.

As soon as we were out, I pushed away from him. "I'm fine," I said. "Go on back inside."

"I'll stay with you," he replied.

My stomach roiled. "Really, Remy. Go on now." It wouldn't be the worst thing to have happened in my life, but I didn't want Remy Granger—or anyone else, for that matter—to see me get sick.

"Ophelia, I—"

My steely resolve and command of my body collapsed in one humiliating eruption. My stomach was the first to revolt, followed by a total spasm of the rest of my body as the moonshine was expelled from my system. I reached out, my arms rigid against the barn in an effort to avoid being pitched over onto the ground.

As the first convulsion passed I felt warmth around my middle as Remy reached his arm around my waist to steady me. His other hand brushed against my neck as he pulled my hair back out of the way.

"I got you, chèr." His voice, barely above a murmur and thick with the Cajun accent that my own dad had spoken with, relaxed me.

I gave up the fight against my sick and let it happen. When I was done, I slumped back into him, too exhausted from the liquor and rejection of it to do much else.

"I'm sorry," I said. The tears from getting sick were taken over by those of humiliation. I accepted the handkerchief he held and dabbed under my eyes.

"For what?" He kept his arm around me and guided me to a bench, where we sat together. Remy's arms stayed firmly around me as we sat.

"This ain't much of an impression."

"It ain't a bad impression," he said in that smooth murmur. "And the first one is the only one that matters. I remember when the school board made my folks send me to school. We went to Breaux's General to get supplies. Your momma helped mine pick out some things that we could afford. I didn't have no interest in any of that, though. I stood at the window watching this little girl on a swing."

I tried to remember the time he was talking about. While Remy Granger had been in the periphery of my life for as long as I could remember, I didn't recall ever having seen him at my family's store.

He kept talking, looking toward the tops of the trees as if he could see that little girl on a swing now.

"The swing was tied to an old oak branch and she kicked her

feet high and leaned back so far I thought she'd tumble right off the back side. Then she tucked them so far underneath her that her whole body pitched forward. That swing cut right through the air. It nearly touched the top of that old tree. I was sure at any time that girl would get scared and scream. But the higher she got, the bigger her smile got. I just knew that was a girl who wouldn't ever be afraid of anything. Now, *that* was an impression."

My mind couldn't think of a decent response. I'd never imagined that Remy Granger might be seeing me, and remembering me, the way I hadn't dared to admit I thought of him.

Remy Granger had always been good-looking. But the Granger family wasn't one that anyone paid much attention to —unless you were the law or looking to break a law yourself.

I looked up into Remy's eyes. In the dark, I couldn't see their caramel color. The dark lashes that lined them and his rich, dark skin—that I'd always thought of as dirty, as in "those dirty Granger boys"—seemed even darker with nothing but the moonlight and shadows to cast light on them.

"And then one day," he added with a quick laugh, "that girl walked right up, kissed me, and then disappeared."

I felt Remy shift toward me.

My face flushed—not from the shine this time, thank the good Lord—and my breath caught.

I was acutely aware of the bitter taste on my tongue and how my breath must smell. I fought the urge to lean in toward him. Then I heard the crunch of footsteps.

"Ophelia!" Dixie giggled and staggered as she tried to walk through the uneven ground in her heeled shoes. "I been lookin' everywhere for you."

"I just needed some fresh air," I explained as I stood and took several hurried steps toward her.

All the kindness Remy had shown me tonight couldn't erase

a lifetime of knowing what people thought of a girl caught in the company of a Granger boy. I couldn't dare draw attention to myself, or Momma. *Like mother, like daughter,* I imagined the old hens network whispering about us. It was only a matter of time, after all.

"Oh." Dixie stopped short as she realized who I was with.

"I got sick," I rushed to explain. "Remy was real nice and made sure I was okay."

"I didn't realize it was you, Remy."

"Yep." Remy didn't seem to be concerned at us being discovered together. Then again, why would he? Remy *is* a Granger boy.

"Eloi was lookin' for you," Dixie said to Remy. "He's got some things that need tendin' to."

It may have been the whiskey muddling my thoughts, but Remy and Dixie seemed to talk to each other as if they were friends. I looked between them, but with no light by which to see their expressions, I couldn't tell if I was right.

Remy stood and I felt his warm hand wrap around mine.

Dixie turned and led us back into the barn. In a back corner was a small area with chairs that the crowd seemed to avoid. Only a handful of people sat there, two of whom were unmistakably Grangers.

As we approached, I noticed Eloi Granger take in Dixie as she emerged from the dancing crowd and walked toward him. Eloi's face remained passive, giving nothing away. The longing in his eyes as she approached, though, was evident, even from a distance.

His eyes shifted as he noticed Remy pulling me along. In a fraction of a second, his eyes flashed on my hand clasped in Remy's and his brows pulled together. The movement was instantaneous, though, passing almost as soon as it happened and leaving behind the same expressionless mask he always wore.

Beside Eloi sat Sirus Granger. The youngest of the Granger brothers, Sirus had the distinct appearance of a Granger, but without the serious, cautious demeanor and confidence of his brothers. His dark hair had the same wave as Remy's, but unlike Eloi's close-cropped style and Remy's oil-smoothed control, Sirus let his waves fall as they may.

His frame was still thin and gangly, giving no sign that he would evolve into the same solid, muscled boys his brothers had become. His face was smooth, without even a hint of the mustache that couldn't be but a year from making its appearance. Sirus obviously revered Eloi and Remy. He watched them with an appraising eye, taking in how they held themselves, moved, and every syllable of their speech. He subtly mimicked what he'd learned in his observation of them.

The thing that stood out to me about Sirus Granger was the smile that played on his lips. I was sure he wouldn't dare a full smile in front of his serious and untrusting family. But Sirus was a boy who was filled with joy and I assumed it was at being included by his older brothers.

"We've got business," Eloi said to Remy when we were close. He had a drink in his right hand and a cigarette dangled from the corner of his mouth. The smoke billowed around his face and he squinted his right eye, leaning away from the plume. He took a deep drag before pulling the cigarette from his mouth with his free hand.

"I'm gonna make sure Ophelia gets home first," Remy told him.

The silent challenge between them was brief but long enough that I knew Eloi Granger wouldn't be denied.

"I'll make sure Dixie gets home, too," Remy added.

At that, Eloi almost seemed to waver. His eyes cut to Dixie, who stood just within the crowd, swaying to the music while she watched the dancers around her.

"Simon Carre gave us a ride here," I offered. "I'm sure he'll take us home."

"Sunshine can take them," Eloi decided, as if he hadn't heard me speak at all.

"No way," Remy said and took a challenging step toward Eloi. "If Sunshine gets caught in town with two white girls in the damn car with him, the judge'll hang his ass where they find him."

I startled at the reference to the judge. Without the benefit of illegal hooch in my body, the tension rendered my muscles rigid again.

Eloi and Remy held each other's gaze. All the energy in the universe seemed to have been siphoned from the room. Almost as if two Olympian gods were about to battle.

"Sirus," Eloi said, his eyes still firmly fixed on Remy's, "take the girls home."

"But I cain't drive in town." Sirus jumped from his seat and reached for the keys Eloi handed him, even as he protested. "I'm only fourteen."

"Then don't get caught," Eloi said. His brows lifted slightly, offering Remy the chance to argue. Daring him.

Remy relaxed his stance with a subtle nod then turned to me. "Sirus'll get ya home."

I looked up into his eyes, desperate to say something—anything—that would make more of a favorable impression than the fact that I had vomited in front of him.

"Okay," was the best I could come up with, and then, "thank you."

Eloi stood and headed toward a back door. "Let's go," he said without a look back. Sunshine Allemond, the Negro boy who'd been a friend of the Grangers since birth, followed Eloi with a nod to me as he passed.

Remy looked as though he were going to say something else. His hands brushed the back of my arms and his head dropped closer to mine.

"Remy!" Eloi called.

"You should go," I said.

He nodded and fell into line behind his brother without a backward glance.

The music stopped.

Dixie stepped beside me. "So," she said to Sirus, "you're lookin' after me again."

Again? I wondered why Sirus Granger would have ever looked after Dixie before this. Was Dixie cavorting with the likes of the Granger boys? I looked at her with my question firmly set upon my face.

She ignored me and wrapped a hand through Sirus's arm.

"What should we do for fun, now?" she asked him as she stumbled.

He tightened his grip on her arm and pulled her up to a solid standing position.

"I'm s'posed to drive you home," he said, which brought on hysterical fits of laughter from Dixie.

"All right then. Let's go, Peeshwank," she said and led him toward the exit.

"Dixie," I chastised, "be nice." Calling Sirus Granger a runt hardly seemed appropriate. Sure, he was smaller than his brothers, but he was only fourteen and I was sure that someday he'd be just as strapping as Eloi and Remy.

"Sirus knows I don't mean no harm," she said as she stepped past the car door he held open. Dixie flopped into the front seat. "We're old friends, now, ain't we, Sirus?"

On the ride home I leaned into Dixie and whispered, "How are you and Sirus Granger old friends?"

She broke up into peals of laughter before slumping back into the effects of the liquor. "Ohh-phelia," she said, dragging out my name. "You been gone so long."

With that, her breathing grew deeper. Her head lolled as the car bounced along the rough road. I let her sleep until we reached my road.

"You can pull up around the corner," I told Sirus.

"No way," he said. "Eloi n' Remy'd have my hide if I didn't see you all get in the house."

He helped rouse Dixie and half-carried her to the front door.

"Thank you, Sirus," I whispered.

It was early morning when Dixie and I snuck into my room. She fell into a corpse-like sleep once she'd lowered herself into my bed.

I lay awake, watching the black of the night lighten to indigo and then lavender, as the sun threatened to rise on a new day.

Determined to get at least an hour of sleep, I rolled away from the window, closed my eyes, and listened to the rhythm of Dixie's liquor-heavy breathing.

I didn't sleep long, but each minute that I was asleep was filled with dreams of Remy Granger.

APRIL 15, 1930

" I could use some help, Ophelia."

Momma's voice cut into my sleep, causing my dream-world Remy to slip from my arms.

"Oh, Momma," I groaned, pulling the pillow over my face as shards of sunlight splintered into my eyes. The fierce tempo of last night's moonshine thumped in my head.

"The sun's been up over an hour now," Momma said. "We have work that needs done."

"I'll be down in a minute," I conceded.

"Dixie, you wake on up, too," she said. "This ain't a flop house. You get down here and start on the laundry bags or get yourself home."

"I'll be sure to tell ma mère 'bout your kind job offer," Dixie said with the hint of a joke in her dried throat. "She'll be upset that I've let another one get by me."

"I'm sure one of them is bound to catch you one of these days," Momma joked back, then turned and walked from my room.

I was miserably aware that the heat of the day was already comin' round. The back of my neck was damp and the air thick and moist.

I pulled on a lightweight dress and twisted my hair up. To keep the hair off my neck I tied my favorite red scarf around my head.

I joined Momma at the laundry buckets after seeing Dixie to the front door. The washing was the most exerting of our tasks. We usually did it just as the sun was climbing high into the sky, but well before the heat crept through the bayou.

My muscles were raw with exhaustion from lack of sleep and too much drink. The sweat beading above my upper lip tasted to be about 90-proof, best I could tell. I didn't dare complain, though. I had my freedoms on the understanding that they wouldn't interfere with my responsibilities. I wasn't about to risk what small liberties Momma had granted me since Daddy passed and we'd returned to Louisiana.

I allowed my mind to drift to Remy Granger, reliving the feeling of his arms around me, his breath hot on my skin.

You were drunk, I rationalized to myself. *And no matter what you felt last night you can't ignore the fact that he is a Granger.*

The Grangers were like an island unto themselves, one that nobody ever wanted to find themselves docked at. I couldn't risk trouble. I couldn't risk distractions. I had to help get Momma out from under the judge's thumb.

With the wash hung on the line, we settled into the shade of the porch to start in on the pile of sewing tasks Momma had taken on.

"Would it be so bad to ask Grand-mère and PawPaw to let us live with them?" I asked.

My fingers were swollen at the tips from the sewing needles, both from pushing them through the sometimes heavy material and the inevitable punctures from when I carelessly stabbed the tender pads. In addition, the fine movement and long hours required to mend countless blouses, dresses, and trousers—and to darn the sweat-stained socks, rigid and discolored by the salt of sweat-drenched workers—turned my fingers rigid. It felt as if arthritis had already claimed my eighteen-year-old joints. Every time I helped Momma with the sewing my mood soured.

"Yes," Momma said. Her fingers flew as her needle and thread rapidly tied together the ragged edges of a frayed hem. "I'm a grown woman, and you're nearly grown yourself. We need to have a home of our own. A space that's just for us. We don't need to be livin' with someone who'll spend all day questioning the choices I made in my life."

When we moved back to Plaquemines Parish, Momma and I had lived with her folks exactly three days before Momma packed us up again. She made it clear she hadn't come back to be judged by anyone. She wouldn't stand to hear talk about the Breauxes or their feud with the Trudeaus. She was in Louisiana only because her husband—and his older brother—were buried here and she couldn't stand to be any farther from him than death had put them.

"But we *don't* have our own home," I said. "This is the judge's house." My mouth contorted around his name—or rather, his title.

Judge Charles Trudeau had grown up with my parents. During that time he was known as CheeChee Trudeau, the eldest son of one of the wealthiest families in town. Upon being granted his first judgeship, people started calling CheeChee by his title—my father had always insisted that CheeChee himself was behind that transition.

"The only reason he went to law school was so we'd stop callin' him CheeChee," Daddy would say, a mischievous glint reflecting where darkness usually settled when talking 'bout the judge.

The fact that we lived in a home owned by the judge disgusted me.

"I pay rent," Momma said, her voice heavy with warning. "That makes this *my* house."

"Which the judge feels free to visit whenever he sees fit."

"I will not have this conversation with you again, Ophelia Beaumont Breaux." Momma dropped her stitching in her lap, then used her forearm to sweep away the beads of perspiration that threatened to roll over her brow, into her eyes. "I wish we had our own house. And with your daddy's insurance money in the bank and what we're earnin' now, we'll have one soon enough."

I knew what she said was true. Momma worked every afternoon as a secretary—for the judge, but I chose to ignore that fact. I preferred to imagine her working for some balding business man, though there weren't many of them left in Point de Concession, since the jobs had gotten harder to find.

She spent mornings, evenings, and days off doing the sewing and laundry for local shrimpers, crabbers, and other laborers. Most didn't have the desire, or wives, to do their own laundry. Some of the laundry was for entire families. Wives were now spending every day, and late into the night, with their husbands trying to catch or grow enough food to feed their family and afford them a surplus to sell.

Momma had also started a garden in the hopes of saving money on groceries. She planned to sell her surplus or use it for trade.

But as much as I admired her for her strength and independence, the one thing I couldn't get past was that Momma, though she didn't know that I knew about the arrangement, allowed the judge to share her bed in exchange for a more affordable rent. The judge had seen her vulnerability and taken the opportunity to claim her.

"Until we can afford our own house," Momma said, "I have to do what I can for us, and not every choice is ideal. I don't want you to focus on all the work we have to do to reach our dream, though." She picked a sock from the pile and laid it in her lap while she threaded her needle. "I want you to focus on the brass ring and not the tail end of the horse in front of you."

"That ain't easy when the horse's ass in front of me is so huge," I said.

"Ophelia!"

"Sorry, Momma," I said, though I wasn't.

It was better for me to imagine that Daddy's death was the end of everything that he was and knew. That it was followed by nothing but darkness and finality. That was a far more acceptable thought than imagining Daddy sitting in Heaven and looking down to see his beloved Emmaline in the arms of the man who'd driven his entire family from the town they loved.

I knotted off my final stitch and set the dress I'd been working on into the basket. "I'm gonna go check on the chickens then go for a walk."

"There's a nickel on the counter," she called after me. "Why don't you go get yourself a cola? Maybe at Piersall's?"

I didn't answer but grabbed the nickel and dropped it in my pocket as I passed through the kitchen and out the back door.

Momma had been tryin' to get me to go to Old Man Piersall's garage since we came back. I hadn't been able to bring myself to go and see the one person in town who'd loved Daddy as much as Momma and I had.

The coop was exactly as it had been when I'd last checked it: eight hens, one rooster, and exactly *zero* eggs.

"I'm 'bout to lose my patience with you freeloaders," I said to the chickens.

They regarded me cautiously and maintained a wide berth, but I didn't think they really absorbed the serious nature of my threat.

"It's been a long time since I've had fried chicken," I said. "Think on that. One egg; that's all it'll take to save your lives for a little while longer."

I wandered the streets as long as I could stand it. Despite the sultry late afternoon, I had no intentions of going home just yet.

The sweat from the day of washing, hanging, and mending laundry covered my body like a film. I tried to stick to the shade of the cypress trees as I walked, reviving my memories of the town I'd spent the first twelve years of my life in.

The people and places were exactly as I remembered them, only a bit more weathered than the last time I'd seen them. There was a comfort in knowing that things in Point de Concession hadn't really changed since the last time I'd lived here. It was like that familiar old tree I'd climbed in my grandparents' backyard. The sturdy trunk and branches remained and the river flowed as close below it as ever. There was new growth, thick patches of moss that existed where the branches had set up residence long ago, and weathered limbs that had fallen or been broken in the passing of time. But the structure was sound and my feet knew the path from top to bottom.

The thing about small towns is that it doesn't take you long to walk from one edge to the outskirts of the other.

As dusk settled in, I found myself standing across the road from Breaux's General Store.

They could have at least changed the damn name, I thought. The Cavern of Things Past, that deep pit that was located just behind the beat of my heart, echoed with the whisper of memories.

The store had been my family's until six years ago when a conflict, rivaled only by the Hatfields and the McCoys, caused my grandparents to sell it and move the lot of us to Charlotte. Despite having left town, Daddy's mère and père had the last laugh. While the Trudeau family was celebrating their good fortune at having driven the Breauxes, and all the money and influence they possessed, from Plaquemines Parish, the Breaux family quietly sold the family store to August Granger for a pittance. Most of the payment he'd probably earned by brewing moonshine during the early years of Prohibition. August Granger was sent to prison not even two years later, but the store still belonged to the Grangers and still carried my family name.

That must burn the judge up, seeing that name every day. Suddenly, a dark kernel of joy sprouted just outside the Cavern of Things Past. My family name had been in town every year that we weren't. It had served as a reminder to the judge that, despite having driven my family from town, we'd taken with us the one thing he'd yearned for more than anything else: Momma.

THREE

The thick stomp of boots on the front porch of the store shook me from my reverie.

Eloi Granger walked around the corner of the store and paused with his hand on the door handle, looking at me. The wide brim of his hat cast a shadow over his eyes, making them unreadable.

I grew uneasy. My skin prickled and a shudder climbed along my spine then scurried across my shoulders. I felt exposed and vulnerable.

Despite his silent demeanor, Eloi Granger intimidated me—even from a distance.

Say something, I chastised myself. But my mouth grew sticky and parched. My tongue swelled, gluing itself firmly to my palate.

Eloi nodded once, a movement so subtle that I thought I may have imagined it. Then he turned the handle and stepped into the store.

The jangle of bells sounded as he opened the screen, and again as it slammed shut behind him.

A gravelly voice called from behind me. "You can look at it all day, but it ain't never gonna change."

I spun around toward the familiar, if not more wrinkled face of Old Man Piersall—or *Vieux* Piersall—Daddy's mentor and my *parrain*, my godfather.

"Mr. Roland." I smiled. I was relieved to finally see him but also filled with guilt that I'd waited so long.

"Pheli!" He smiled and held out his arms.

Before I'd had the chance to think, I'd moved in and wrapped my arms around his large frame. Immediately, the comfort of pleasant memories washed over me.

"You be careful, Pheli," he said as he unwound from my embrace. "I got grease all o'er me. I'll ruin ya' dress."

I stepped back and smiled at him. "I ain't worried 'bout this old thing," I said.

"Whyn't ya come on o'er at the porch and tell me what's been goin' on wit you n' your mère." The words rolled out of his mouth in a warm, garbled glob of Creole comfort.

The one thing I'd never gotten accustomed to while living in Charlotte was the precise drawl of the people we'd lived near. Their speech seemed practiced and particular in its enunciation unlike the loose and free pattern of the Louisiana bayou. I'd loved the familiarity of words, loosely based on generations of people coming together to meld their lifestyles, traditions, and languages.

I sat on the old swing that hung from the shaded corner of the porch. As a young girl I'd spent many afternoons swinging from this bench while Daddy helped Vieux Piersall work on a car—or any other project that had been brought in to the garage. Daddy had always liked to work with his hands, no matter how that had upset his parents.

Vieux Piersall went into the shop and then came back out with a Coca-Cola bottle in each hand.

"Oh," I said and reached my hand into my pocket. I held the nickel toward him.

His brows met and then raised as he looked at me as if he'd never seen such a thing in his life.

"Wha'dat?"

"For the Coca-Cola," I said. "Momma gave it to me so I could buy one."

"Nah, you put dat away," he said with a gruff laugh. "An old man never went broke from buyin' his goddaughter a drink."

"Thank you," I said. "I'm thirstier than I thought."

"Why you out walkin' about in dis heat?"

"Just wanted to get out for a bit. I been workin' with Momma all day and needed to rest my fingers."

"Ah," he said. "I hear she been doin' laundry n' sewin'. Didn't know she had a helper." As he spoke, he looked out across the street and along the tree line. His eyes were always on the move. He nodded at people who walked and drove past.

"Yes, sir. We can get twice as much done if I help, which means we earn twice as much."

He brushed a rag across his forehead, wiping away the beads of perspiration that were gathering across the growing bald patch on his head.

"You keep up wit' your momma, then? She musta taught you good." The left side of his mouth curled into a grin and a glint gleamed in his eye.

"Well, maybe we don't do *twice* as much with my help," I admitted with a smile of my own. "But I definitely help her get more done."

"I 'ave no doubt 'bout dat, Pheli," he said.

The good-natured banter subsided and I felt the weight of unsaid things begin to press between us.

Vieux Piersall blew the hesitation from his lungs and wiped

his brow again. "I was sure sad to hear 'bout your defan pauvre," he said.

The sting was immediate in my heart as well as my eyes. Tears fought their way to the surface and my throat constricted. I turned my gaze toward the moss-covered trees and focused all of my attention on the cypress that lined the dirt road until I could control the emotions that threatened to bubble over. I imagined the Cavern of Things Past with its doors burst open. Pain and sadness spilled out beyond it, infecting the light with its heavy darkness. I took a deep breath, pushed it all back into the cavern, and secured the doors.

I looked back at Vieux Piersall. This wasn't a conversation that either of us was comfortable having.

"I loved my daddy, Mr. Roland," I said, "but he wa'nt no saint." The admission fell heavy in my chest. It was one of my greatest conflicts with Daddy's memory.

"Your père was a good man." His voice had dropped, taking on a smooth and reflective tone. "I'll never forget the day he walked over here n' started workin'." A laugh erupted from deep within him. His belly strained against his shirt as it heaved with the joyous memories.

"His père told him dat it was time he started workin'. He was expected to work as hard as everyone else in da family and he was to start in da store dat very day." He laughed again. His eyes began to tear with humor. "But your daddy had no plans to ev'r work for da family. He told your gran'father dat he'd get a job, but he'd first die than work in da store. He walked straight 'cross da road and started pumpin' gas into a car dat had just pulled up. I didn't even know I was needin' any help," he said, "but I ain't 'bout to turn away someone wit dat much gumption to work."

I smiled. I'd heard the story before, from Daddy as well as my grandparents and Vieux Piersall. That was the first day in a long friendship that resulted in Mr. Roland Piersall, a man who'd never stepped foot in a church in his life, being asked to join my family at St. Mary's Church to become my godfather. That was much to the shock of the rest of the Breaux family and the genteel society in Point de Concession.

We sat in companionable silence for several minutes, each lost in our own memories.

The clang of the bell across the street caught my attention. I looked up as Marie Granger walked out of the door, followed by her eldest, Eloi. She called an order to whoever remained in the store, and then followed Eloi to the truck.

She was far thinner and more aged than when I'd seen her last. I suspected that raising three boys and running a store, while her husband languished in prison, would be hard on any woman. More difficult, though, when those three boys were Grangers.

"Was a shame when your family sold dat place," Vieux Piersall said with a shake of his head.

"Yeah." I'd been young, and my family had tried to shield me from the problems. I knew nonetheless, the way I'm sure all kids know everything their parents try to shield them from.

"I don' blame 'em, though," he said. "Phillipe came alive when Emmaline agreed to marry him and then they had you. He would've done anythin' to save his family from dat feudin' nonsense."

"And now we're back." Bitterness rose up in me. "We're here, Daddy ain't, and the judge and the whole Trudeau family are back in control."

He rubbed the rag over his head, several times, as if wasting time while he searched for something to say to ease the sting of my words.

The sun had dipped below the horizon. The last of the light was quickly vanishing into the encroaching indigo sky.

"Phillipe Breaux was a good man," he said. "That was a heavy burden dat he was tryin' to shed."

"A heavier burden than leaving his wife and daughter behind?"

"Das somethin' he gonna have ta take up wit da Lord," Vieux Piersall said, his voice quiet.

Despite the internal struggling my daddy had endured since the terrible accident, his suicide would always loom over our last memories of him like an ominous storm cloud on a late October's day.

A loud clatter rang out from inside the garage, followed by a curse. "Damn this thing!"

"Who is that?" I asked. I hadn't considered that anyone else would be in Vieux Piersall's garage. The only person I'd ever seen in there, besides its owner, was Daddy.

He shook his head and groaned as he stood. "Ah, I had to take on a boy to help out." He started toward the door and I followed, carrying our empty cola bottles. "I'm gettin' too old to do it alone."

I noticed, then, the stooped posture he'd settled into over the years since I'd seen him last. His breath was heavy with exertion and he hummed a low tune that sounded happy, but I realized was done to mask his labored breathing.

We stepped into the lighted main room of the garage that served as his office. He called into the doorway that led into the shop, "Sun's gone down. Clean on up now. You c'n work on dat t'morrow."

"Yes, sir," came a muffled reply.

I assumed his shop boy must be underneath one of the beat-up cars I saw outlined in the darkening garage.

Vieux Piersall pointed through the opposite doorway as he eased himself onto a stool and took a deep breath.

"There's a bucket of fresh rhubarb in da kitchen," he said. "You take some home fer your mère."

"Yes, sir." I made my way into the living area that was attached to his garage. It wasn't a large area. The front room and kitchen shared the same space and at the back were doors, which I assumed led to Vieux Piersall's bedroom and toilet.

"Check da pantry next to da window," he said. "Go on and grab some cabbage and turnips to take home too. Your mère can make a nice soup. And some of da oranges."

I came back into the office area, fresh crops teetering in my arms.

Vieux Piersall reached into a closet and pulled out a wooden produce box. I loaded the rhubarb and fresh vegetables into it.

"Thank you, Mr. Roland, sir. Momma'll be real pleased."

"You cain't walk home wit' all 'dat," he said. "I'll make da boy drive you home. He's got a delivery ta make anyhow."

"I'm sure I can make do," I objected.

He didn't answer, just leaned toward the garage area again and yelled, "Bring the truck 'round and give Miss Breaux a ride home."

"Yes, sir." The reply was immediate; I was impressed that his employee was so quick to respond and do as Vieux Piersall ordered.

"Now that we've gotten over the first hurdle, I 'spect I'll be seein' you more often," he said.

Despite the lack of accusation in his voice, shame rushed over me.

"Nothin' short of a hungry gator sittin' at your front door would keep me away." I laughed and he pulled me in for a hug. Before we pulled away I saw he'd slipped another bottle of cola into the box.

I heard the truck being driven around the corner and pulled

up by the steps. I gathered the box in my arms and backed out through the screen door.

As I turned toward the rackety sputter of the engine, I nearly dropped everything. There, leaning against the side of the truck next to the open passenger door was Remy Granger.

One leg was crossed over the ankle of the other and his arms were folded across his chest. His shirt was covered in dirt and grease, and I noticed it clung nicely to the muscles in his chest and his arms. The grin on his face had been placed there by the devil himself and hinted at nothin' but trouble.

"Miss Breaux," he said and stood to give me a cursory bow.

"I shoulda known," I said. "Trouble always does seem to follow me."

He stepped forward quickly to relieve me of my armload. He placed the box in the back of the truck.

"Now is that any way to talk to a fella after he showed you nothin' but kindness?" He feigned hurt feelings.

Last night rushed back to me with embarrassing clarity. I'd allowed Remy Granger to get uncomfortably fresh with me—or was it me who'd gotten fresh with him?—and then I'd gotten sick in front of him.

The screen door slammed closed behind me then I heard Vieaux Piersall's low hum and heavy breath. "You be sure and get that delivery taken care of, son."

"Yes'sir," Remy answered. He guided me into the truck with a gentle lead.

Remy closed the door and I waved out the window to Vieaux Piersall. "Thanks again, Mr. Roland. Momma and I appreciate your kindness."

We rode in silence for several minutes before I finally spoke up.

"I owe you gratitude for lookin' out for me last night," I told him. "I may have had a bit much to drink."

He chuckled. His amusement grew into a full-on laugh. Remy wrapped one arm around his belly, holding the steering wheel expertly with the other. "I think you passed 'a bit much' about two drinks in," he said.

I was incensed at being the source of his ribbing. "Are you saying I can't hold my liquor, Remy Granger? I'll have you know I drank plenty in Charlotte. I've drunk men twice your size under the table."

He straightened and assumed a serious demeanor. "I don't mean to doubt you, Miss Breaux," he said, using the name— and tone of voice—that Vieux Piersall had used to address me at the garage. "But those fine cordials you were undoubtedly accustomed to in Charlotte are nothin' compared to Louisiana hooch."

"I'm sure I don't know what you're talkin' 'bout," I said. "I was simply tired last night from puttin' in a hard day's work. Perhaps you've heard of those?" I asked with an angelic rise of my brows.

"I think what you're referrin' to is a *day's* work," he said, apparently intent on matching me barb for barb. "You spend a day doin' *hard* work—*men's* work—and gettin' all dolled up before a few drinks won't even enter your mind."

"Stop the car," I demanded.

He looked over at me, his brows knit in surprise. "What?"

"Remy Granger, you stop this car right now," I raised my voice, adopting the voice Momma used when I'd done something she disapproved of.

He slowed the car and brought it to a stop.

I opened the door and swung my legs out.

"You can't get out," he said.

"Oh, I assure you I can." I stood and slammed the door then reached into the back of the truck for the box of rhubarb and vegetables.

I heard the driver door open and close again as Remy got out. "It's dark," he said.

"That tends to happen when the sun goes down," I retorted. I scooped up a wayward turnip with my fingertips, turned, and began walking down the road. My ankles rolled as I stepped into the ruts and I fought to stay upright while holding my items.

"Ophelia."

I continued walking, determined to put as much distance between Remy and myself as possible. What had I been thinkin' even entertaining thoughts about Remy Granger? Had I really almost kissed him last night? Had I spent the past twenty-four hours daydreamin' about him? *Once a Granger, always a dirty Granger*, I thought.

"Ophelia!" The scratch of his shoes scraped across the dirt as he rushed to follow me.

He rounded in front of me as I turned the corner. He held up his hands, as if warding me off. "Please, stop. I'm sorry. I didn't mean to offend you."

I stopped—not that I had a choice, he was standing directly in front of me—and glared at him.

His eyes were wide and imploring as he urged me to return to the car with him, but the devil was back in his grin. Maybe he hadn't intended to push me so far, but he was enjoying the fact that he had. And that I'd responded to his jibes.

"Please let me drive you home," he said, already reaching to relieve me of my armload.

I released the crate and flung the loose turnip onto the top of the pile, swinging it dangerously close to his jaw.

"Fine, but I'm not about to tolerate another wayward word from you, Remy Granger."

I turned on one heel and walked back to the car. I did my

best to maintain my impressive haughty demeanor, without rolling my ankles and falling into a rut.

Remy put the fruit and vegetables into the back of the truck then climbed in. He pulled the door closed and turned to me. "I really didn't intend to upset you, Ophelia. I was just ribbing you. I shouldn't have."

I nodded, hoping that would indicate that I accepted his apology. My feelings were more bitter than I could admit. My eyes stung with the salt of tears, though there was no way I intended to allow them to spill. I hadn't cried since the day the uniformed men walked up to our front porch in Charlotte and told us that Private Phillipe Breaux—my daddy—had taken his own life with his service revolver.

Remy started the car and drove in silence.

It was a small town and I'd only been back two months. I knew enough to know that Momma and I were the subject of talk all over town, and that Remy, as well as the rest of town, would know where I lived.

He pulled up out front and jumped out to get my door. I stepped out and waited while he gathered up the rhubarb and vegetables and carried them to the porch.

As we approached the steps I heard a loud cough and looked through the windows to the lighted interior. The large frame of Judge Trudeau was occupying the space inside the front room. He stood, coat in hand, and I saw Momma reach for his hat. My heart sank. As if it weren't bad enough that the judge was in my house, Remy Granger had to be here to witness my humiliation.

I noticed the stagger in his step as he recognized the man in my front room. He paused.

I held out my arms for the box. "I'll take them," I said and gave him an apologetic smile.

He remained still for only another moment. "No," he said.

I noticed that his voice was much lower than before and as

he stepped onto the first step, and each one thereafter, it was with a soft step, so as to not draw attention to his presence.

He set the box on the small table and seemed to float back down to the walk path.

"Thank you," I said. "For drivin' me home and for helping with the produce." I wanted him to stay, and yet, wanted him to leave as fast as possible. What would he think of the judge being in Momma's home this late? What would Momma think if she found me with Remy Granger?

He stepped close. He was a full head taller than me and I had to lean my head back to meet his eyes. "I really am sorry that I made ya' mad." His voice was a near whisper and I felt the heat of his breath on my cheek. "I never had any intent on makin' such a bad impression."

"*That* wasn't a bad impression." I smiled up at him, reviving the conversation from last night. "The boy who held my hair and looked out for me when I was sick...now *that* was an impression."

He smiled. A low chuckle rumbled from his throat.

My eyes held his. My chest swelled with the anticipation of what could come.

In the periphery, I noticed a car driving down the road. We pulled to a respectable distance seconds before the light from the car illuminated our close proximity.

Remy smiled at me.

From the house I heard music start. As the raw jazz sounds floated out through the windows, I heard Momma giggle.

My stomach soured. I knew Remy heard the sounds and understood their implications.

"I should probably go," he said in a hushed voice.

I nodded.

He turned back toward the truck and walked a few paces before he turned back around to face me. "You could come with me," he said. "Just for a while." His head inclined briefly to the house, letting me know we'd be gone just long enough to avoid whatever it was that was happenin' in my front room.

"But you're still workin'," I said even as I walked toward him with a buoyancy in my step.

Remy looked confused.

"The delivery? Vieux Piersall said not to forget."

"Oh, right." He nodded as if remembering something long forgotten. "Well, the good thing about that delivery is that I can do it any time before the sun comes up," he said and led me back to the truck.

I jumped in, both eager to be avoidin' the judge and to spend more time with Remy.

"Where should we go?" he asked.

"I hadn't really thought that far," I said with a smile. The farther we drove from my house, the more relief seemed to wash over me and loosen the stress I carried in my muscles and joints.

"Are you hungry?"

"I haven't really eaten all day," I admitted. I'd woken this morning with a sour stomach from the night before and spent the day working nonstop with Momma. I'd had a slice of bread and a plum but nothing else.

"Well then, let's get somethin' to eat."

"Where?" I couldn't imagine where we would go this late at night.

"Trust me," he said with a smile.

I relaxed into the seat as we traveled farther from my house. The windows were open and the wind caught my hair, pulling it from my scarf and whipping it about.

The speed of the truck caused the evening bayou air to feel cool. The stickiness of the long day dried, and my skin prickled at the sensation of the cooler wind.

Remy turned the truck down a succession of narrow dirt paths until we finally pulled to a stop in front of a weather-beaten shack. Boards hung from the top of the porch. The steps out front seemed to bow dangerously.

A tire hung by a frayed rope from a cypress at the edge of the swamp.

The air was filled with a cacophony of swamp sounds. Toads sang their gravely songs and hounds barked, their calls reverberating along the bayou. It seemed as though the noise was carried on the currents of the water that flowed just feet away from me.

There wasn't a single car or streetlight to disrupt what Mother Nature had intended the evenings to be like.

We were at the Granger house, and my body stiffened. Though I felt sure that Remy wouldn't hurt me, I'd spent a lifetime hearing about the evil deeds of the Granger clan and being warned away from them. Was I really about to walk straight into their lair?

The door swung open and Remy held out a hand to help me.

My own hand trembled as I laid it in his.

"It's okay," he said. "We quit eatin' wayward souls two years ago."

I inhaled in surprise, my nervousness gettin' the better of me.

Remy laughed softly and pulled my hand to his chest so that I was close and forced to look into his eyes. "You're okay, Ophelia. Trust me."

And I did.

Remy held my hand as he guided me through the front yard. He navigated me around the bicycles and pirogues that littered the yard.

"Watch the third step," he said as he stepped over it himself.

Remy pulled the handle on the screen and stepped through, pulling me along with him.

"I'm home," he yelled.

Three people were seated around an oval table. They all turned toward us and stopped in surprise when they saw me.

My heart thundered. Right there, not even ten feet away were Eloi and Sirus Granger. Their mère, Marie, stood holding a pot that steamed as though it had been pulled straight off the stove as we'd walked in the door. Maybe it had.

It was Eloi, though, who made me the most uncomfortable. While Sirus and Marie Granger were obviously shocked to see me, Eloi's expression didn't betray him still. It was as if he had some suspicion all along that I'd walk into their house tonight on the arm of his brother.

Sirus was the first to recover. He stood from the table. "Well, ain't this a nice surprise?" he asked, as if prompting his mother and Eloi. "Ophelia Breaux has come to visit." He stood aside and offered me his chair, indicating with his hand that I should sit.

Marie recovered quickly. "I didn't know we was havin' guests tonight," she said. "It's good to see you, Ophelia." Her voice, though kind, hinted at an irritation that Remy had brought me into their home unannounced.

I'd never been this close to Marie Granger and fought hard to not stare at her. I could see that she'd been beautiful in her day. She still had a certain beauty, but it was tempered by the cautious, hard look of a woman who'd lived on the outskirts of the law for so much of her life.

Marie Granger was obviously the source of the Granger boys' dark, gypsy coloring. Her black hair was thick with waves, tamed only by the kerchief she had wrapped around her head. Although Remy's eyes were caramel-colored and warm, Marie's were black and unnerving in their intensity. They seemed to take in every aspect of my being as if she was committing me to memory in case she had to use that information someday.

"I don't mean to impose," I said finally.

"Nonsense," she said. "There's always enough room for a friend of my boys at the supper table."

She indicated for me to take the proffered chair and swatted at Remy's arm as he stepped past her to claim his own seat. She would be polite, but we all knew I didn't belong in their home.

Eloi said nothing, only continued to watch me with silent, unwavering caution—or was it judgment?

Once I sat down, Remy handed me a bowl and pulled a chair close to me before sitting down himself. His leg was pressed against mine as we gathered around the small table.

"Thank you," I said, as grateful for the bowl as his proximity to me.

"I hope you don't mind rabbit gumbo," Miss Marie said as she ladled a spoonful into my bowl.

The steam carried the spicy aroma to my nose. My stomach answered with a low growl and churn.

"No, ma'am," I said. "It smells wonderful."

She filled all the bowls before sitting to her own. I waited, hands in my lap, unsure of the proper protocol in the Granger home. I'd been raised to wait for Daddy—and, after Daddy had gone into the service, PawPaw—to say Grace before eating.

Miss Marie, Eloi, Sirus, and Remy bowed their heads for only a moment before sayin' "Amen" and proceeding to plunge their spoons into their gumbo.

"Amen," I muttered, a moment too late, then picked up my own spoon.

I blew on the thick, steaming stew. The heat warmed my lips before I'd even touched them to the stew. I knew from the rich smell that Miss Marie's gumbo would be spicy. It'd been six years since I'd eaten a true Louisiana gumbo.

Momma had tried to make it a few times when we were in Charlotte, but she seemed unable to mix a decent roux once we'd moved from Point de Concession. Once we were settled in Charlotte, my grand-mère had refused to cook, act or speak in any way that reminded her of the place she'd turned her back on.

Although the Grangers all made a show of enjoying their supper, their eyes cut repeatedly to me. I made sure that, as I took small bites of my gumbo, my face reflected my enjoyment of it.

It wasn't difficult to do. The stew really was wonderful. The rich broth warmed my tongue and all the way into my belly. The peppers and onions were perfectly cooked and the rabbit tender and juicy with broth.

"This is very good, Miss Marie," I said. "I ain't had a decent gumbo since I was little."

She set her spoon into the bowl and sat back in her chair. "Thank you, Ophelia."

She wore her cautious demeanor like Eloi, but pride flashed across her face at my compliment.

Remy pushed his thigh tighter against mine and cast me a quick smile before he lifted another spoonful to his mouth.

"I hear you and your ma been back a couple months now," Miss Marie said.

"Yes'm," I answered between bites.

"I ain't got nothin' bad to say 'bout your ma," she said.

I nodded, unsure why she would feel the need to clarify such a thing.

"And I was sorry to see your père's family move, but I'm grateful for the chance they gave my family." She stood and took her bowl to the sink, grabbing a pitcher of dark purple liquid and returning to fill the empty glasses. "Nobody else woulda ever given a Granger that same chance."

43

I knew she was referring to the sale of the store and I was burning to ask about Breaux's General. Why'd they kept the name? How were they still runnin' it when there were so few customers able to pay for store-bought groceries and other sundry items? I'd even heard tell that the Grangers were just givin' groceries to the poorest folks in town. They couldn't keep the store open if they were just givin' away food. Didn't they know anything 'bout runnin' a business? But I didn't dare ask any of those questions out loud.

I lifted my glass to my mouth. The purple liquid was sweet and grape-flavored. It flooded my mouth and attacked all the areas that had been heated by the spice of the gumbo.

The surprise I had at the drink must have been evident on my face. All the Grangers, save for Eloi, smiled at me as if witnessing the funniest thing in seven parishes.

"Ain't you ever had Kool-Ade before?" Sirus asked.

"No," I answered. I took another sip. The backs of my inner cheeks tickled when the sweetness rushed into the back corners of my mouth. I swallowed and smiled. "But, I think I like it."

Remy, Miss Marie, and Sirus laughed.

Eloi stood suddenly, placed his bowl on the counter, and poured coffee into a cup.

He returned to the table and I smelled the bitter, comforting aroma of chicory coffee. "Don't you have a delivery tonight?" he grumbled toward Remy.

Miss Marie and Sirus both looked at Remy. The momentary good-natured mood had been snatched away.

Remy sat up straighter, leveling his gaze to Eloi. "I'll get it taken care of," he said. "Have I ever missed a delivery?"

"You see to it that you don't miss this one," said Eloi.

Remy stared at Eloi but didn't answer. Both of them sat rigid, as if they'd been carved from stone.

Miss Marie's jaw pulsed and her eyes flicked from Eloi to

Remy and back again. Sirus focused his attention to the rice and peppers that remained at the bottom of his bowl.

"I should probably be gettin' home," I said and bumped Remy's leg with my own, hoping Eloi didn't notice my movement. I pushed my chair back. "Thank you for the meal," I said to Miss Marie as Remy stood to pull my chair further. "It was delicious."

"Was my pleasure," Miss Marie said and wrapped her hands around a dish towel.

She'd be polite, but wouldn't shake my hand. The unspoken message was clear: Miss Marie and I were not friends and I didn't belong in the Granger home.

Sirus stood, smiled at me, and said, "Was good ta see ya again, Ophelia."

"And you," I said. I thought better of thanking him for gettin' Dixie and me home safely yesterday. He was only fourteen and Miss Marie was probably unaware that he'd been driving.

Eloi remained seated. He lifted his cup to his mouth and sipped his coffee.

Remy placed a hand on my lower back and led me to the door.

CHAPTER
FOUR

"You should probably drop me off 'round the corner," I told Remy as we neared my house.

He pulled the truck to the side of the road and turned off the lights.

An occasional wisp of cool wind blew in from the water, offering a reprieve from the sticky night air. Songs of crickets and frogs filled the silence of the late evening, interrupted only by the occasional howl of a hound from somewhere off in the distance.

"I'll walk you," Remy said before opening his door.

Remy stood beside me as I surveyed the house from the street.

The lights were still on in the front room and the judge's car remained parked on the opposite side of the road.

"I might just sit on the porch for a while before I go in," I said to Remy. "But thank you for dinner."

He looked nervously from me to the house. His eyes drifted to the upstairs window, which was also lit. "I cain't leave you sittin' on the porch this late at night," he said. "I'll sit with you."

I knew from his nervous demeanor that he had no interest

in waiting for the judge to come out of the house. Everything in Remy Granger's very being had been groomed to stay far away from the law. Or so I imagined.

"We could go for a walk," I offered. It was an effort to save both of us the humility in admitting why we didn't want to wait on the porch. "Might help supper digest."

It'd been six years since I'd seen Remy Granger and time hadn't diminished my feelings toward him. I was intrigued by him. Perhaps even obsessed. It felt as if there was some invisible thread that bound my attention directly to Remy Granger. I couldn't imagine letting him walk off into the night.

He stood and offered me his hand. I slid mine into it, a surge of electricity sparking between us.

Remy Granger wound his fingers between mine and held me so close that our arms pressed firmly together.

I was grateful for the dark of the night; a blush burned a path from my neck to the tips of my ears.

We talked about inconsequential things: favorite foods, the best breed of dogs, and whether jazz music could ever replace zydeco. We both agreed that it couldn't.

I stole glances at him as we walked and flushed when he caught me gazing up at him. Each time he leaned toward me and gave me a sultry, heavy-lidded smile. I leaned closer into him, assuring that our arms stayed in contact as our pace slowed.

"Can I ask you a personal question, Remy?" I stopped walking and leaned one shoulder against a moss-covered oak that had grown into the walkway.

"Ain't nothin' to stop ya from askin'," he said, leaning across from me. "But it might not be in my best interest to answer." A smile spread across his face.

My heart fluttered at his close proximity and the boldness I felt in his presence.

"Is it true what everyone says?" I was nervous now, unsure of how to ask him but not wanting to offend him.

"What does everyone say?"

"Are you a bootlegger?" Well, there was certainly no preamble with that. Straight to the point it is, then.

He smiled. "Well, I guess that depends."

"On what?"

"On who's askin'."

He leaned over me with a devilish grin and added in a whispered voice, "If you're a revenuer or a prohibition agent? Then no, I definitely ain't no bootlegger."

Remy Granger had just—almost—admitted to me that he was in fact, a bootlegger. The breath that had carried his admission warmed my cheek. My heart gave a thrill as I thought about the fact that I'd just spent an evening with a criminal.

A smile took up residence on my face as he pulled me back onto the walkway and we continued our side-by-side amble.

"What was Charlotte like?" Remy asked once we'd gotten a fair distance from my house. His voice was low and the words rolled from his lips like warm honey.

I had to stop my mind from imagining my own lips pressed against his, tasting their sweetness.

"It was fine," I said. "We lived next door to Daddy's parents. I went to school and had friends. Wasn't really no different than Point de Concession, other than there wasn't no feud."

"Yeah." Remy shook his head. "That was somethin' else. People still talk about the big feud between the Breauxes and Trudeaus. That was the most spectacular battle to happen here since the Union Aggression."

"It wasn't nearly so excitin' when it was your family that was run off," I said.

The memories rushed back: Momma bruised and crying as she packed our things quickly in trunks. Grand-mère Breaux yellin' at Sheriff Alberti that she just wanted her son's body for burial. Leaving town in the dark of night and sittin' on the side of the road outside of town while we waited for Daddy to meet up with us. And then there was that drive. The long, silent trip to Charlotte with everyone lost in their own thoughts.

"Why'd you come back?" Remy asked. "I mean, after your père—" He stopped.

Most people had a hard time saying the words "passed", "died" or "killed himself". Normally I would help them out by saying the words myself, throwin' them out into the world with jarring clarity. But I didn't feel like bein' that person with Remy for some reason.

"My grand-mère and grand-père always blamed Momma for my uncle, Louis's death," I told him. "And then, when Daddy died, they seemed to blame her for that too. Momma and I were a daily reminder that their sons had both loved her more than life itself."

Remy didn't say anything. What could he say? The troubles with the Breaux boys, CheeChee Trudeau, and Emmaline Beaumont were legendary in Southern Louisiana.

We walked in silence until we came to the truck again. We paused. Remy leaned against it, not seeming to want to turn that final corner to take me back home. I didn't have any desire to leave him either. I dropped his hand and turned to lift myself onto the back edge of the bed of the truck.

Remy stepped in quickly, wrapped his hands around my waist, and boosted me as I slid onto the tail end of the truck. As I slid into position Remy's hands lingered at my hips. He stood between my knees, his hands warming my hips and the top of my thighs through the thin material of my dress.

My dress! I suddenly realized I'd spent the entire evening with Remy while wearing the old, shapeless work dress I'd been wearing while I helped Momma with the laundry and sewing.

Not only had I been seen wearing it by Remy, I'd eaten supper in his family's home dressed this way.

"I'm glad you came back." His voice dropped again and the soft, jumbled words seemed to fall out from between his lips.

Those lips! I watched, mesmerized as they moved in a sensuous dance around whatever words he was sayin'.

The moonlight was soft and cast a gentle glow across Remy's face, making his skin appear soft as velvet. My fingers ached to reach up and touch him.

His body was suddenly closer. His hips pressed against my inner thighs while his hands snaked farther up my hips, pulling me toward him.

My own body responded, sitting up straight, my chest reaching to make contact with his.

The rhythm of our breaths became heavy and synchronized again, rising and falling with increasingly heavy anticipation.

I lifted my lids, looking up at him and the look of desire that clouded his face.

Remy placed two fingers gently below my jaw line and lifted my chin so that I was forced to look directly into his eyes.

I let my gaze drift across his face and down to—

Those lips! They moved toward me and I reached up to meet them. The soft warmth of his mouth met mine in a silent greeting for only a brief minute before urgency overtook us.

My breath became rapid and I allowed my lips to part, tasting the sweetness of his kisses.

Remy pulled me tighter to him and I reached behind his neck, pulling him harder into me.

Warmth flooded through my body. Heat traced the path of Remy's hands as they moved from my hips, up my back, then down again to my legs.

I felt the heat of his hand on the bare skin of my leg, then gasped as his hand followed a path under my dress and higher on my leg.

"I'm sorry," he said as he yanked his hand away.

I reached for his hand and placed it again on my bare skin, but just above my knee, below my hemline. I looked directly into his eyes, letting him know that I didn't want him to stop touching me. Then I pulled him back into another kiss.

Remy's hand moved to the back of my knees. He pulled me closer into him. His hands traveled back to the top of my thighs, but still just below the hem.

Remy Granger was, undoubtedly, an island and I had run well and thoroughly aground.

I don't know how long we continued. Our intensity increased with every moment we were locked together.

It was Remy who pulled away first.

I gasped, my breathing fast and my chest still heaving. I reached for him again.

"I can't, chèr," he said, grasping my wrists in his hands and pushing them on my own abdomen. He leaned slightly forward, taking deep breaths.

I tried to get control of my own breaths. "Remy?"

He stepped closer to me and placed a soft kiss on my mouth. His fingertips traced the line of my jaw before brushing away a wisp of hair that was stuck at the neckline of my dress.

"I have to make that delivery," he said. "I should go." He kissed my jaw then I felt a soft nibble on my earlobe.

He made a soft sound, like a growl. "I don't want to leave you, chèr," he whispered.

"Then don't," I whispered back and kissed the space just under his lower lip.

He pulled me into him so tight that I nearly couldn't breathe. Then, he pulled back, lifted me from the truck, and led me around the corner to my house.

Remy left me at the screen door with one last sweet kiss. He watched from the walk path as I went in the house and closed the door behind me.

I leaned against the door as I closed it. I allowed the feeling of excitement and urgency to linger in my chest for a few moments more. I nearly ran up the steps, desperate to get to bed so that I might find Remy Granger lingering in my dreams again. If nothing else, I'd lie awake for hours and remember the feeling of his hands as they moved along my back, my hips, my skin—

The sound of Momma's door opening as I opened my own bedroom door startled me from my reverie. I spun around to find Momma and the judge standing in the hallway. The judge looked formidable in his wrinkled suit and straight posture.

Momma was wearing only her housecoat. Her face flushed and her eyes darted from me to the judge.

"Ophelia," she stammered, "I, uh, the judge was kind enough to help get my bedroom window unstuck."

I looked from Momma to the judge. Between us was an unspoken understanding: there had been no problem with the window.

Momma's eyes dropped to the floor, her cheeks flushed. "Thank you, Judge. I certainly hate to take up any more of your time."

"Any time at all, Emma." He turned to me and reached for my hand. "And, Ophelia, if there is ever anything I can do to ease your burdens." He lifted my hand to his cool, moistened lips. His kiss lingered and my skin seized up, recoiling to escape his clammy touch.

Momma pushed her way between us and pushed me back toward my own bedroom door. "I'm sure Ophelia won't have any reason to be a bother." She turned to me. "Now you go and get on to bed."

I backed into my room. The frigid feeling of the judge's lips remained on my hand and seemed to spread farther up my arm. I picked up a cloth from my dresser and scrubbed away the lingering offense.

As I climbed into bed, I forced the thoughts of Momma and the judge from my mind. Thoughts of them together, thoughts of his lips touching my skin, thoughts of his lecherous behavior. I closed my eyes tight and forced the memory of Remy to return. The heat of Remy's touch chased away any lingering chill from the judge. I found myself relaxing into the heated memory of what had been my first real kiss.

That night, I dreamed only of Remy Granger.

CHAPTER
FIVE

Momma didn't wake me the next morning.

The smell of coffee tickled at my nose, pulling me from the arms of my dream Remy. I lay quietly in my bed for a while, thinking about the lustful inclinations that I couldn't seem to control when I was with him. I'd just come back to Point de Concession and barely knew him. Was that kind of electricity really possible between two people? Was this what love at first sight was about: an indescribable pull to be with someone else?

I pulled on a fresh dress and went downstairs. Momma was out in the back with the wash tubs scrubbing laundry. I could see by the amount of wash already hangin' on the lines that she'd been at it for quite some time.

Remembering the sight of the judge in Momma's doorway and his kiss on my hand, I poured a cup of coffee and watched her work a while longer.

I sipped the bitter liquid, thinking about the things I'd always known about Momma. Not the things that a daughter knows about her mother—like the stories she tells at bedtime, her best recipe, or the way her whisper filled my ears when she cuddled me as a small girl—but the things I'd heard all my life about the enigma that was Emmaline Beaumont Breaux.

My mother had somethin' that most girls dreamed about. Some indefinable characteristic that caused men to fall in love with her.

"How could I have ever resisted her?" Daddy said to me. "I loved her from the minute I saw her, and I would've waited for her forever if that's what it took."

It wasn't a skill that Momma had, nor a trick or some bit of magic that only she knew how to perform. It wasn't even somethin' that Momma used to her advantage. Momma always implied it was as much a curse as a gift, for as easily as men seemed to fall for her, she would also fall in love with them.

Momma had the ability to see the good in even the most horrible people. She could find the parts of every person that were worthy of love, as if some songbird part of her soul would alight and return with the best part of another person. And she'd love them and feel bound to them for those best parts of themselves.

"You let me sleep late," I said in an accusatory tone when I finally stepped out into the yard.

She looked up at me, sweat already gathering at her brow line and her arms elbow-deep in the sudsy water. "You were up late last night," she said. "I figured you could use some more sleep."

"I wasn't up any later than you." I let the accusation hang in the air between us. Waited to see if she'd reach out and grab for it or if it'd hover on the breeze.

"No," she said in a quiet voice, "I don't guess you were."

She pulled a shirt from the water and wrung it out. She

carried it to the line and hung it up before returning for another. And then another.

Realizin' that Momma wasn't willing to talk about the fact that I'd found the judge in our house—in her *bedroom*—late at night, I set to work myself.

We spent the rest of the morning washing, wringing, and hanging laundry in complete silence.

While Momma started her sewing tasks, I folded the piles of laundry and stacked them into old potato sacks to be delivered to their rightful owners.

I had seven deliveries to make, and with the weight of each, I wouldn't be able to carry more than two at a time. I considered the position of the sun in the sky and the murky, sticky air that already clung to my skin. I cursed that we had to resort to this kind of work in order to survive.

"Make sure that Vieux Desbois doesn't get his laundry until you've got the coins in your hand," Momma warned.

"Yes, ma'am," I said as I reached for the first two laundry bags.

Vieux Desbois had a long and crafty skill at avoiding payment for services. His tactics ranged from leavin' delivery people standin' on the porch and never returning with payment, feigning a heart attack, and, my personal favorite, cryin' about his long-dead hero son who'd passed away while servin' our military overseas. Only Vieux Desbois had only ever had daughters; he hadn't known how to react when I started cryin' about my own pauvre defan who'd also, and just recently, passed away overseas. I got my coins that day, much to Vieux Desbois's surprise.

Despite the heat of the job, doin' the deliveries was my favorite task. It gave me a chance to get out of the house and see the people I'd grown up around.

My path frequently led me past the school. I'd sometimes

stand in the shade of a tree for a few minutes, watchin' the students as they stretched out in the grass readin' their books in the shade of the trees. I imagined them stretched out, studying for a test on some great philosopher or memorizin' the lines of an epic poem about the magic of love.

A poem came to my mind, one I'd studied while I was going to school in Charlotte: *The fountains mingle with the river, And the rivers with the ocean; The winds of heaven mix forever With a sweet emotion; Nothing in the world is single; All things by a law divine In another's being mingle-- Why not I with thine? See, the mountains kiss high heaven, And the waves clasp one another; No sister flower could be forgiven. If it disdained its brother; And the sunlight clasps the earth, And the moonbeams kiss the sea;-- What are all these kissings worth, If thou kiss not me.*

I'd loved that poem from the moment I'd first read it. It seemed a promise to me: that all love was connected, which meant that someday, I would find my own love—one to rival the power of the ocean. One that would reach to the heights of the mountains and skies. My thoughts turned to Remy and my heart revved in my chest. I felt the stretch of skin across my mouth as it spread into a smile and I remembered last night.

"You plannin' to go back to school?" Dixie had stepped up beside me and my heart leapt in surprise.

"Nah," I said. "Not until Momma and I have our own house."

She nodded and stepped to walk beside me as I continued with the laundry sacks.

"Where you headed?" I asked her. It seemed strange for Dixie to be out in the heat of the day. As I looked more carefully at her, I saw that she was made up real nice for so early in the day as well. Her snow-white hair had perfect finger curls. Her makeup was applied perfectly, right down to her ruby-red lipstick.

I stepped back and appraised her more thoroughly. "Dixie Bajolière, are you wearing stockings?" I gasped. "And new shoes?"

She giggled and pulled my elbow, leaning in conspiratorially. "Well, don't tell my parents, but I've kind of got a job," she said. "I'm on my way now."

"Why wouldn't you want your parents to know you got a job?" I asked. That was a surprising thing to consider, especially since so many people were lookin' for decent work these days.

"They wouldn't approve," she said. "But don't worry, it won't be a secret long. Half the town's already talkin' 'bout it. It's only a matter of time before my family knows."

"Where are you workin'?" I couldn't imagine her working at a job that could be as scandalous as she was making this seem.

"Breaux's General."

I gasped. "You work for the Grangers?"

"Yep." She giggled.

"Doin' what?" I couldn't keep the shock from my voice. In all my life I'd never imagined that anyone I knew would voluntarily get into business—or spend any time, for that matter—with the Grangers. *Well,* I reminded myself, *except for the time you spent with Remy Granger last night.*

She stopped and pulled away from me. "Well, Ophelia." She filled her lungs with a fresh breath of air before she continued. "I just lie naked on a bed in the back and wait for the urge to strike one of 'em."

My mouth fell open and one of the laundry bags slipped from my grasp, dropping onto the walkway.

"Oh, good grief, Ophelia." She slapped my arm and crossed hers across her chest. I saw the hurt in her azure eyes. "I sweep, I replace stuff on the shelves, and I'm learnin' to do some of the bookwork."

Relief took up a place in me and assured that I was breathing in a manner that would support life.

"I'm sorry," I said. "I should've known you was just jokin' with me."

I picked up the bag I'd dropped and we continued walking. We paused our conversation long enough for me to drop off the Millett's laundry and collect payment.

"I thought Mrs. Millett was doin' laundry services herself," Dixie said as we walked on.

"Nah, she's been helpin' with the shrimpin' now. She and Mr. Millett been tryin' to do all their business in N'Orleans."

As we neared Breaux's General, we paused in the shade and I asked Dixie the one question I hadn't yet been brave enough to broach. "How'd you come to work for the Grangers?"

She shrugged. "Eloi offered me the job."

"But…" I struggled with the best way to broach my deeper question. "Why?"

"What do you mean?" Indignation flashed through her eyes. "Are you askin' why anyone would dare give me a job?"

I didn't want to hurt her feelings. I decided that it was best to tell her exactly what it was that had been lingering in my thoughts since the night at Miller's Point. "Dixie, are you and Eloi Granger an item?"

"What makes you think that?" Her answer was smooth and well-rehearsed. But a flicker of truth sparkled in her eye and in the expertly concealed tug of a grin at the edge of her mouth.

"I was just curious," I said.

"Eloi was nice enough to offer me a job so that Marie wouldn't have to work in the store all day anymore. And that's all there is to that story." The way she ended her statement was without emphasis, leaving me to think that I'd been right.

She looked me directly in the eyes with an open and honest expression. She wasn't tryin' to convince me of anything. I knew she was just repeating the accepted-and-agreed-upon story about her work at Breaux's General.

And I also knew then that, whether the feelings were shared or not, Dixie had feelings for Eloi Granger.

"Just be careful," I told her.

Everyone in town knew that Eloi wasn't simply the owner of the store. He and his family had a long history of dealing in stolen property and, if the rumors were true, they were still in charge of one of the top bootlegging businesses in Southern Louisiana.

"I could say the same to you," she said. She waved and stepped off the sidewalk toward the store, calling over her shoulder, "You be sure and tell Remy that I said *hello*."

I realized very quickly that Dixie and I had perhaps fallen into very similar situations with very similar people. Only, it was her beau who scared me the most. Where Remy was mostly open and approachable, Eloi Granger seemed to have a lot of secrets. And I imagined, as the head of his family, he was willing to do anything to protect those secrets.

Momma was sure to wonder what had taken me so long with my first two deliveries, so I rushed back home.

As the screen door slammed into place behind me, I found Momma in the kitchen stirring a pitcher of lemonade. "You have a caller," she said and raised her brows at me to indicate that she was less than thrilled. "Back porch."

I stepped out onto the porch and right there, with a grin to rival the most perfect image of happiness ever conceived, sat Remy Granger.

He stood as I approached, hat in his hand, and offered me a slight bow.

"Ophelia," he said and reached to open the screen door as Momma came through with the tray of lemonade and glasses. "I hope you don't mind that I've come to call on you." He said it with all the innocent flourish of a true gentleman caller, and I ignored the fact that this was the same scoundrel—endearing though he may have been—who'd had his hand up my dress just the night before.

"I must say, this is quite a surprise, Remy Granger," I said. I sat primly on my chair as he held it for me, then he helped Momma into hers as well.

"I assume you're the one I have to thank for bringing Ophelia home last night?" Momma asked as she poured the lemonade. "Late," she added and threw me a caustic glance to let me know that she wasn't the only one harboring secrets from last night.

"Yes'm," Remy answered. "I do apologize for the late hour. I took her to my mère's for supper," he explained.

Momma's head tilted , her eyes burning with questions. "Supper?" The question was directed to me and so much deeper than the simple words she spoke out loud. "That was nice of your mère to invite Ophelia," she said pleasantly. "Please offer my thanks to her."

We engaged in small talk and, once I felt Momma had put Remy through a thorough inquisition, I tried to excuse myself. "I have more deliveries to make," I said, standing. "If I don't get back to it, I'll be delivering all night long."

"I could help," Remy said. "I've got Vieux Piersall's truck. We can just throw everythin' in the back and be done with it in short order."

"Could I, Momma?" I knew she'd be reluctant to allow me to get in a car with Remy Granger. I hoped her compassion would win over.

"I would hate to put you out, Remy," Momma said.

"It's really no trouble," he said. "I was hopin' to be able to spend some time with Ophelia. I'd be pleased to help her with her deliveries."

Momma looked at us both, pressed her lips together, then seemed to realize it was silly to insist I haul the bags all by myself.

"All right then, but you be home by supper."

"Yes, ma'am," I said and rushed to grab the other laundry bags.

"And, Remy," she said over her shoulder.

He stopped and turned back to look at her.

Momma turned in her chair and looked at him with her brows slightly raised. "I'm trustin' you with my daughter. I expect you'll prove that trust was well-placed if you ever want me to trust you again."

"Yes, ma'am," Remy answered. He reached out his right hand to relieve me of the two sacks I carried and scooped two others with his free hand.

"I'll be just one minute," I said to him as we passed through the front room. I ran up the stairs, dragged a brush through my hair, and secured several bobby pins in place. I smeared on a light red lipstick and shed my sweaty work dress for a lighter one with a wider neckline that exposed my collarbones. The dress skimmed across my hips and I imagined Remy's hands doing the same. My heart fluttered at the thought. I ran back down the stairs, scooped up the last bag of laundry, and called, "Thanks, Momma" as I burst through the screen door.

Remy waited by the truck, the door open in anticipation of my arrival. He let out a low whistle as I bounded out the front door, down the stairs, and tossed the laundry bag into the back of the truck.

I paused in front of him, grazing his body as I maneuvered past him to get into the truck. He leaned to my ear. "How'm I s'posed to keep my word with your momma when you come out here lookin' like that?"

I giggled as I sat on the front seat of the truck and he closed the door.

He leaned through the window. "You're even more beautiful in the daylight."

I turned to smile in appreciation.

Like magnets, our lips were drawn together. The urgency and excitement of last night returned, unhampered by having the truck door between us. We both pulled away, breathing heavy.

"Let's get your deliveries done," he said. "I can't stand to not be alone with you for another minute."

SIX

With Remy driving it took less than thirty minutes to deliver each and every bag of laundry.

"Where we headed?" Remy asked.

"I don't really know." As excited as I'd been to see Remy again and to be able to spend time with him, I hadn't really thought about where we would go.

"I s'pose a man with good intentions might take you to the library and read you some poetry or somethin'," he said.

"But where would *you* take me?" I asked.

He laughed. "I got an idea," he said and started the truck.

Moments later, we pulled up in front of Breaux's General and Remy helped me out of the truck. He held my hand as we walked up the stairs and into the store.

Eloi and Marie stood at the front counter. Their eyes sought each other out as if in confirmation of some earlier discussion.

"Well, there." Marie tried to put an airy tone in her voice. "What're you two gettin' up to?"

"I just helped Ophelia drop off her laundry jobs and thought we might take a picnic up the river," Remy said.

"That so?" Eloi asked, though he didn't really seem interested. He turned his attention back to the receipts he'd been counting.

"Well, that sounds nice," Marie said. "We got some nice apples from the orchards. You could take a potted hash and cook it up on the fire."

"Just be sure you pay for anythin' you take," Eloi grumbled without looking up from his work.

"Well, ain't this somethin'." Dixie walked through the doors from the back of the store. She had a broom in one hand and a canning jar of sweet tea in the other.

She set the tea in front of Eloi. He looked at her, gave a subtle nod, then turned his attention back to his work.

"Hey," I said. I was feeling uncomfortable in the store. It was more than the knowledge that this place no longer belonged to my family and hadn't for the past six years.

I felt in the core of my being that neither Eloi nor Marie would ever welcome me into their lives—or Remy's. I wished I could share the same comfortable sense of belonging that Dixie seemed to have there in the Grangers' store.

"Let me get a box put together for you," Marie said, then set about to do just that. She walked up and down the aisles, tossing in cans and packages of who knows what. She handed the box to Remy and slid in two bottles of cola as an afterthought. "That ought'a take care of anything and everythin' you got a taste for," she said.

"Thank you," Remy said before placing a kiss on her cheek. He walked to the door and leaned into the screen, holding it open for me.

"Yes, ma'am," I said, "thank you."

She smiled and followed me to the door.

"You have fun now," Dixie called, a lilt in her voice.

"I'll deduct the cost of the groceries from your pay," I heard Eloi's gruff voice call to Remy.

"You do that," Remy responded as if he hadn't a care in the world.

With the groceries in the back of the truck, Remy closed my door for me. As he turned, I was able to see across the road. Remy stopped briefly, seeming to have noticed the same, solitary figure sittin' on the swing outside of Piersall's Garage.

Though he was sitting in the shade and his features were difficult to make out, I saw Vieux Piersall nod. I wasn't sure if it was to me or to Remy, though. Remy nodded back and I waved to him as the car started and we drove onto the road between the businesses.

It only took a few minutes to get to the dock. Remy led me to a boat and held my hand as I stepped in. I took a seat at the front of the boat, facing back so that I could more easily talk to him. He leaned over, handing me the box, which I slid into place at my feet. He used the push paddle to shove away from the dock and maneuvered the boat until we began to skim over the rolls of the waterway.

After several turns through a labyrinth of channels I felt impossibly lost. The lilies and trees seemed to shift with each passing minute, exposing passages that were previously hidden. Remy negotiated a narrow outlet that opened into an overgrown waterway. The water was calmer and the boat glided gently across its soft crests.

Remy was strong. His chest rippled as he strained to propel us through the channel. The muscles of his arms flexed, straining against his shirtsleeves as he navigated the boat around the boscoyos and into deeper waters.

The paddle ruffled the water as Remy pushed us along. Fallen tufts of moss danced on the surface of the waves. In the distance a whooping crane trumpeted a warning to its mate. The songs of smaller birds paused as if they, too, were heeding the warning.

I leaned my head back, determined not to stare at him. I closed my eyes and let the sun warm my face. A cool breeze skipped over my skin and loosened the waves of my mahogany hair. The wisps caressed my neck and shoulders and I shivered at the tickling sensation.

Lord, how I had missed the bayou, I realized. Despite all the trouble my family had experienced, I was convinced that every good thing in the world started and ended in Southern Louisiana.

Remy turned the boat into a narrow channel. There were hand-painted signs warning trespassers away. *You WILL be shot*, they all read.

My startled response must have been evident because when I looked back at Remy he smiled and said, "It's okay. This is our camp."

There were a number of houseboats and fishing camps that had obviously been abandoned for quite some time. Small houses on the banks barely stood, teetering on stilts and straining under the weight of branches and debris that hung from all sides.

"The hurricane in '26 ruined most of 'em," Remy said, acting as tour guide, which I appreciated since it had been six years since I was last in Plaquemines Parish. "Houma got the worst of it, but we took a wallop."

Remy lifted a hand to shield his eyes from the sun. He scanned the ruins, shook his head, and resumed piloting us across the waterway.

"The flood in '27 finished off the rest," he said.

It was sad for me to see that, even in such humble surroundings, everything could be taken away in a moment.

After navigating several more turns, Remy pulled the boat up to the one camp we'd seen that had weathered the storms and the passage of time. It seemed to be barely standing, but there it was nonetheless.

The house was similar to the ones I'd been to with Daddy and my uncle—Nunkie Louis—when I was young. The exterior walls had once been painted red. Now they were simply grayed slats with pink veins spidering along the cracks.

Branches rested atop the roof, shielding it from the sun. Gray metal spanned the rafters to cover the porch along the front of the house. It was the only thing that looked as if it'd been added recently. In the bayou, a good porch covering is important. You never know when you, or a passing fisherman, will need to take refuge from a storm.

The boards on the dock were each bowed to different degrees. It seemed they could fold upon each other like the bellows of an accordion. I reached for the dock as we neared and the end of a slat crumbled away in my grasp.

"*Mais, jamais d'la vie!*" Remy exclaimed as he reached out a hand to slow the boat as well. "You broke the dock."

I leaned forward, my jaw tensed—I was ready to defend myself. I was fueled by indignation—and embarrassment. How could he think this was in any way my fault?

He held one hand out, as if to ward off an attack, and chuck-led. "I'm jokin', chèr."

I eased back onto by seat. I was surprised at how quickly I'd become defensive. *Why should I care so much what Remy Granger thinks of me?* But I did. I cared a lot more than I was willin' to admit.

Remy angled the boat alongside the dock and tied off before offerin' me a hand. My sea legs had long since abandoned me. While living in Charlotte I hadn't had much opportunity to go on boats. I grabbed Remy's hand tight as I heaved under the gentle rolling waves.

He pulled me close and mumbled in my ear, "Maybe I should carry you in, chèr? Make sure ya' get in safe."

I smiled, losing myself in the warm color of his eyes. "If you think that's best."

I squealed as Remy scooped my legs out from under me and carried me through the door, into the camp structure. He set me gently on an old couch that had been covered in worn quilts. His body followed mine, pressing softly into me and claiming a kiss for his effort.

My hands slipped behind his neck, pulling him closer. My body was desperate to resume the connection we shared last night.

"Chèr," he said, "I have to get the stuff." He pulled away.

"Leave it," I begged, pullin' at him.

He laughed as he extracted himself from my arms and stepped onto the dock to get the groceries.

When he came back inside, Remy seemed to go to great lengths to keep a respectable distance between us. He unpacked the box, which contained a hodgepodge collection of food items. There was canned meat, crackers, cheese, and snack foods.

"Well, there's definitely a variety." He laughed.

Remy carried the tins out to the porch where a makeshift kitchen had been set up under the awning. He lit a burner and placed the opened canned food into a pan on top of the flame to cook. While it did, we settled into a porch swing and watched the food begin to steam and then bubble.

We talked again about inconsequential things, Remy's arm resting across my shoulders and me pressed firmly into his side.

After we ate, we sat again, swingin' and watchin' the rise and fall of the water as it passed by us on its great journey to bigger places and greater adventures.

"Why is your momma sleepin' with the judge?"

The question was as shocking as it was intrusive. I pulled away from him immediately, putting as much distance between us on the swing as I could.

"I don't know what you're talking 'bout, Remy Granger." My voice was high and full of what I hoped was indignation, but realized was more like panic. "How dare you insinuate—"

"Ophelia." He slid to me as quickly as I had pulled away. "I ain't judgin' your mère. I was just wonderin' why."

I opened my mouth to deny the accusation again but stopped when I saw Remy shake his head, letting me know that he already didn't believe the story I was planning to make up.

The truth settled warmly around my shoulders like a knit wool shawl on a winter night. Ever since I'd come back to Plaquemines Parish, I'd denied Momma's involvement with the judge to everyone, including myself. I was tired of lookin' away from the truth when it was sitting so high and wide in front of me.

"Because we can't afford the rent otherwise," I said. Shame softened my voice and pulled my head low. "We're tryin' to buy a house. We just need a little more money, but Momma ain't gettin' paid like she thought she would."

Remy didn't respond, just wrapped his arm around my shoulder again. His fingers trailed along my shoulder and neckline as I spoke.

"The judge offered to let her move in without paying for the first few weeks. When she couldn't get a job, he offered her one, but it still wasn't enough to pay the rent. We've taken on the laundry and sewin' jobs to help. Momma is talkin' about takin' on some boarders now. She and I will share a room so there's room to take on two boarders. If we make them lunches and include laundry services we can get a better room charge from them. With that we should be able to get our own home before the year is up."

I cast a glance at Remy to see if my humiliation had done anything to change how he looked at me. I'd left Plaquemines Parish as a member of one of the two wealthiest families in town and returned six years later nearly living the life of the destitute.

Remy leaned into me and placed a kiss at my temple.

"But why *him*?" he asked. "Wasn't he the reason your family left to begin with? Why would your mère give in to him? Certainly someone else would have helped."

"He was the only one who offered a glimmer of hope," I said. As angry as I was at Momma for the choices she'd made lately, deep down, I understood her reasons. I understood her.

"He's always loved her and she thought he'd really help us. Momma just can't seem to see the bad in people." Even now, Momma didn't seem to be able to tell that the judge didn't have her best interests in mind so much as his own. The judge was driven by the same desire to claim Emmaline Beaumont, as he'd been all those years ago when he was little CheeChee Trudeau. It wasn't love for her that had ever driven him, it was a desire to lay claim to someone he'd always wanted, and who'd denied him.

"She seen the bad in me," Remy countered.

I turned to him. "I don't think there really is any bad in you, Remy Granger. I ain't seen none yet." I placed a hand along his cheek, trailing it down his neck and letting it rest on his chest. I leaned into him and laid my head on the other side of his chest. I marveled at the soft pillow of muscle that twitched below my cheek.

"I guess that makes me your judge," he said. "Because I'm full of bad, and for some reason, you ain't seein' it."

I looked up at him, appalled that he'd say something like that. "You ain't nothin' like him." I described my encounter with the judge the previous night after Remy had left me at home. "It was downright creepy," I said. I recoiled at the memory of the judge's mouth pressed against my hand. "Like he was propositioning me, right in front of my own mother."

Remy's body grew rigid. "You can't stay there," he said. "I don't want you anywhere near him."

"Anywhere else would be my choice, believe me. But that ain't gonna happen until Momma and I can buy our own house."

We sat quietly again. The sun had moved across the sky and was starting to drop into the western horizon.

"What if I could help you and your mère?"

I sat straight and looked at him. "Do you have six hundred dollars in your pocket that you're offerin' to give me, Remy Granger?"

"I don't have it right now," he said. "But I can get it, and it won't take the year."

"There's no way we could borrow that kind of money from you." I shook my head emphatically. "Momma wouldn't even consider it, anyway."

"It wouldn't be nothin'," he said. "I got no need for it right now."

"It's *six hundred* dollars, Remy," I said. "People on Wall Street killed themselves on Black Tuesday for losin' far less than that."

"But they needed it," he said. "And you and your mère do too. I ain't got no need for it right now. If it gets you out of the reach of the judge, I'd consider it a wise investment."

"We couldn't accept your money," I said. No matter how much I wished that weren't true.

In the back of my mind, I could imagine yelling "Yes" to Remy, collecting the money, and moving Momma into a house of our own the very next day. A house that had been paid for, and for which we'd only have to work to pay for the groceries and such. A place where we could have a fair chance at the life we'd had before Daddy died.

"I want to help." He was begging me now.

I could see in his eyes how it tortured him to know what the judge had done and said to me. I regretted having said anything.

I marveled at how simple it seemed for Remy to think about getting six hundred dollars. I'd never once thought that would be a simple thing for Momma and me to accomplish. Not even with both of us working toward the goal and me havin' dropped out of school to help.

Of course, Momma and I had never considered bootleggin' as a means to earn money.

I nearly laughed. Me as a bootlegger. Who'd ever believe that?

Suddenly a single clarifying thought filled my head. *Who would ever believe that I was a bootlegger? Even if I were standing in front of a revenuer with flasks of moonshine tied to my thighs, nobody'd believe it.*

I held his hands in my own and looked straight into his eyes. "Remy, could I work for your family?"

He considered for a moment. "I suppose we could put you to work. Of course, there's no way Eloi would let you take over any of Dixie's jobs."

"Not in the store," I said, shaking my head and holding his gaze until I saw understanding blow away the confusion that had clouded his eyes.

I nodded in confirmation of his silent realization.

He jumped up and walked away from me. "No." He leaned against the railing, shifting his weight from one foot to the other. He folded his arms across his chest, then dropped them and gripped the rail, before he crossed them again.

I watched him. An imploring look settled firmly on my face.

This was the one opportunity I'd found that would get me and Momma out from under the judge's thumb before it was too late.

"No way," he said.

"Why not?" I asked. "It would solve all of our problems. Momma and I could get enough money to get a house. We could get away from the judge—"

"No way, Ophelia," he said. "You got no idea what you're thinkin'. Bootleggin' ain't just a fast way to get your money. It's dangerous. You could get arrested. You don't know enough to stay out of other gang's areas, or how to even drive a car to avoid the Prohibition authorities. What're you gonna do the first time a revenuer pulls you over and questions you?"

I didn't offer any answers, and he didn't wait for any because we both knew I didn't have any to offer. I truly didn't know anything about being a bootlegger.

"Do you even know how to drive a car?" He was pacing now, the flight of ideas that scuttled through his brain carrying him from one end of the porch to the other. "It don't matter if you do, because it's a far bit of difference between drivin' to church on a Sunday and outrunnin' a bunch of cars filled with lawmen bent on makin' you an example for all the other bootleggers in the state."

He finally paused and looked at me. I could see in his eyes that he wished he'd be able to convince me to abandon my hopes of joinin' him in this pursuit.

"So, have we reached an understandin' then?" I asked with a bit of a quiet threat in my voice.

"An understandin' about what?" He was well and truly confused.

"That you are, in fact, a bootlegger." It wasn't a question, just a simple statement. There was no accusation in it, no excitement or judgment. It was a simple statement of what I, and everyone else in Plaquemines Parish, knew to be true: The Grangers ran a bootlegging enterprise.

"I can't put you in that kind of danger," he said. "I'll get you the money, but I can't involve you."

I stood up from the bench and walked to him. He was leanin' against the railing again and I leaned into him. I wrapped my arms around his waist and laid my head on his chest.

"I can't take money from you, Remy. It wouldn't feel right. And the only way for Momma and me to get away from the judge is for *me* to get the money for our house. I'm gonna do this, and the only way I can do it, the only way I can be safe, is if you help me."

I looked up at him and knew I'd put a ton of pressure on him.

"I can do this," I whispered and kissed the hollow place at the base of his neck. "I'm a smart girl. I'm not scared or prone to be impulsive." Well, I knew that to be a lie, but I could work on that. "And I can look out for you as much as you are lookin' out for me." I placed more kisses along his jaw line, up to his ear, and then across his cheek to his mouth.

Our kisses were hungry. Filled with a new edge of danger and resolve.

"I have to talk to Eloi and Sunshine," he said. "They have to agree."

"I'll go with you," I said.

"Maybe you should wait. There's bound to be yelling. A lot of yelling."

I thought about what a confrontation with Eloi Granger would be like. Sunshine had always been quiet and had a friendly air about him. I knew that he was as much a Granger as the boys who'd been born from the union of Marie and August

Granger, but he didn't carry the same dangerous, threatening air.

I couldn't decide what was more terrifying, the thought of being in a room with Eloi Granger's silent, unwavering judgment, or the thought of him yelling in rage.

"I'll go with you," I reaffirmed. "We'll go first thing in the mornin'. This is all to help me and my momma. I can face whatever your brother has to say."

I should've known that would be more difficult than I'd ever imagined.

CHAPTER
SEVEN

"What the hell are you thinkin'?" Eloi exploded before all the words had come from Remy's mouth.

Dixie was at the door to the back room immediately, broom in hand, pulling the doors shut. The store was closed and there was no risk of any customers overhearing us. Nonetheless, I heard a transistor radio switch on in the front of the store and the crackle as Dixie searched for a station. The sounds of zydeco echoed around the store walls.

Sunshine leaned forward on the table, shaking his head in disbelief, but he remained silent. He reached for a crumpled pack of Lucky Strikes and shook a bent cigarette from the pack. With one quick motion he struck the lighter against his leg. Yellow and orange danced together as the flame engulfed the tip of the cigarette. He drew deep, pulling the smoke into his lungs.

Sirus reached for the pack and followed suit.

"I already told you what was goin' on," Remy said.

I understood then that, although he had kept his promise to approach Eloi together about me working for them, Remy had already told Eloi about what had happened with the judge.

"I understand that ain't a good situation," he said, his voice still raised. He stood and his solid form and anger combined to make the threat of Eloi Granger seem far greater than it ever had before. Now, he wasn't just assessing me, he was furious and I was one of the root causes of that fury. "But what the hell are you thinkin' comin' in here—to *my* store—and talkin' this nonsense 'bout runnin' shine? Are you lookin' to get the dry raiders in our door?"

"Nah," Remy said. "Ophelia ain't gonna tell anyone."

From the other side of the table, Sunshine finally spoke up. "She might'nt not mean to tell anyone, but she got no reason to be trusted with the store business."

I noticed that, although the bootlegging was only being alluded to, all of their talk still centered firmly on the store. It was as if they were just talkin' about me workin' at Breaux's General.

"She might be just perfect," Remy said, pushing his point again. "Eloi, everyone's been lookin' for us lately. We cain't get by on any route to N'Orleans anymore 'cuz of the Moret Gang and the damn revenuers. Maybe if we had a moll to help us get through and set up some more drops, we could expand back over to the city. Them docks been sittin' empty since the businesses dried up. You know we need a way to get in there and set up buyers."

"You're talkin' crazy," Eloi warned. "There ain't no way your gaienne's got it in her to be on the outs with the law."

Did Eloi just call me Remy's girlfriend? More importantly, I knew he doubted me.

"Let her help me do some local runs. She can learn, Eloi. She's smart and she's got a solid reason to want to make good."

"The only one with a solid reason for this idea is you. You can get what you're wantin' from her without takin' the rest of us down with ya."

Remy lunged at him. Eloi stood tall, bracing for an impact he didn't seem entirely concerned would land. Sunshine jumped up and threw himself in front of Remy. He wrapped his arms firmly about his friend and pressed him back toward me.

"Everyone just sit down," Sunshine said. "Let's talk this over like men."

Remy untangled himself from Sunshine's arms and held out a chair for me. He and Eloi sat across from each other, and Sunshine sat between them, across from me.

Eloi pulled a cigar from his pocket. He bit through the end and spat it on the floor before lighting it. "I understand you wantin' to help her," he said to Remy. "But right now, the Grangers ain't nothin' but an annoyance to the authorities. You're talkin' 'bout settin' up a bigger operation, which'll bring more risk to us."

Remy shook his head, but Eloi continued. "And runnin' to N'Orleans? Don't you think every road from here to that city ain't already got at least five carloads of agents sittin' there, waitin' on runners? You're talkin' 'bout somethin' that'll put us square in the sights of the state and federal agents, not just the local boys."

"I'll get through," Remy said without a hint of doubt in his voice.

"*We'll* get through," I added, leaning forward so that everyone knew I wasn't just along for the ride. I intended to be a full participant in everything. This was my only option; I wasn't about to lose the chance.

I swallowed down every bit of terror that threatened to rise up in my chest as I looked Eloi Granger straight in the eye. "This ain't just about gettin' some spendin' money for a nice pair of shoes or a new dress," I said with as much conviction as I could muster. "This is about gettin' my momma away from the judge. It ain't no secret what's happened between my family and the Trudeaus. I got more reasons than anyone to make this work."

Although his expression didn't change, I saw a slight relaxation in Eloi's shoulders as if the degree of the fight in him had just been drastically reduced.

"I know you got your reasons," he said, "and I admire your being willin' to do anything to look out for your mère. But gettin' those deliveries up north ain't no easy thing."

"I know that." I let some of the fight out of my own posture. I had to get Eloi's support. I couldn't be in opposition of him.

"I got nothin' to lose at this point," I said. "I ain't gonna give up. It's in my blood to do whatever it takes."

He puffed on the cigar and then seemed to play with the smoke as he pondered. It swirled in his mouth for just a moment before he blew it out. "Your daddy ever talk to you 'bout what happens when people decide to start runnin' shine?"

Why would Daddy ever talk to me about that? Just because we lived around it didn't mean he knew nothin' about it.

"No," I said. "Why would he?"

"No reason." Eloi shifted in his chair, leaning back and assessing me silently. The cigar was lodged in the corner of his mouth. The smoke wafted around his face. He squinted one eye and leaned away from it, never breaking his gaze from where I sat.

"Look, I'm willin' to risk everything to get my momma away from the judge. *Anything*," I emphasized.

"There's certain things that I ain't willin' to risk," Eloi said. "People are relying on me."

"And I know you'd do anything for your family." I tried to appeal to some emotional side that I wasn't even convinced Eloi Granger possessed. "Just like I'm doing."

"It's more than his family," Sunshine said. "You ever notice that there ain't no families starvin' in Point De Concession? That ev'ry family's got food and a roof o'er their heads?"

I hadn't thought of it before, but what Sunshine said was true. Across the country, people were losing their homes and starving to death. Some folks had it so bad that they'd rather end it all than live another day in the grips of this crisis. But in Point De Concession, while money was tight, I couldn't recall seeing any empty homes or any families without a home.

"I didn't know," I said.

"Why would you?" Eloi looked at Sunshine, who lifted his shoulders in surrender. My spirits lifted. Sunshine and Remy were both on my side, I knew it. I only needed Eloi to consent.

"All right," Eloi said. "But the final decision ain't mine." He looked at Remy. "Did you ask the Old Man?"

"No," Remy said. I sensed reluctance in his voice. "I wanted to get your okay first."

Eloi turned to me. "We run our own operation, but we ain't in this alone. We run the business just like we learned the business—comme les vieux."

Just like the old people. I nodded. So much of the way everything was and had ever been in the bayou was based on what we'd learned from the generations before us.

"You gotta get the Old Man to agree to this," he told Remy. "And I ain't gonna be the one to ask."

Remy nodded. "I'll ask him."

"No." I stood up. "I'll ask him."

The eyebrows on every one of them stood up in surprise.

"Where do I find the Old Man?"

Dust turned up as I crossed the lot in front of Breaux's

General. The heels of my shoes wobbled on the small bits of gravel that were still covering the old lot. Neglect had settled into the land several years ago.

The wooden sign that hung across the street swayed in the cool breeze blowing in from the waterways. It was early and the wind would be warm soon, if it continued at all. The words on the sign had been chiseled into that oak long before I'd ever graced the earth. The white-painted letters had cracked and peeled away, leaving gapping flakes in the lettering. The sign was still clear, though. Even if I hadn't seen it a thousand times before, I'd know it: Piersall's Garage.

I saw him, swinging in the shade of the porch, before I'd set one hesitant foot on the road between us. One of his legs rested on an old wooden crate, the other pushed his large frame on the swing. Back and forth, the pace was unhurried.

Vieux Piersall neither called out to me, nor gestured in greeting. It was then I knew that Remy hadn't waited for me to talk to Eloi. And Eloi had, in turn, told Vieux Piersall.

My legs shook and resisted as I climbed the steps. They threatened to pitch me to the ground, to keep me from this ridiculous path I was determined to follow. I gripped the handrail; raw splinters of wood bit into the web between my thumb and first finger. I knew that the pain should've been immediate and intense, but I only registered it as a dull reminder that I was still capable of feeling.

"Mr. Roland," I finally greeted him.

He nodded once but said nothing. The tempo of his swinging didn't change at all.

I sat next to him without saying another word, keeping a good distance between us on the swing. *He ain't gonna attack ya'*, I chastised myself.

The silence exploded around me. I couldn't think of anything to say.

Vieux Piersall finally saved me the turmoil of startin' the conversation.

"So, you think you gon' be a runner?"

The words rolled from his mouth, one word melting warmly into the next. There was no malice in his voice, not even an air of disbelief, just a simply stated question.

"Yes, sir."

"An' how's it dat you came ta this plan? Dat Granger boy tell ya it's a good'un?"

"No, sir," I said, trying to relax my throat so that the quaver in my voice wasn't so evident. "I need to help Momma. I got to help get her away from the judge."

"That damn Trudeau boy." Vieux Piersall's gruff voice cut through the quiet. "He been noth'n but trouble since he learn't to walk on his own."

"I need to help Momma get her own house."

He resumed his silent swing, his lips pursed together as he contemplated.

As an impulse I said, "I never knew you was a bootlegger."

He turned his chin in my direction, and his right eye squinted while his left brow rose in question. "I look like I'm in any condition ta be runnin' shine?"

I didn't want to say "no, sir" for fear of being rude, so I stayed silent and let the rise of my own brows pose the question.

"I done my share, but I ain't no runner now."

"But the Grangers answer to you," I dared.

"And you do too," he said. He used one hand to lift the propped leg off the crate and lowered it to the floor. With both feet firmly planted on the groaning slats, he pushed himself off the swing, emitting a groan of his own. He placed the palms of his hands on his thighs and pushed himself to a full standing position.

"I do?" I asked.

"Yep." He assumed a slow, shuffling gait as the kinks of inactivity were worked out. He reached for the porch door and opened it then looked back at me. "I get three dimes for ev'ry dolla' you bring in. Eloi Granger gets two."

I'd done it! I'd convinced Vieux Piersall—and the Grangers—to let me work for them. I was gonna get Momma out of that house.

"Yes, sir." I tried to stand without leaping from the swing. I felt a strong urge to run over and hug him. Vieux Piersall had offered me my own personal salvation.

"You get nabbed by the rev'nuers, ya on ya own." He didn't give me a chance to reply. He stepped through the door. The sound of his hum was the only thing left in the wake of his slow, shuffling exit.

I forced my steps to be even and on par with my regular pace. Inside, though, I was jumping up and down, throwing my hands with wild abandon in the air.

There was no way to control the grin on my face. I felt the corners of my mouth pull up tight, tucking up under my cheek-bones. I was certain that each of my teeth was visible to anyone who might walk past.

I looked at the store as I crossed the road. Sunshine sat on the railing and Remy leaned over the top of the rail right next to him. Eloi sat in a chair just outside the door. All of their eyes were watchin' me for some clue as to whether I had secured the permission of Vieux Piersall. By the time I stepped into the street, they must have known for sure by my smile.

Sunshine clapped Remy on the shoulder and Remy took the stairs two at a time and met me before I'd crossed half the lot. I finally let my elation take over. I jumped into Remy's arms, wrapping my arms and legs firmly about him as he spun me around.

"You did it," he said. "You're in."

I kissed him deeply. "I couldn't have done it without you." The longer I held his gaze, the hungrier my body was for his. I forced myself to let go of him and resumed standing on my own two feet. It wouldn't do any good to be seen molesting him right here in public.

And, I thought, my rational and brand-new business sense taking over, *I won't be any use in helping their business if everyone in town knows I'm Remy Granger's gaienne.* If I couldn't help the Grangers with their business, I wouldn't be helping myself none either.

I looked at the store. Eloi Granger hadn't moved from his chair and his face still didn't betray his thoughts.

Dixie stood quietly just inside the screen door, watching everything as we approached. I wondered how long she'd been there—and how much she knew about the Grangers' business outside of the store.

Remy and I approached the bottom step and stopped to wait for Eloi's lead.

"Well, we best get in and make a plan," Eloi said, standing. He entered through the screen door without waiting to see if anyone else was coming.

There was no doubt in my mind, while Eloi might answer to Vieux Piersall about some things, he was firmly in charge of what happened within the Grangers' business.

We followed Eloi through the door—first Sunshine, then Remy and me.

In the back room of the store, we sat around the table. Dixie walked in silently. I hadn't heard or seen her, but Eloi's eyes, carefully watching her movements, let me know she was there.

Dixie set a jar of lemonade in front of each of us.

"Thank ya'." Eloi's voice was soft. He looked at her directly for the first time that day and offered her a nod. I knew in that instant that Eloi Granger was sweet on Dixie.

Dixie smiled at him before leaving the room and pulling the door closed behind her. *Is Dixie sweet on Eloi as well?* The thought nearly distracted me from the reason I was sitting in that room. I focused all of my attention on the room and the table, and each person surrounding it. This was it, that moment I had been searching for. This would be my only chance to save Momma from the influence of the judge.

I was about to become a bootlegger.

EIGHT

"Y ou're gonna work for Vieux Piersall every afternoon for a few hours," Eloi informed me that afternoon.

We were out behind the store in the shade of the old storage shed.

"Oh no, I'm not." I stood straight up from where I'd sat on the running boards of an old car. I boldly crossed to where Eloi sat, leaning against a post in his chair. My first finger, seeming to have developed a mind of its own, stuck straight out in his face. "Y'all told me that I was in. I'm a member of this gang now, and I didn't hire on to work in no garage. You ain't cuttin' me out already."

Eloi tilted his head just enough that I could see his piercing black eyes from under the brim of his hat. I obviously didn't intimidate him, even in my fury. I thought I might've actually seen a spark of amusement in his eyes.

"Relax," Eloi said. "Ain't nobody cuttin' you out." He pulled out a knife and began to clean under his fingernails like he didn't have another care in the world. "You may have noticed that ev'ry one of us has a job. How you gonna explain the money you'll be bringin' home if you ain't got a job?"

I had to admit—to myself at least—that I hadn't considered how to explain my sudden income. But what would I do in a garage?

"Why can't I work in the sto—"

"There ain't no jobs in the store," Eloi answered before I'd even finished my question.

"But if it's just for show. If I ain't really workin' in there, it won't hurt none to say—"

"No," Eloi said, leaving no doubt that he wouldn't change his mind or listen to my reasoning.

"Miss Ophelia," Sunshine spoke up. He'd been sitting quietly beside Remy on an old hitching post just inside the doors. He slid off and brought one of the old chairs nearer to me. "Ain't nobody tryin' to keep ya from workin' with us." It was rare to hear Sunshine speak so many words. His voice was smooth and warm, and I felt deep inside like everything that Sunshine Allemond spoke was the truth. "We just tryin' to be smart 'bout how you can work with us, so we all stay safe. If a nice girl from a good family suddenly starts runnin' round with the Grangers, people gonna talk."

"I understand that," I said.

"Your daddy worked for Vieux Piersall," Sunshine continued. "Stands to reason he'd give you a job to help you out."

"But Remy works for Vieux Piersall, too," I said.

"I'm gonna start goin' in the mornin's," Remy said. "I'll leave at lunch time. You ain't expected until three. We shouldn't have no cause to be seen there at the same time."

"Nobody should have any cause to put you together with the Grangers," Sunshine said. "So long as that's the case, you might just be our shinin' star."

"As long as the two of you ain't seen runnin' all 'round town together," Eloi said. The gruff tone in his voice jangled my nerves.

Remy explained—more kindly than Eloi would have—that they were goin' to teach me to run shine. The plan was that I'd be fully on my own. "Nobody'd suspect you. No revenuer's gonna detain a good girl from an upstandin' family on her way to her poor old auntie's house in N'Orleans."

I nearly laughed at his characterization of me. A good girl from an upstanding family? I was running with bootleggers. My momma was sleepin' with a man in exchange for a roof over our heads. And I was falling crazy in love with a member of one of the most notorious families in Louisiana, who as it turned out, wasn't as bad as I'd always been led to believe. *Maybe Remy is just as wrong about me as I've been about him.*

"The only way to pull this off is if nobody knows that ya'll are an item," Sunshine said.

Remy hung his head, as if he could neither bear to ask me to do this, nor stand my answer should I refuse.

I nodded. I understood the need to be discreet, but I hated it nonetheless. For all the years I'd spent avoiding the Grangers and fearing them, I wanted nothing more now than to yell from the courthouse steps that everyone had been wrong and that I was in love with Remy Granger.

"Who all knows?" Eloi asked. "It may be too late already."

"We was together at Miller's Point the other night," Remy said, shaking his head.

"That could be written off as a drunken night," Sunshine said. "And Sirus drove them home that night. Was a one-time thing far as anyone knows."

"Remy met my momma," I said to them. "Just once."

"Be sure she knows you ain't got nothin' nice to say 'bout him and that you never plan to see him again," Eloi ordered.

"Anyone else?"

"Dixie," I said.

Eloi's eyes snapped sharply to me.

"But she knows everything, right?" I couldn't imagine that Dixie could work in such close proximity to the Grangers and not know what they were up to.

Eloi set the front legs of his chair down, leaned forward, and leveled his eyes at me. "Don't you ever talk 'bout any of this with Dixie, you understand?"

The vein that ran along the thick muscles of his neck pulsated as he waited for my answer. Everything soft in his body was rigid, as though he might leap to attack if he didn't hear the words he wanted to hear.

I stared open-mouthed at him. Did he really think that Dixie didn't know? More importantly, how could he deny Dixie that knowledge? Shouldn't she be told so that she could make a decision on her own about whether she wanted to work for a man like him or not?

"Understand?" he demanded again.

"Yes," I said, almost breathless in fear at his intensity.

He stood and walked from the shed, toward the store. He didn't look back. In the distance, I heard the clang of the bell as he entered.

I looked at Remy and Sunshine for support.

"He's just lookin' out for her," Sunshine said. "Same as Remy here's gon' be lookin' after you, I assume." He clapped Remy on the shoulder.

Remy pushed him lightly. "Just like you look after *all* the girls, ain't that right?"

Their pushing evolved into several minutes of good-natured wrestling and shoving before they dissolved into laughter.

"So, I work for Vieux Piersall," I said. "And Remy works for him too. Eloi and Sirus work at the store."

Remy and Sunshine nodded.

"Where do you work, Sunshine?"

The smiles fell from their faces. Both shifted their weights and neither seemed to want to answer.

"What?" I asked. "Eloi said everyone has a job."

"He works for us," Remy said. "He works for our family just like his daddy did, and his daddy before him."

I was confused. Everyone in town knew that Sunshine's family had been tied to the Grangers for years, but nobody seemed to know what the Allemonds did for the Grangers or what the relationship was.

"Sunshine does whatever we need him to," Remy said. "It's been that way since they became free men and his great-granddaddy was killed tryin' to get a job that no white man would take."

"So, he works for you," I said and nodded to show that I understood and had no more questions on the matter.

"It's more than that," Remy said. "They're family." He said it so emphatically that for a moment I thought Eloi had come back in and said it himself.

Sunshine smiled at Remy then looked at me. He raised his eyebrows and grinned further. "And they never let me forget it, no matter how hard I try."

Remy gave him a gentle shove. "Okay," he said, turning to me, "it's time to turn you into a bootlegger."

He held the door to the car open and I climbed in. Before he closed it, he handed me a large hat with a wide, floppy brim. "Put this on," he said. "Don't want nobody to recognize you when we're driving."

I pulled the hat on, making sure the brim fell low over my eyes and along the sides. Thinking better, I unrolled the scarf I'd used to secure my hair that morning, tied it low across my brow covering my hair, then pulled the hat back on.

Sunshine climbed into the back and Remy pulled the car

slowly out of the shed. He jumped out to close the doors and secure them with bailing twine.

Remy drove carefully through town. It seemed that everyone recognized the Granger car and their curiosity was only increased when they noticed the unidentified lady in the front seat.

I was careful to keep the brim low and avoided looking at people directly.

"The most important thing about not being noticed," Remy said, "is to look like you belong. If you try too hard to not be seen, it only makes you stand out more."

"You're the one who picked the hat," I reminded him.

He smiled. "Well, for right now, we need you to *not* be seen with us. When you're on your own, though, don't ever drop your gaze when someone looks at you. You look them in the eye and smile like you got no problem and they'll doubt themselves more than they doubt you."

Once we left the center of town Remy picked up speed and I looked out the windows at the surrounding area.

"We're gonna drive around for a while," he said. "You gotta get to know all the roads in Plaquemines Parish. Who lives where, which land you can trespass on and which you better not be caught anywhere near. Then you gotta know Jefferson, Orleans, and Saint Bernard Parishes."

For hours we drove throughout Plaquemines Parish. We drove the main roads, back roads, old fishing trails, and places where I didn't even see how a car could stay on the road. At one point, Remy drove the car right through a low stream. The bouncing and jarring of the uneven surface caused my back to stiffen and my head, being tossed from side to side, felt like it might fall right off my spine.

We stopped at a diner and Remy went in to buy us each a cola. I opened the car door and stood just outside the car to stretch my back while I waited. "You want out?" I asked Sunshine.

"No, Miss Ophelia, I'm just fine here. I don't hardly get out this far from Point de Concession."

I hadn't thought much of the risks associated with being a Negro man in a place where he wasn't known. Suddenly, I felt the weight of being the one person standing between Sunshine and people who might like to do him harm.

I closed my own door and turned to lean against it. I met the eyes of everyone who looked from Sunshine to me with confidence burning in my eyes. I silently dared anyone to question the man in my car, and nobody dared give me a second look. I wondered what I would do if someone had asked.

"Remy's coming," I said over my shoulder to Sunshine, "then we can get going."

I nearly jumped in the car when Remy was halfway back.

"You in a hurry?"

"Yes," I said. "Don't you realize how dangerous it is for Sunshine to be left out here?"

He gave a quick laugh as he started the car and backed out onto the road. "That's why he stays in the car. Ain't nobody gonna mess with him if he tells them that he was told to stay in the car."

I was shocked at how little it seemed to bother either of them that Sunshine could be targeted at any minute, just because someone thought he was in the wrong place.

"I been lookin' after Sunshine longer than you, Ophelia," Remy said with a bit of warning in his voice.

"I thought I was lookin' after you?" Sunshine quipped.

As we drove farther from town, with the windows down and the breeze blowing through the car, I relaxed again.

Several miles away, Remy turned into a lot. A sign dangled by one rusted chain: *Fortunate Farms*. The slight breeze caused the sign to sway like a drunken old man, and I was sure that it would topple to the ground any second. Remy maneuvered the car through a narrow fence and onto a gravel and dirt—though now, mostly dirt—road. No Trespassing signs hung from the fence and trees.

I looked at Remy, concern etched on my brows.

"It was abandoned long ago," he said. "The flood wiped it all out, destroyed the buildings and the house. It brought in debris from up river and left it here. Not very fortunate after all." He shook his head at the irony.

He pulled the car to a stop a short way up the road. "We should be far enough from the road that nobody'll see us here."

Remy got out of the car, walked around, and opened my door. I took the hand he offered and stepped out onto the dirt. He held my hand and as we walked, I immediately felt dirt kick up and slide into my T-strap shoes. I knew the grains of dirt would rub and blister. The shoes were Momma's old ones and hardly fit my feet properly.

As we reached the other side of the car, Remy dropped my hand and reached out to run his own over the dark metal fender of the car. "This beauty is a 1927 Ford Model A," he told me. "I spent months making sure this is the fastest car in Plaquemines Parish." He laughed. "Hell, this might just be the fastest car in all Louisiana."

"That's what he tells ev'ryone anyhow," Sunshine quipped as he crawled from the back seat. "It is fast, though," he admitted and winked at me with a mischievous smile.

"It's very nice," I said, unsure of the proper etiquette when discussing automobiles or why Remy had brought me here.

"You're going to drive it," he said as if he sensed my question.

"But I don't know how to drive," I admitted. My nerves fluttered at the thought of being in control of such a huge piece of machinery.

"Well, Ophelia, that's gonna be important if you're plannin' to be a bootlegger." He reached for my hand, placed the key in my open palm, then folded my fingers over it. "Or were you just plannin' to carry all those jugs of moonshine in your arms and walk across the Louisiana bayou country and up into N'Orleans?"

"I guess I hadn't really thought about it," I said.

Remy and Sunshine cast a look at each other and then at me. I knew they were both waitin' for me to change my mind, to admit that I was in no way meant to be a rumrunner, and that they should probably take me home.

But there was no way that was going to happen.

I wasn't doing this for myself or for some fun. I needed the money to save Momma from the judge, I reminded myself. I was committed to doing whatever it took to make sure Momma got away from him.

"Where do I put this?" I asked and let myself into the car. I found the ignition easily, slipped the key in, then rested my hands on the steering wheel as I waited for Remy and Sunshine to jump into the car with me. I'd met the limits of my skill level rather quickly, and my stomach flittered high under my ribs. I gripped the steering wheel so that the shaking in my hands wouldn't be so apparent.

I tried to pay attention as Remy explained which pedal was the clutch, which was the brake, and which was the throttle. Next, he explained how to change gears.

"How do I know which one?" I asked.

"Which one what?"

"Which gear to use?"

He looked back at Sunshine and, in the mirror, I saw

Sunshine shake his head and wipe his hands across his head. At least they were smiling...for now.

Remy went over the gears with me again, and the succession of each. We covered how to gear up as well as down.

It took some time, but I finally felt comfortable. I could quickly answer every question that Remy and Sunshine asked me about operating a car, shifting, braking, and steering. I was filled with pride at how much I'd accomplished already.

"All right," Remy said, "fire it up. Let's see what you've learned."

"What?" All the confidence fled from my body like a herd of rabbits fleeing a ferocious lion.

"Start the car, Ophelia," he urged.

"Oh no, Remy Granger." I opened the door, got out, and slammed it shut. "There ain't no way I'm drivin' this thing."

He laughed as I stood there, arms crossed and fuming.

"Don't you realize that talkin' about doing somethin' and actually doin' it are two very different things? You're gonna get me killed," I nearly yelled, my fear swelling.

"You ain't gonna kill us, Ophelia." Remy was tryin' to control his laugh as he saw how much madder I was getting. He switched to a begging tone. "Please, Ophelia, get in the car. Trust me, you can do this. I *know* you can."

Fear had caused me to grow roots. I stood my ground.

Remy crawled across the front seat and let himself out through the driver's door. He stood close; my arm brushed against his chest as he leaned in and whispered in my ear, "You can do this, Ophelia. I *know* you. I *know* what you're capable of when you set your mind to a thing."

The heat of his breath and the warmth of his words in my ear melted my resistance. I leaned slightly into him.

"You can do this, mon chèr." His lips brushed against my ear as he spoke, melting away any resistance that lingered in my body.

He took my hand and crawled back into the car, pulling me with him.

I sat in the seat and reached to close the door.

My palms were sweaty as I gripped the cool, rigid steering wheel. I took a deep breath and blew it out slowly, trying to conjure all that I'd learned only minutes ago about driving a car. It seemed as though every bit of information had flown from my mind the minute I realized I would be putting that knowledge to use.

"Push in the clutch." Remy's voice was soft.

My leg shook as I did. Not from the effort of pushin' it, but from my nervousness.

"And now the key," he said.

I turned the key and the engine rattled and then caught. The sputtering of the engine eased my nerves. I allowed my heart to settle into the hum of the engine, to feel its consistent purr.

"When you're ready," Remy said. "Just take it slow."

I nodded, still unable to speak, but my thoughts were coming back. *The gears*, I slipped it into first gear and lifted my foot from the clutch as I pushed my other foot gently against the throttle. The car lurched forward and then stopped with a jarring suddenness, nearly throwing my forehead into the top of the steering wheel. The engine was no longer running.

"It's okay," Remy said. "You just let up on the clutch too fast. It takes some practice, but you'll get it."

I tried again. And again. And then again.

After several more attempts—and failures—I threw my hands up, frustrated. "I'm gonna break the damn car!"

Remy and Sunshine were both smiling, tryin' to support me. I could see in their eyes, though, that they wondered if I would be able to do it.

"Just relax," Remy said. "I *know* you can do this."

I closed my eyes and tried to relax my breathing. I had to quell the fury of frustration swelling in my chest.

I imagined Momma in her own house; in my mind she was sittin' on her porch, rocking and enjoyin' her evening. There was no washing or stitching to be done. No renters to cook for or clean up after. Most importantly, there was no judge. Just me and Momma.

I opened my eyes, nodded in determination, and turned the key. The engine hummed to life again. I lifted my foot from the clutch while applying an equal pressure to the throttle. The car rolled slowly. I felt the tug as the engine tried to pull us along. The tires were rolling, the engine noise increased, and then the car jerked and lurched. I tried to push the gas, then changed and pushed the clutch back in. The lurching stopped, but the engine was still running.

I looked at Remy.

"You moved us," he said, smiling. "We moved."

I laughed. It hadn't been that much of a success. "We're a solid five feet farther than when I started," I said.

"Well, then you're five feet closer to bein' a rumrunner." Sunshine laughed from the back seat.

It was only a few more attempts until I managed to get the car started and shift through the next gear. We practiced goin' up and down the old farm road several times before I felt comfortable to try adding speed to my skill list.

The straight roads were fine but navigating turns, especially with any amount of speed, proved difficult. A few times, Remy took over to show me how fast it could be done. I was impressed by how smoothly Remy handled the car, both on the straight roads and around tight corners. He never panicked, even when the wheels spun under us and seemed to go in the opposite direction than we intended.

"The most important thing is to not panic," he told me as I tried the rapid corners again. "The car will respond the way it's s'posed to, it's you who needs to learn how to respond right when it all seems to be going wrong."

The sun was starting to slip low in the sky.

"I think you done pretty good for your first day," Remy said.

"Can I drive us home?" I didn't want to stop. The feeling of being in control of such a big and powerful machine was intoxicating.

"I s'pose," Remy said, "but on the roads you gotta mind the laws."

All the way back to Point de Concession, Remy told me everything he could think of about driving and what could go wrong and how I should respond if it did. He also pointed out the roads just outside of Plaquemines Parish that I was to avoid.

"That's Moret territory," he said. "Don't ever get caught on their routes. They'll shoot you without asking questions."

I made it a point to remember which roads he'd pointed out.

Remy handed my hat to me before we entered the edge of town and I pulled it tight over my head again so that nobody would recognize me.

When we got to the store, we pulled into the shed and Sunshine climbed out to close the doors behind us.

Dusk had settled over town and it would be hard for anyone to see that it was me who was coming from the shed, so I left the hat in the car.

"We have a run later," Remy said.

My heart leapt. A real run. It was official; I was about to become a tried and true criminal.

"It's a small one," he said. "We pick up. We drop off. We ain't gonna see nobody. It's as simple as they get."

"Okay," I said. "When do we go?"

"Not until late. Why don't you go get somethin' to drink? I'll wrap up some things then drop you home to rest a bit." He pulled me in for a kiss. My body, already alight with energy and excitement, nearly exploded at his touch.

"Go on in and tell Dixie I'll square up for whatever you want." He smacked my rear end, then went to pull the doors closed behind me.

I was so filled with excitement, I nearly ran all the way to the store and up the steps. It was only the knowledge that I shouldn't draw attention to myself that helped me maintain a natural gait and demeanor.

"What can I get ya?" Dixie asked as soon as the bell jangled.

"I'm so thirsty I'll drink anything you got," I told her. "Remy said he'd take care of it. I don't have any money on me."

"Don't you worry about it." She smiled. "Eloi ain't gonna go broke from a glass of lemonade. And if he does, he can blame me."

She went behind the counter on the side of the store and returned with two glasses of lemonade. "Let's go sit on the porch," she said. "Ain't nobody coming in this time of night, anyway."

We carried our drinks to the porch and sat side by side on the swing that my grandfather had hung the day after he married my grandmother. He'd hung it so that she'd always have a place to sit when she visited him at the store. It was also meant to entice her to be there as much as possible—he always said he just couldn't stand knowing she was out in the world being beautiful without him there by her side. Grand-mère was soon spending all of her time at the store, working alongside Grand-père, right up until each of her babies was born.

"Where you been all day?" Dixie asked.

"Just around town, tryin' to learn where everything is again."

"How nice that Remy was available to take you out to do

that." She took a sip of her lemonade. A small smile played about her lips.

Eloi's warning came back in my head like a warning siren, *Don't you ever talk 'bout any of this with Dixie. You understand?*

"Yeah," I said. "It was nice he was available today. It'll make it easier for me when I'm tryin' to get around town myself." I sipped my own drink. "I'm gonna be doin' deliveries and whatnot for Vieux Piersall."

"Mmm-hmm," Dixie said.

I sipped at my drink again. I hated to keep secrets from Dixie, but I also understood where Eloi was coming from. Keeping Dixie in the dark was the only way to keep her safe. She couldn't be implicated in the Grangers' illegal activities if she didn't know about them.

"I'm not so stupid as everyone thinks, ya know," she said. Her voice was low, but I didn't sense any anger in her tone.

"What do you mean? Nobody thinks you're stupid."

She set her lemonade at her feet and turned toward me. She reached for one of my hands. "Ophelia, I know you're sweet on Remy, and that he's sweet on you."

I blushed. I couldn't control my reaction to her statement any more than I could control the rush of my blood when Remy stood near me or the thrill of my heart when he touched me.

"I'm happy for you," she said. "Remy is so good. He'll look out for you forever."

I smiled. "He's amazing," I whispered. "But I can't tell anyone else, Dixie." I had to keep the secret as Eloi and Remy had told me, and I had to start by controlling what Dixie knew about us. "He's a Granger, and Momma wouldn't understand."

"Your momma's been in love before," she said and rubbed my arm. "If anyone knows what it's like to love the wrong person, it's your mère."

Had anyone else said that, I would've immediately been

101

furious. But I knew Dixie didn't judge my momma. She was just speaking the facts.

"I don't think she'll be happy that I'm with Remy," I said, trying to take control of the conversation. "I'd rather she just not know."

"I think she'd accept the fact that you're in love with a Granger better than she'd accept the fact that you're bootleggin' with them."

The lemonade I'd just sipped swelled into my upper throat, nearly choking me. I controlled the flow of the fluid and swallowed it down, but I couldn't stop my eyes watering and the citrus burning my nasal passages.

"What are you talkin' about?" I whispered.

"Please, Ophelia." She shook her head. "I told you I ain't stupid."

I turned away from her and pushed myself farther down the swing. "I ain't s'posed to be talkin' to you about this," I hissed at her. "I can get in trouble."

"With Eloi?" She smiled and shook her head. "He's just tryin' to protect me, but I got eyes and ears, Ophelia. I knew what I walked into when I came here."

I couldn't help but feel relieved. "Are you and Eloi...?" I didn't know how to finish the question.

"He kissed me," she said. She looked up at the sky like she was remembering it, perhaps reliving it. "Twice." A sad look came over her. "But, he won't touch me beyond that. He's afraid I'll get hurt. Or arrested. It's a dangerous business, Ophelia."

"I know." Our whispered conversation only enhanced the feeling of danger that lingered around me since I'd decided to join up in the Grangers' business.

I felt a sadness settle over me. I'd known when I'd seen Eloi Granger watching Dixie that he had feelings for her. I'd known that first day I saw them in the store that those feelings were shared and ran deep. What I didn't know was that Eloi Granger, the hardened, expressionless man who caused me to quake in my shoes any time he looked at me was so deeply in love with my best friend that he didn't dare act on it for fear of hurting her. But, I realized, he also couldn't bear to distance himself from her either. It was why Dixie was working in his store, a job that Marie Granger had always, and could certainly still hold.

The heavy boot steps came around the corner. Eloi stopped suddenly. Remy, who'd been following close behind, nearly ran into him. Eloi took in the sight of Dixie and me sitting together.

"What's going on here?" he asked.

"Nothin' much," Dixie answered airily. "It's just been such a hot day we were sittin' here havin' some lemonade. Let me get you some." She jumped up and disappeared through the door before he could object.

Not that he would. If Dixie tells him he needs a drink, I have no doubt he'll take that drink. I smiled to myself, warmed by the knowledge that Dixie was loved. I only hoped she was truly protected from the danger that existed in being loved by Eloi Granger.

I smiled at Remy and realized we weren't very far different from Eloi and Dixie. At least for now, we would be hiding our relationship.

"Let's get you home," Remy said and reached for my hand.

"You get that delivery on time," Eloi said as we walked down the steps. "No second chances."

Remy didn't answer but led me around the back of the corner to the old truck.

"He doesn't think I can do it, does he?"

"He's just bein' cautious," Remy said. "Eloi's the head of the family. If anyone gets nabbed, we're all at risk, and the fault will be on him."

"Why would it be on him?" I asked as I climbed into the truck.

Remy stopped, his arm resting over the door. "Because that's the way Eloi is. If he can't keep everyone safe, he'll think he failed." He closed the door and walked around to the driver side.

I'd learned more about Eloi Granger in the last twenty minutes than I had in my entire life. Suddenly, he wasn't such a scary figure—he was a man who took responsibility for everyone else on his own shoulders. He looked out for his family, and he looked out for his friends and their families. He even looked out for the people who lived in his town. And he was willing to forgo the fulfillment of love to keep the girl he loved from being entangled in the danger that went along with being near him.

Remy pulled the truck to the side of the road and parked around the corner from my house. "I'll pick you up at one," he said.

"I'll be ready."

Exhaustion had suddenly settled over me and I gave Remy a chaste kiss—well, maybe not chaste, but certainly more so than all of our previous kisses—and walked to my house.

CHAPTER
NINE

"**O**phelia Beaumont Breaux, where have you been all day?"

I'd tried to sneak into the house, but Momma was sittin' at the kitchen table darning socks.

"I'm sorry, Momma," I said.

"I could have used your help today," she said. "I ended up with twice the laundry to wash this mornin', and Mrs. Oliver offered to pay me to can her tomatoes this year. I've got boxes of jars on the back porch that need to be rinsed."

Guilt washed over me. Not only was Momma depending on me to help her work, I had to lie to her about where I'd been all day.

"I'm sorry, Momma. I didn't realize you'd have so much work today."

I felt like I could drop from exhaustion, but I sat at the table, grabbed some stitching, and got to work.

"I got a job," I told her.

"You did?"

"It's only part-time," I said. "But it'll help some."

"Well, I suppose anything extra helps, doesn't it?" She

smiled and looked at me with pride in her eyes. So far as Momma knew, I had gone out and gotten a regular job to help out.

I could never tell her that I was learning to run shine. *Maybe after I get the money for the house?* No, not even then. I knew she wouldn't accept the money if she knew where I'd gotten it. She might just walk out of any house we bought if she found out I'd earned my money illegally.

"Where're you gonna to be working?" she asked.

"For Vieux Piersall," I said.

She set the needle and the sock she'd been working on in her lap. Her eyes narrowed and she studied me.

"Daddy used to work there," I said, as if that were my sole purpose for working there.

"Yes, I know," she said. "And what will you be *doing* for Vieux Piersall?"

"I don't know for sure yet," I said. "Anything he needs, I suspect. I'll sweep and clean up. Maybe I'll even learn to pump gas and put on a tire." I laughed, trying to divert her questions with humor.

She stared at me, a look of worry firmly etched on her face.

"It's a job, Momma. I ain't worried if I get dirty, and you shouldn't be either."

"I know," she said and picked up the stitching again. "I just wish you didn't have to work. You should be in school."

"Worryin' about what should be ain't gonna do us no good," I told her. "We do what we need to in order to get by. No regrets," I said, mimicking something she told me once before.

"No regrets," she said with a nod.

After excusing myself to go to bed, I pulled my chair up to the window in case I fell into a deep sleep and eased myself into it.

Sleep didn't come easy. My toes tingled and cramped,

longing for a release of pent-up energy. I tapped my toes to the steady beat of some unseen metronome.

My mind raced with a whirling tornado of thoughts. *What am I thinking? I'm no bootlegger. Is it worth a lifetime in prison if I get caught?*

I thought of Momma being forced to rely on the judge for a home. As determined a woman as Momma was, I knew she was vulnerable, too. Losing Daddy had damaged her. She only saw the judge as a friendly port, somewhere she'd be safe. She forgot that he was the tempest that had cast us into this storm to begin with.

The tingling in my feet rolled into bigger waves and spread up into my belly. I didn't want to risk going to jail and leaving Momma. *But I'll be damned if I leave her at the mercy of that bastard.*

Through the milky light of the moon, I saw the clock face. It read 11:08. I had to rest, so I leaned back, closed my eyes, and tried to exhale my swirling thoughts. Then I did the same for the roiling energy in my body.

A dog barked down the road and I sat up, shrugging the sleep from my bones. It was 12:45. I ran my hands across my eyes and a brush through my hair. I grabbed a sweater and snuck down the back stairs.

Remy was waiting behind the bushes.

"You ready?"

I nodded. "Nervous," I admitted in a hushed voice.

Remy grabbed my hand and led me around the corner to where a car sat. I hadn't seen this car before and, for a moment, I worried we'd already been caught by the revenuers.

"You got no reason to be nervous," he said and opened the door on the Buick sedan for me. "This is gonna be an easy one. The drop changed a bit from what we was expectin' to run tonight, but it'll be okay." He closed my door, got behind the wheel, started the car, and pulled onto the road. A few blocks away, he pulled over into the lot of a boarded-up tavern. "If anything does happen," he said, "I'm gonna do my damnedest to get us as far away as possible."

I nodded.

"Always remember that we can get a new car and we can get more liquor. What's important is that we look out for ourselves. You gotta listen to me, Ophelia. If I tell you to run, you take off and you don't look back."

"Okay," I said. I tried to portray confidence, though I didn't feel it.

What was I thinking? I'm not an outlaw. I'm a poor girl from a privileged family. That don't make me ready to live on the outskirts of the law. I pressed my palms together and held them between my thighs to control their shaking.

"Promise me that you'll run," he said.

"I'll run," I said. "I promise."

He started the car and we pulled out of the lot slowly. "We're picking up fifteen gallons of shine from one spot and transporting them to another. There ain't a lot, but it's enough to go to jail. If you're ever nabbed, you don't know nothin' about the shine. You just say some man paid you five bucks to drive a car and leave it. That's all you say, got it?"

"Yes," I said a little more forcefully than I'd expected. I knew Remy was trying to prepare me, tryin' to do everything he could to make sure I was safe if either of us were caught. But the constant stream of instructions was doing nothing to settle the jangling in my nerves.

A mile outside of town, Remy pulled onto a small road, barely noticeable for the overgrowth that covered it. He turned off the lights and continued driving until we'd crested a hill at the line of trees. On the back side of the hill he pulled the car over and turned it off. We sat quietly, listening for any indication of the law.

Bullfrog calls and the symphony of sounds from the bayou filled the night. Remy's eyes scanned the tree line and the road ahead of us. His gaze slowed as he took in every motion—from the fluttering of leaves, to the flight of winged creatures hunting for a meal.

I scanned as well, using the silence in the car and peaceful surroundings to help calm my nerves.

"Do you see anything out of place?" he whispered.

"No," I said, "I don't think so."

"If you ever see anything—or just *feel* like somethin' is off—you leave right away," he said.

I nodded. I knew that if I spoke, my nerves would rise to my throat again and I might just get sick right then and there. *What kind of a bootlegger gets so nervous she pukes?*

"All right," Remy said, opening his door. "Let's go."

I opened my own door and followed him to the base of a group of oak trees.

Remy reached under dried moss that had fallen and accumulated at the base of the trees.

"Give me your hand," he whispered and reached for me.

I leaned closer, giving him my hand, which he grabbed by the wrist. He pulled my arm until my hand was under the moss with his. I had to lower to one knee as he pulled at me. And then I felt it.

A rope.

I looked at Remy and he nodded, indicating that I should lift up on it.

With my legs stabilizing me, I pulled up. The moss rolled aside and a heavy board tipped up from underneath it. Remy helped push the board aside. And there, in a shallow culvert, clear as it could be in the moonlight, were fifteen gallon jugs of moonshine.

I gasped. The thrill of adventure sped my heart. For some reason, when I looked at those jugs, I found them to be beautiful, and I cherished them immediately. They signified everything that I needed and wanted. They were my hope, my chance, and Momma's freedom.

"Grab what you can," Remy said and gathered several jugs in his own arms, "but don't take so many that you can't handle them. If we break 'em, we have to pay for 'em."

I lifted one. It was surprisingly heavy, so I chose to carry one in each hand. The uneven ground made carrying them more difficult, as did the shadows cast by the moonlight.

At the car, Remy set his jugs beside the tire, leaned in, and pulled at the back seat until it lifted. He pushed the seat to the side, revealing an empty box that had been concealed underneath.

I grinned at the cleverness of hiding the moonshine under the seat. I'd imagined we'd just be putting the jugs in the back and hoping for the best.

It took several trips to retrieve all the jugs. Remy pulled a blanket from the floor. He shook it open and proceeded to tuck it over and between the bottles.

"Cuts down on any noise if they bump together," he said.

Bootlegging was far more involved than I'd expected. Would I ever be able to anticipate—and prevent—everything that could possibly go awry?

Remy slid the seat back in place then handed me a cigar box from under the front seat. "We leave this," he said and handed it to me.

I lifted the lid. "There's so much," I whispered. I could've taken that money and probably made up the difference in what Momma needed for a house. I knew that I couldn't, of course—

that money belonged to whoever brewed the shine. I placed the box in the hole, we heaved the board back in place, and then pulled the moss to cover it.

Remy picked up a fallen branch and wrapped a bit of moss around the end. He used it like a broom, erasing our footprints and mussing up the leaves and twigs that lay nearby.

"Always cover your trail," he said. "A drop location is only good for so long. No sense making them obvious to revenuers and do-gooders before we've gotten our use out of it."

As we drove the darkened roads, I tried to keep track of the turns we'd taken and where we were.

Remy turned left onto a familiar-looking road.

"Isn't this Moret territory?"

He smiled. "It was, until Claude Moret sold some of his liquor to a revenuer yesterday mornin'."

"But he still has his people operatin', right? They'll find out that we crossed lines."

"Claude Moret cain't supply his buyers, so someone has to," he said. "Don't worry, we'll be in and out of there before anyone knows who we are."

"They'll know you," I said.

"Maybe," he said. "If they see my face clear."

My heart lurched. Then I had an idea. "They won't know me," I said.

Remy didn't answer.

"Tell me what to do," I said. "Tell me what I say to them."

"No way, you ain't doin' this."

"You said yourself that if they get a good look at you, they'll know who you are. They won't know me from Eve," I said. "If you tell me what to say, I can do this, Remy."

"There ain't supposed to be nobody there when we drop," he said. "We drive in, we unload, and we drive right back out."

"But if there's someone there?"

He didn't say anything for the longest time. Each minute he was silent, I knew with more certainty that this was more dangerous than even Remy had anticipated.

I also knew two other things: this was my chance to see if I had the nerves to be a bootlegger. And this was the biggest chance I'd have to prove to each and every one of the Grangers that I was the biggest asset their gang currently had.

"How long have you known this was the drop?"

"It just came up this afternoon," he said. "We was told that if we could fill the first order, we'd have a shot at the big buyer in Lafayette."

"But if Claude Moret gets out of jail or his gang figures out that it was the Grangers who sold to his seller, it'll cause trouble."

He nodded.

"They don't know me," I said again. "And we're not plannin' on anyone in Plaquemines Parish bein' able to put you and me together any time soon."

I don't know how, but in the course of five minutes, I'd come up with a plan and convinced Remy that it was the only option if, in fact, the buyer had people waiting. I said a silent prayer, hoping we'd pull up to find the shed as empty as we were expecting.

The small town was dark as we approached. No lights shone through the windows of houses or the businesses on the main thoroughfare. At the end of the town was a rundown restaurant. The windows were boarded up and warning signs were posted on the covered windows and doors. I didn't have to read the signs to know what they said: Closed for Violation of the National Prohibition Act. That same sign clouded the windows of thousands of businesses in Charlotte, Plaquemines Parish, and every town Momma and I had driven through between the two.

Remy pushed in the lever to turn off the lights and drove slowly around the building. In the back of the restaurant was an old barn, as expected. Both of us strained our eyes as we approached the structure.

"I don't see anything," I said and let out a relieved breath. "It's just the barn."

Remy stopped the car just short of the doors.

"I'll get it," I said and jumped out of the car. The doors were heavy and took a decent amount of effort to swing them open. Once they were both open, Remy pulled the car in and rolled to a stop.

I heard the click of a gun an instant before I felt the hard, cool metal pressing against my temple.

I raised my hands immediately. My heart sped up. I felt a sense of complete awareness wash over me. My brain began to categorize every noise and object that surrounded me, assessing the threat.

"Quiet, girlie," a gruff voice said. A man's strong arm wrapped around my shoulders and pushed me into the barn.

Lights from a truck, parked just inside, flipped on and flooded the interior with brightness. The truck was parked directly in front of Remy; he was effectively blinded.

"Let me see your hands," another man ordered.

Remy held his hands up and then placed them at the top of the steering wheel. I could see from the angle and movement of his head that he was checking the rear mirror for sight of me.

I had to take control of this situation before these men did.

"So, am I under arrest, fellas, or what?" I pulled my shoulders back and let my hips swing a bit more than I would ever dare under normal circumstances. "I'll need to call my lawyer. He's in Baton Rouge, but I'm sure he'll be able to get me by mornin'."

By the looks being passed around the six men surrounding

Remy and me, I knew that these men weren't revenuers. I just had to figure out if they were with Moret or the buyer. I was at a disadvantage having never seen the Morets—oh, and the fact that I was just puttin' on airs and had no real idea what I was doing.

"Well then," I said and dropped my hands to my hips. I looked around at the group of men then walked with as much confidence as I could toward the one man who was leaning against an old stack of hay and not holding a gun.

His trousers were in good repair. The buckles on his suspenders were polished, as were his shoes. While all the other men wore worn boots, this fella wore fine leather wing tips, which he'd probably picked up on a spending spree in New Orleans. With some girl he was tryin' to impress, I imagined.

I stopped in front of him, arms crossed and one hip pushed out in my best irritated stance. "You ain't the law, so how 'bout you tell me just who you are and why you're interferin' with my business."

"Since when is this your business?" he asked, challenging me as much as I had challenged him.

"Since Claude Moret got pinched and I have the product he can't supply."

"And who are you exactly?" he asked. He stood upright and stepped closer, circling me. He was close, his gaze moving up and down my body, lingering.

I refused to let him intimidate me. I looked him in the eyes, not letting my gaze waver at all. "My name is Marline Fortune, and I'm either your supplier, or I'm the supplier that you almost had the chance to work with." I paused. "Either way, I don't take kindly to bein' held at gunpoint by my customers."

He pulled back a bit, creating a more respectful distance between us. "Who's the fella in the car?"

"My driver," I said, mustering up an irritation and indignation in my voice.

"Why don't he get out of the car?"

"Well," I said, "I assume it might have somethin' to do with all the guns your boys are pointin' at him."

"Let him out," the man said to his boys.

"No," I said and spun at him. "He don't get out of the car." There was no way I could risk anyone getting a good look at Remy or recognizing him.

The man looked at me, his brows pulled together as if trying to piece together a puzzle.

"I didn't catch your name," I said to him.

"James."

"Well, James," I said decisively, "Sonny there is my driver. That's his job and he's the best driver in Charlotte, North Carolina. I don't involve him in any of my other business, nor do I need anyone else sticking their noses in it."

James looked at Remy, who remained still in the car. His eyes were straight ahead, hands on the wheel, but I knew he was aware of where each and every person in that barn was and that he heard everything I was saying.

"Now, I'm either gonna complete my business here, or I'm gonna leave. If I go, I'm takin' my product with me," I added. Then I leaned into him, dropped my voice to a low sultry voice, and said, "I'm bettin' there's someone down the road who's waitin' on you to bring them their liquor. And when you don't, I'm bettin' that manual labor ain't how you thought you'd be spendin' the rest of your days." I leaned in closer yet, pressing myself against his arm to whisper, "You don't seem the type."

I stepped away, turning my back to him and walking to the other side of the car as if I were going to leave. "Now, is someone gonna unload this whiskey or am I takin' it with me?"

James signaled for his men to get the liquor.

"Help the men, Sonny," I said to Remy and saw him tuck a pistol into the back of his pants as he got out of the car to expose the hidden compartment in the back of the car. He got back into the front seat and allowed James's men to unload the jugs.

When they were finished, James approached me and handed me several stacks of bills.

"No hard feelin's, I hope," he said.

"We're all tryin' to cover our own," I told him. "But I do expect a warmer reception next time we cross paths, James." I smiled and winked as I climbed into the car next to Remy.

James closed the door for me then leaned against the open window. "I guarantee it," he said, though I barely heard the words as Remy started the engine at just that moment and began to back up the car.

James had just enough time to lift his foot from the running board. He lifted his hat and tipped the brim as we pulled away.

Once the car hit the road and I felt the tires slip as Remy throttled, my nerves caved in around me. My hands shook and my breaths grew more rapid. Tears filled my eyes, and I wiped them away.

"You okay?" Remy asked.

"I...I don't know." My nerves had been so calm only moments ago. With men pointing guns at me, I'd felt calm and serene. But now, with the danger finally behind me, I was collapsing into a hysterical mess.

Remy reached for my hand and held it tight, his other hand on the wheel. I felt the speed of the car increase.

"Remy, slow down," I said. "You'll draw attention."

"There's nothin' we can get busted for now," he said. The car bounced along the road faster yet.

When we'd put a fair distance between us and the drop

spot, Remy turned onto a smaller road and then another. He stopped the car and pulled me into him.

I was still shaking, and the comfort and safety of his arms caused me to finally let go of the terror of the situation I'd just been in. I cried and clung to him until my tears had been spilled and I was too exhausted to shed another one.

"You're all right, mon chèr," he whispered in my ear as he pulled me closer to his chest. "You're safe. I'll never put you in that kind of danger again."

I pushed away, but only slightly, not ready to let go of the comfort and warmth of his arms. "What do you mean?" I asked in surprise. "I'm goin' again, Remy Granger. I may've had my wits scared out of me, but I was *good*. I got us out of that mess. Not you, and not your brothers, or Sunshine. Ophelia Breaux just saved your life, fella."

I settled into my seat and crossed my arms. Secure in my realization that, with no experience in bootlegging or any other criminal endeavor, I'd just pulled off a major scam and delivered the liquor we were supposed to deliver.

Remy laughed. He bounced in his seat. "That was the most amazin' damn thing I ever seen. Those fellas are prob'ly scratchin' their heads right now wonderin' what the hell just happened." He laughed again then turned to the window and let out a loud *Whoo* into the night air.

"And I saved your life," I reiterated.

"That you did. But please don't make me sound so pathetic when we tell the fellas 'bout this." He reached for the key, but I stopped him.

I turned to him, the excitement of what had happened in that shed coursing through me. All of my nerves were alight with energy. I pulled myself up to my knees on the seat, facing him.

"I want you to know," I said, "that when I saw those men

pointing guns at you, I knew I'd do whatever it took to protect you. In that instant, Remy Granger, I knew I would die tryin' to save you."

I reached for his face and pulled him into a kiss.

His hands were around my waist, but he pushed me back. "I don't ever want you to risk yourself to save me again. I'd rather spend eternity tormented in hell than one minute on earth knowin' you'd been hurt to save me."

I looked at him and wondered if he could see just how deeply I loved him.

I leaned into him and kissed him with all the passion that had blossomed in my chest. Remy responded, the heat of his lips burning a path from my lips to my jaw line. I met his mouth again, hungry to absorb him in every possible way.

Remy leaned back against the door, his hands traveling up the back of my thighs and under my skirt. Heavy breaths pressed against my chest and I leaned into him, needing to feel him firmly against my body. My fingers found the buttons of his shirt and I unfastened each one until I was able to push the crisp material over his shoulders. The heat of his skin against my hands caused another surge of electricity to shoot through me. I pushed at the shirt, trying to free his arms.

Remy sat up, shrugging his arms from the shirt and wrapping them around my waist. He picked me up and laid me back on the seat, careful to avoid hitting my head against the door.

Hot kisses trailed along my neck and down to the neckline of my dress. Remy fumbled with the buttons, managing to open only two before his mouth explored the newly exposed flesh.

I leaned back, arching into the pleasure of his touch. My fingers wound through his hair. I wanted so badly to hold him in place and yet wanted to pull his attention back up to my mouth, hungry again for the deep kisses that lit a fire in my belly.

I grasped at his hips with my legs, pulling him toward me as I clung around his shoulders. I craved him with a deep and animalistic yearning.

"Remy," I breathed. "I love you." The truth slipped out on a breath without even a thought.

I felt him slow his attention. He buried his head in my neck, and his hands pulled slowly up my thighs, to my waist. He gained control of his breathing and lifted his head, placing a slow, sweet kiss on my lips.

My own breath was still too rapid to control. My single driving impulse right now was to be with Remy in every way possible. *Why is he pulling away again?*

"Remy?" I asked in a heavy breath. "What's wrong?"

"Nothin'," he said and sat up, pulling the hem of my dress down and reaching for his shirt.

I sat up, embarrassed. I straightened my clothing, buttoning my dress.

A thought suddenly occurred to me. Had I been so stupid to mistake Remy's interest and friendliness for deeper feelings?

"You don't love me," I said.

"What?" he asked and turned toward me.

"That's why you pulled away from me at the fish camp and now," I said.

He shook his head and reached for me, scooting closer. He held one of my hands in his and pushed the hair that hung in my eyes with the other hand before resting it on my cheek. "I do love you, Ophelia," he said, his voice quiet and sincere. "And *that's* why I stopped."

Humiliation washed over me. I was embarrassed at doubting him and also at how badly I still wanted to surrender myself to him.

He leaned over and laid a soft kiss on my lips. "I love you, Ophelia Breaux," he whispered again. "Don't ever doubt that."

The ride home was quiet. Remy reached for me and I slid under his arm. We rode that way all the way back to Point de Concession.

Once we arrived at my house, he parked the car and walked me to the back door. We stepped quietly to avoid waking anyone up.

Remy kissed me again, sweet and gentle, as he left me at the back steps.

"I'm so proud of you," he whispered. "You were amazing tonight."

I smiled, but there was something else on my mind. "Remy?" I slipped my arms under his to absorb his warmth in the early hours of the morning. "Why don't you want to—you know—*be* with me?"

He shook his head slightly and pulled me closer. "Is that what you think? That I don't want to be with you?"

I shook my head. "Each time we got close, you stopped."

"I assure you, Ophelia, that I want nothin' more than to be with you." He placed a kiss on my forehead. "But only when the time's right."

"Remy," I said, "have you ever been with a girl who was so desperate to be with you?"

"No," he said. "You'll be my first—and my only."

We kissed again, and he waited until I went into the house before leaving.

It was hard to sleep. The night played repeatedly in my head, over and over again—my first bootlegging job and every minute I'd spent with Remy.

I'd only slept a few hours when the sun began to rise. I knew I'd have to get up and help Momma. I couldn't let her know that I hadn't been asleep in my room all night. She couldn't be allowed to suspect anything.

The wash work was torturous. My mind buzzed due to the

lack of sleep, and the sun beating down on my back rendered my muscles nearly useless.

"What time are you expected at Vieux Piersall's?" she asked.

"Three o'clock," I said. "I was hopin' to finish up my chores so I can go by and see Dixie before I start."

"She's working at the store?" Momma hadn't been able to refer to the store by its name since Daddy's family had sold it. "For the Grangers?"

"Yes, ma'am," I said, trying to keep my tone neutral.

"What does she do for them?"

"Cleans up mostly," I said. "Sweeps the floors, stocks shelves. I think she runs the counter when Marie Granger ain't there."

"And what about that Granger boy who came here?" she asked. "Remy?"

"Oh," I said with a wave of my hand. "He was nice enough to help me make those deliveries, but I ain't got time for runnin' around with boys. I've got work and I've really missed Dixie. My days are plenty full." I snuck a look from the side of my eye to see if I'd offered a convincing act.

She considered what I'd said. "Well, it's been a while since you've seen Dixie; the two of you have a lot of catchin' up to do. I'm glad she's still here for you. Why don't you finish hangin' that load then you can get cleaned up for work. You should have plenty of time to visit with Dixie before work."

"Yes, ma'am," I said and hung the laundry in record time.

I was dressed and out the door by lunch time. Despite the thick, damp air that hung around me, I nearly ran all the way to Breaux's General.

Dixie was at the counter when I bounded in through the door. "In the back." She smiled and waved me past. "Hurry."

I rushed toward the back and rounded the corner to find Remy and Sunshine in the back room playing cards. A cloud of cigarette smoke hung in the heavy air and half-empty glasses of clear liquid sat on the table between them. Remy dropped his cards, crossed the room in only a few steps, and scooped me up into a deep embrace. When he kissed me, he tasted of stale cigarettes and moonshine.

I was nearly bent over backward by the pressure of his attentions.

He pulled back and looked into my eyes, smiling. "Hi there," he said.

I couldn't help but giggle at the intensity of his greeting. "I thought you was workin' mornings," I said.

"Oh, yeah," he said, "I'm on a delivery." His fingers encircled mine. "Can I get you a drink?"

"No, I'm fine right now."

The bell clanged as the door opened and again as it closed.

"In the back," I heard Dixie say and knew it was Eloi.

He walked in a moment later, followed by Sirus.

Sirus offered a wide grin to everyone, including me. "I hear you're a natural." He laughed as he took a seat.

Eloi assessed me silently—as usual.

"You should've seen her," Remy bragged. "It was amazing."

"It was dangerous," Eloi said. "You had no idea who you were dealin' with."

The smiles disappeared from everyone else's faces and they shifted in their seats.

"You wouldn't have known them either." I decided that I was done cowering to Eloi Granger. "As a matter of fact, you *didn't* know them either, did you? That was a Moret sale— someone set it up and you moved in on it. I walked into that deal as blind as you would have. And I walked out of there, didn't I?" I demanded.

He stared at me silently, and for a brief moment, I worried he'd pull that pistol I could see peeking out from under his shirt and silence me once and for all. Instead, he leaned back into his chair. "Was ya' scared?"

"Hell, yes, I was scared," I said just as directly as he'd spoken to me. "But I didn't let them know it."

He looked at Remy for confirmation.

"No way," Remy said. "Nobody in that place would've known that she wasn't runnin' her own crew. It was flawless."

"All right then," Eloi said. "We've got a short time to set up some more runs. Moret is still in jail, and his crew ain't managed to put nothin' together since. They're too scared to stick their heads out for fear of gettin' pinched themselves."

"There's just one thing," I said. "I'd like a gun. And I'd like *you* to teach me how to use it," I said to Eloi.

For the first time, clear, unmistakable confusion clouded Eloi Granger's features. He recovered in seconds, but I'd caused him to drop his carefully crafted demeanor, and inside I was thrilled.

"What you think you need a gun for?" he asked.

"In case I'm ever in a situation, like last night, but I can't talk my way out of it."

"Why me?"

"Because you're the only one who will tell me if I ain't doin' it right, and what my options are if the gun don't work."

"*Hmph*," he grunted with a single nod. "Tonight, after you're done at the garage."

"I'll be here," I said.

We spent an hour discussing the different drop spots they'd used too many times lately, which needed to be dried up, and which old spots could be revived again.

"Who supplies the shine?" I asked. Certainly, if we were putting ourselves in this much risk, Eloi knew who it was for.

"That ain't none of our business," he said. "We run, that's it.

If we get caught, the less we know, the better. The less they know about us, the better."

I understood the caution involved in the moonshine business, but I had a burning desire for more knowledge. I was already tired of relying on the little information Eloi allowed me.

"Do you know who the supplier is?" I asked Dixie.

We were sitting on the porch before my shift at Piersall's Garage. The sun was attempting to scorch everything it touched and the hand-held fans Dixie found offered little relief.

"You know I ain't got nothin' to say about Granger business. Not even to you."

There was a heavy warning in her tone. She was as protective of Eloi as he was of her.

Dixie and I redirected our attention to the fashions in the latest issue of *Women's Weekly.*

At three o'clock, I crossed the road to Vieux Piersall's.

I swept and picked up old newspapers. I even pumped gas a few times. But as busy as I stayed, the time dragged. This job was a distraction from where I wanted to be and what I wanted to be doing. But I needed the job to justify the money I'd be bringing home, so I did it without complainin'.

Just before five o'clock, a truck pulled up behind the garage. Eloi Granger sat at the wheel. I looked out, wondering what he was doing. He reached a hand out, pointed a finger at me, and bent his thumb.

"Eloi is gonna teach me to shoot," I told Vieux Piersall, who had joined me at the window.

"Probably a good thing to know," he said and turned around, returning to his spot on the stool in the counter. "You'd better get a move on," he said.

I left by the back door, pulling an old ball cap I'd found low over my eyes. I climbed into the truck.

Eloi didn't say anything, just put the truck in gear and drove.

We'd only been driving five minutes when he pulled off the main road and took a series of turns.

"Ain't nobody out here to hear us," he said and handed me a pistol.

I didn't move. I had no idea what to do with it or how it worked. I knew I would have a lot of explaining to do if I accidentally shot it and it hit Eloi—and God forbid if I accidentally shot him and he lived.

"It ain't loaded and it don't bite," he said gruffly.

He demonstrated with another pistol how I should hold it.

I mimicked everything Eloi did. I opened the barrel, closed it, pulled the hammer back, aimed, and pulled.

The only time Eloi spoke was to tell me how to time my breathing with the pull of the trigger.

After I'd practiced firing a number of times, Eloi handed me six bullets and demonstrated how to load them into the gun. The bullets slid easily into the cylinder and I snapped the cylinder into place. I pulled the hammer back, sighted in my target—an old Frigidaire that someone had left behind—and pulled the trigger.

The jolt of the firing knocked me backward. I took one step back but recovered my stance quickly. Ringing filled my ears and my teeth ached from the jarring impact of pulling the trigger.

"A little too much?" Eloi asked.

"No," I said and stepped up to line my sights again. "I'm just fine."

Although I couldn't seem to get over the apprehension of the kick and noise that came with each shot, I was able to line my shots up and hit in a consistent pattern.

"That should do," Eloi said and started back to the truck.

Eloi didn't wait for me to get in the truck before he'd started it and had it in gear. The truck was rolling forward as I pulled my foot from the ground and closed the door. He returned me to the same place he'd collected me.

"Thank you," I said when he stopped the truck. "I appreciate it."

"Didn't have much of a choice, did I?"

I turned to face him, anger propelling me. I hadn't done anything for Eloi to continue to hate me as much as he did. If anything, I thought I had proven my worth to the Grangers. And then I remembered Dixie. If Eloi was too afraid to let Dixie into his heart and give her a permanent place in it, there was no way he would find room for me.

"I know how you feel about Dixie," I said quietly. If there was somethin' we had in common it was our love for Remy and Dixie. "And I know that you keep her at a distance because you think it protects her."

"That's enough," he said.

"Eloi, let her know how you feel. Tell her. She deserves that much. Even if lovin' you is dangerous for her, she should know."

He turned and leaned toward me, one finger pointing at my face. "I been real patient 'bout you bein' here." His teeth were clenched and the muscles in his jaw pulsated. "But once you get the money for your momma's house, I don't ever want to see you again. You're the one who's dangerous."

I felt myself blanch at his accusation.

"You're a danger to my family, to me, and to Dixie. You're gonna be the reason someone dies. So you get your money and then disappear, even if you have to take my brother with you."

I was stunned into silence. "How could you think I'd do anything to hurt any of you?"

"You won't mean to," he said. "It's just in your nature. Now get out."

I got out of the truck. He was already pulling away when the door clicked closed.

My eyes burned with tears. How could Eloi distrust me enough to think I'd hurt anyone? Hadn't I already proven myself? I'd risked my life to save Remy.

Vieux Piersall peeked through his window then turned, letting the curtain fall across the glass.

I walked around the garage and sat on the steps, looking across at the store. Through the window I saw Dixie sitting at the counter readin' a book.

How could Eloi say that it was *me* who was a danger to Dixie? He'd been a criminal his entire life; *he* was the one who would end up bringing the law or another gang near her.

I knew one thing for certain: I would get my money and then I *would* walk away from Eloi Granger. He was a means to an end. That man and I would never see eye to eye.

CHAPTER

TEN

APRIL 19 TO JUNE 9, 1930

The runs we made after that first one all paled in comparison to my first. Nothin' went wrong, nothing unexpected happened and nothing exciting either. We picked up the shine, delivered it, and collected our pay.

I was making far more money than I could bring home to Momma. Each week I brought home three dollars and handed it to Momma. I stashed the rest in a cigar box under my bed.

"Vieux Piersall's payin' you that much? For just a few hours work?"

"Is that a lot?" I feigned ignorance. I knew it was a lot for what I was doin'—or rather what I'd told her I was doin'—but for the work I actually did, I was earnin' far more than I'd even hoped. I could have Momma out of the judge's house in months.

Exhaustion was catching up with me, though. I did runs with Remy, Sirus, and Sunshine every single night, late. Sometimes we ran all the way to New Orleans and into Saint

Tammany Parish. With Claude Moret in jail, all of his customers were desperate for someone else to fill his quota. Eloi told us that if we didn't do it, they'd start bringin' in shine from up north. We had to meet the demand or we'd lose the runs altogether.

"Can your supplier meet the need?" I'd asked. "What if he runs out or brews a bad batch? Maybe we should make some other contacts." It seemed a prudent concern to me.

"You been short on a run yet?" Eloi asked, thus ending that line of discussion—not that I'd had a discussion with Eloi since that night in his truck.

Every morning I was up early with Momma doing laundry and stitching. I'd started leaving early for the garage, telling her that Vieux Piersall had asked me to start earlier. In reality, I went to the store and slept in the barn out back. Dixie made sure to wake me up in time to go to my shift at the garage.

Vieux Piersall never asked me questions about working with the Grangers, nor did he mention it. He simply tucked the cash into the pocket of his overalls as I handed it to him then went on about his business.

My third week runnin', we came across my first revenuers.

We were doing a long run to Lafourche Parish for a buyer who was paying a premium price in order to have some liquor in time for his daughter's wedding.

We had ten gallons of shine under the back seat. Remy was driving. I sat next to him and Sirus and Sunshine were in the back.

We rounded a corner and Remy braked quickly—had he not, we would have driven straight into the side of the car that was parked across the road. Two other cars were parked on each side of it, preventing anyone from driving around one to avoid stopping.

"Everyone relax," Remy said as he stopped and leaned one

arm out the window. "Hello, gentlemen," he said in an amiable voice, "what can we do for you tonight?"

I counted six men—two per car. Two sitting ready at the wheels of their cars in case they had to give chase. Three had guns drawn and aimed at us.

I smiled. "My goodness, you gave us a fright," I said. My insides were tumblin', but I willed my muscles to assume a relaxed manner. "We thought you was bandits when we came 'round the bend."

"Where you folks headed?" The man who had taken charge was in no mood for small talk.

"Headin' north to Thibodaux," Remy said. "My girl's auntie has taken ill. Her mère phoned and said she should come right away."

The light shined into the back seat. "And what about you all?" he asked Sirus and Sunshine.

"I'm just along for the ride, sir," Sirus said. "My brother and I ain't been north in quite a while. Figured I'd see what Thibodaux has to offer these days."

"And the Negro?" He nearly spat the word.

I saw Remy's grip tighten on the wheel.

From the corner of my eye I could see that Sunshine remained still, looking at his hands.

"Oh, him," Remy said, putting on the airs of a moneyed family. "He's been workin' for my family all his life. He's a good worker. Ain't no reason to go givin' up a hard worker just because the law says we gotta pay them a fair wage now, is there?" He laughed in an overly boisterous way that I'd never heard from Remy—or anyone in Plaquemines Parish for that matter.

The man studied Remy and then Sunshine. "I 'spect not," he said, though he didn't sound convinced. "Where's your luggage?"

"What's that?" Remy asked.

"If you're headed to Thibodaux, you're gonna need a change of clothes. Where's your bags?"

"Ah, hell," Remy said. "You got me. This ain't my girl and we ain't goin' to Thibodaux. My brother and I picked her up in town. We was lookin' for somewhere to take her. You know, have a little private party."

Remy was lucky for the presence of the lawman at that moment or I would've scrambled across the car and knocked the teeth from his mouth.

The revenuer's eyes narrowed. "And the Negro?"

"That was true. He's been in our employ practically since he was born."

I could barely breathe as we waited for the agent to make a decision. Finally he pulled his shoulders back. "You're gonna have to take that girl back to town," he said. He focused on me then. "And you be more careful 'bout drivin' around with men you don't know."

"Yes, sir," we all said as Remy started the car again and backed away. He pulled onto the side of the road and turned to drive in the other direction.

"You ready?" he asked. "We get around this corner and we are takin' another road. If they see, they're gonna know we're runnin' and they're gonna come after us."

I nodded.

"Woo-hoo, let's drive!" Sirus whooped.

"They're gonna see us," Remy said to me, "and they're gonna chase us."

I nodded again, planted my feet firmly on the floor, and braced my arms on the dash and door.

Before I knew it, Remy shifted, turning onto a small, under-used road. I felt the gear engage as he released the clutch and pushed the gas pedal to the floor. The car bounced over a small rut that had dried long ago.

Remy maneuvered the car through the trees, up the slight rise of a hill. As we crested the hill I looked to the right and saw the revenuers' cars still lined up across the road. I heard yelling and then the lights to their cars flooded the hillside as they started them in a scrambled attempt to give chase to us.

The road angled away from the other road and narrowed. I braced myself, certain we would lose control at any moment and slam into one of the trees. But Remy expertly navigated the road. He slid around corners, without even slowing, almost as though he'd simply willed the rear wheels of the car to follow along with the front tires.

The lights behind us grew farther and farther away until we knew for sure they'd given up the chase.

"Woo-hoo!" Sirus whooped again.

"They never stood a chance," Sunshine yelled, laughing.

Remy drove fast for another mile or more before he finally slowed.

"You okay?" He looked at me and I realized I was still braced for impact.

I could feel the flush of blood in my cheeks and my mouth was set in a rigid smile that I couldn't relax. My heart thundered in my chest. I couldn't remember a time I'd been so happy and I couldn't wait to do it again. "That was the most thrilling thing I've ever experienced," I said.

It was the nights when we came close to the revenuers, or were forced to outrun them, that I had the hardest time falling asleep. With so few hours between the time Remy brought me home and I had to wake up to help Momma, I couldn't afford to waste any of my sleep time, but I constantly lay awake reliving the rush of sitting next to Remy and outrunning the law. Feeling so in love, and so invincible, was powerful—more intoxicating than the shine we were runnin'.

"You need more sleep," Dixie said one afternoon. "You're starting to look tired all the time. If I see it, you can bet your mère does too. And the fellas too. You can't keep your head straight if you're tired."

"I'll get sleep," I said. "It's just hard right now. It's all so exciting."

"It won't be exciting if you're dead," she said. "And those revenuers been shootin' people all over the country. They don't care who you are, they just wanna stop the shine."

"I'll sleep," I said. "Don't worry."

The very next day Eloi announced that we were going to start running during the day.

"The revenuers are out every night," he said. "They know that's when the shine is bein' run. We've got six drops this week, all in the daytime. We'll have to run two cars to each drop and one decoy car to be lookout."

I assumed I'd be driving the decoy since I was the least experienced driver.

"Sirus, you'll take the truck," Eloi said. "Remy and Ophelia in the big car. Sunshine, you're with me. Our first drop is tomorrow. Be here by sunup. Remy and I are goin' to scout now."

By sunup? I thought of my obligations. Vieux Piersall wasn't a concern; he knew our business and when we ran shine, he got paid too. He wouldn't care if I worked. But Momma, on the other hand, I couldn't abandon to do a run.

"You have a scheduling conflict, Ophelia?" Eloi asked.

"You know she works for her mère," Remy said.

"Then maybe she should just focus on that from now on and leave us to our business."

"I'll figure it out," I told them. "I'll be there."

By dinner time I still hadn't figured out how to tell Momma

that I couldn't help her in the morning. I couldn't say that I had to work at the garage—she could easily check up on that. I couldn't say I was spendin' the day with Dixie because she would certainly be covering at the store.

I sat on the porch, watching the sky grow dark and prayin' that an answer would fall in my lap.

And then, one did.

I didn't recognize the car that pulled up in front of the house. In the darkened interior, I could only make out a lady's hat. Then the door opened, and I nearly fell off the stoop when Marie Granger stepped out and headed up my walkway.

My initial reaction was panic. Why would Marie be at my house? Her presence here went against everything Remy and I were trying to do in avoiding the people in town making any connections between us.

"Miss Marie?" I stepped quickly down the stairs to meet her on the walkway. I heard the screen slam behind me as Momma stepped out behind me. "What're you doin' here?" I whispered.

"Hello, Emmaline," Miss Marie called over my shoulder.

I turned to look at Momma. She looked as confused about why Marie Granger was standing in her front yard as I was.

"Marie," Momma called in greeting. "To what do we owe the pleasure of your visit?"

"Well"—Marie stepped around me and addressed Momma—"I hope you don't think I'm being presumptuous, but I've heard around town that Ophelia's been pickin' up odd jobs to help out. My boys have business out of town tomorrow, and I'm in desperate need of someone to deliver groceries out to the island in the mornin'."

Momma stood with her arms crossed.

"It's a big order," Marie said. "I could pay her five dollars for one good day's work."

"Five dollars?" I turned to Momma and stepped closer so I

could lower my voice to a near whisper. "It's five dollars, Momma, for one day."

"Just deliverin' groceries?" Momma was notably skeptical.

"It's a big order," Marie explained. "I only deliver to the island once a month."

"All right," Momma said. "But just this once."

"Thank you, Emmaline," Marie said. "Ophelia, I'll need you to start loading the orders by sunup."

"Yes, ma'am," I said and followed her to the car. "And thank Remy," I whispered to her.

"It wasn't Remy," she said. "You can thank Sirus. And you'd better bring five dollars to pay yourself with, because she'll be wanting to see that when you get home."

Even though I was excited for the run, I slept the entire night. I dressed quickly in the morning and nearly ran all the way to the store.

Three cars were parked behind the shed when I got there.

Eloi explained the route and the pickup and drop-off details. "Remy and I parked at one end of that road and there was hardly more than three cars in the two hours we sat there. The liquor has been sittin' there for three days—it was a planned run that the Morets used to run, but they ain't been able to shake the law for weeks, so we're gonna deliver."

"We have to be quick," Remy said. "There's old houses across the channel. They're mostly abandoned, but anyone could be living there still. The longer we stay, the more attention we'll attract."

"Sirus is going first," Eloi said. "You see anything suspect on the way up, you pull over. Act like you're checking the engine until we've both passed then come right back here. If not, you go to the top of the hill and sit on the hood with this sandwich and this book." He handed the items to Sirus. "You stay there until lunch time. Anyone asks, you're just enjoyin' the afternoon. If nothin' happens, you eat the sandwich then head back."

Sirus nodded, took the keys from Eloi, and drove off.

"If anythin' does go wrong," Eloi said, "get to the top of the hill and find Sirus. You only have until he's finished with that sandwich, so you'd better hurry."

Remy and I left before Eloi and Sunshine. The morning sun cast yellow and orange hues across the horizon. White clouds scattered across the sky, punctuating the color of the new day. If we hadn't been facing such a serious task, it would have been a peaceful morning drive.

"How many gallons?" I asked. I knew, if we were bringing two cars, that there had to be a lot. I didn't know how many Eloi's car could hide.

"Fifty," Remy said.

"*Fifty gallons?* We can't hide fifty," I said, shocked that they would even consider running so many.

"They won't all be hidden," he said. "But we've got to deliver it all at once. We got no choice."

A dark feeling settled into my stomach. It wasn't nerves, I could tell because I wasn't fidgety and my heart wasn't racing. But my skin prickled, and I felt a sense of dread.

"We can't do this, Remy," I said. "Somethin' is gonna go wrong."

"Don't say that, Ophelia. You're just nervous 'cuz it's daylight. We'll be just as careful as we are any other time."

I nodded. I trusted him yet I couldn't shed the dark feeling of doom.

My eyes strained as we drove up the road. I was hoping to see Sirus pulled over to the side of the road inspecting his engine, but we didn't. We reached the turn and Remy followed the road as it dropped down along the water line.

The houses were run-down. Several had shutters drawn,

others had boards nailed over the windows and doorways. Many had obviously been abandoned long ago. Old dogs lay on porches, barely lifting their heads in curiosity before laying them back down as we drove by.

We passed the cabins and crossed a bridge to the other side of a channel. I held my breath as we crossed, certain it would resist the weight of the car at any moment and pitch us into the water below.

"It's too quiet here," I said. "I don't like it."

"It's abandoned," Remy said. He reached over and took my hand. "There's nobody around to make noise. We'll be out of here before you know it."

Over my shoulder I saw Eloi's car making its initial descent down the road.

Remy stopped the car and opened my door. "We're just a young couple looking for a nice spot to picnic." He pointed as if he'd discovered the perfect spot. We looked about, but I didn't see anything that looked out of the ordinary.

"The drop is right next to the car," Remy said. "If there's anyone in the houses, they won't be able to see what we're doin'."

Eloi pulled up and Remy set a foot on the running board, leaning forward as though they were talking. Remy scanned behind the cars while Eloi looked ahead. I leaned against the passenger side of our car and scanned the houses and tree line behind them, up the hill. Nothing looked suspect.

"Let's do this as fast as possible and get out of here," Eloi said.

Sunshine and Remy found the camouflage and pulled back the wooden planks that covered the drop holes.

Quickly and quietly, we carried the jugs to the cars, first filling the compartments under the back seat, then the one that had just recently been installed under my own seat. Then we moved on to Eloi's car. Not only did he have false seats, but a false bottom in the back of the car as well.

In less than ten minutes we had all the jugs loaded and we jumped back into the cars.

I breathed heavily from the exertion and wiped the thick sweat from my forehead and upper lip with the hem of my dress.

"I told you," Remy said. "Not a bit of trouble."

I smiled and nodded, but the dark knot pulled tighter in my belly. I closed my eyes and said a silent prayer, begging for the Lord to see us back safely.

The word *Amen* had barely fluttered through my mind when I heard Remy utter, "Oh shit," and felt the car veer to the right.

When I opened my eyes I saw cars driving quickly from the tree line behind the old cabins. Eloi's car veered left, narrowly avoiding a car intent on preventing passage on the road. He accelerated quickly and the dirt and dust kicked up from the back tires.

Two other cars raced alongside us. Remy swerved to avoid the car that had tried to cut off Eloi. I flew off my seat, hitting my head on the roof as our car left the road.

"Hold on!" Remy yelled. He dropped the gear low and tried to power around the pursuing cars, but they were so much faster than our car. I smashed into the dashboard as he slammed on the brakes. The cars flew past us as Remy reversed and spun our car around. The revenuers caught up again quickly.

I looked around madly. We were in a valley, a deep funnel in the middle of the hills, and there was nowhere to go.

Remy spun the car around again, driving between the houses, but our pursuers were right on our tail the entire time.

"We're gonna have to run, Ophelia." He looked at me

quickly as he maneuvered the car away from the water and back toward the hillside. "Okay?"

"Yes," I said. My heart thumped in my ears, drowning out the sound of the cars as they collided and bumped off each other, trying to push us from our course. I braced myself in my seat.

Remy stomped on the gas and jerked the wheel, spinning us round and round. When he stopped the car it was facing the revenuers.

"Now!" he yelled and I jumped out. I heard him rev the engine just before he leapt out.

I rolled as I hit the ground. Sticks and rocks scraped my bare skin as I tumbled over them. I scrambled to get my feet under me.

Remy ran up beside me, scooped his arm under mine, and pulled me into a run alongside him.

The hill was steeper than it had appeared from the bottom. My legs and lungs both burned as I pushed myself farther up the hill. We leapt over roots and fallen trees. We couldn't afford to fall now; we could hear the revenuers as they chased us up the hill.

"Keep going," Remy said through his heavy breaths. "Keep going."

And I did, I pushed on, ignoring the pain and the exhaustion. Ignoring the branches that reached out to nab me as I ran by, winding their long fingers into my hair and dragging me backward.

"We're almost to the top," Remy said. He reached back for me.

I was slowing and I knew it but there was nothing I could do—I was exhausted, and my body refused to cooperate.

Remy pulled me along, over, under, and around as we made our way through the trees and the overgrowth. Each time we had to duck under the bushes, it became that much harder to keep up with Remy. Every time he would reach back, seeming to sense exactly where I was, to grab my hand and pull me along.

"There they are!" I heard a voice behind us—much closer than I would have guessed.

I'm slowing Remy down, I thought, panicking.

"Freeze—now!" another voice commanded.

"Keep running, chèr," Remy begged, pulling me down again to crawl under a thick growth of bushes.

This growth was far deeper than the others. My knees ached and my feet refused to come up under me once we'd reached an opening in the tunnel of overgrowth. I stumbled and scrambled for my footing again before I felt a sharp bite in my back.

My first thought was that this was a horrible time to be stung by a bee. A sharp, burning sensation ripped into my upper back. Heat tore through my shoulder blade and filled my left side.

A second sting burned into my left cheek and the tinny taste of blood flooded my mouth.

Remy hadn't seen me fall behind. He was still running, his hand grasping behind him over and over again, waiting for my hand to find it.

Remy slowed and turned his head just as my legs gave out. I crashed to my knees and a cough erupted from my throat. Bright red liquid splattered across my hands. Fear seized me.

"Ophelia!" Remy ran back toward me. His eyes were wide and his skin ashen.

"Run," I pleaded with him. Each of my breaths came with the gurgle of fresh blood. Tears stung my eyes. My fear for Remy was at least as ripe as my fear for myself. "Go!" I screamed.

He shook his head as Eloi and Sunshine burst through the bushes. They grabbed him from behind and pulled him into the overgrowth.

"Get down!" men's voices yelled.

I held my hands up. I was vaguely aware that I was crying hysterically, unsure if I was dying and knowing for sure that if I didn't die, I was most certainly going to jail.

I had failed the Grangers. I had failed Remy. And I had failed Momma.

CHAPTER
ELEVEN

JUNE 10 TO JULY 15, 1930

Pain was the first thing I recognized. Before I'd even opened my eyes, I felt a deep burning ache tear up my back and into my jaw.

"*Unngh*," I groaned and tried to roll away. I wasn't sure where the revenuers were, but my most animal sense knew that I had to get to my feet and run.

I rolled to my right, away from the pain. I immediately felt resistance.

"You're not going anywhere, young lady," a strange female voice said. "May as well make yourself comfortable."

I opened my eyes, squinting against the harsh glare of the sunshine and antiseptic, white surroundings of what I assumed to be a hospital. "Which hospital am I in?" I asked. "You have to tell my mère."

I heard the woman snicker. "Hospital? Welcome to the Plaquemines Parish women's jail infirmary," she said. "Your mère is *quite* aware that you're here, as is everyone else in the Parish."

Jail?

My body grew numb—except for the deep throb in my back and cheek. A chill swept over me.

I'm in jail. Despite the risks I'd taken, I'd never truly believed I'd lose my freedom. I felt the reality of confinement now.

I rolled toward the guard's voice. She was far prettier than I would have guessed from the hateful tone in her voice.

"When can I see her?" I asked. I was desperate to see Momma. I wanted her to know that every choice I made was for a good reason: to help her get away from the judge and get a home of her own.

"I would imagine she'll want to come see you sentenced," she said. "There's a lot of folks interested in seein' that. You have the distinction of bein' arrested in one of the biggest dry raids in the history of the parish. Your mère must be proud."

I glared at her.

She smiled an overly sweet and completely false smile.

With no way to talk to Momma, or Remy, my mind obsessed over the possibilities. I was fairly certain Remy had gotten away. Sunshine and Eloi had dragged him off when he started to come back for me.

He came back for me. That realization made me both happy and terrified at the same time. Remy loved me enough to come back for me, but at the same time, Remy had risked himself just to save me.

One of the first things Sunshine and the Grangers taught me about bootleggin' was to run. Each and every one of us was entrusted to look out for ourselves—that and to not rat out the others if caught. I knew Remy had spent his entire life honing his ability to evade the law. A few months with me and he was prepared to run right into their grasp.

It was nearly a week before I could get out of bed without the use of a cane or some form of assistance. A bullet had torn through the top of the muscle in the side of my back and another had gone through my cheek. While the back muscle prevented me from moving without pain, the hole in my cheek made it near impossible to eat without pain. My tongue was continuously searching out the hole and rubbing the strange new tissue.

"The risk of infection has nearly passed," the doctor said. "You'll have to use the muscle as much as possible if you want it to heal correctly. I'm going to discharge you from the infirmary."

"I can go home?" I asked.

"No, darlin', you'll go into the women's housing unit. You do realize that you're in jail, don't you?"

I did know. But it still seemed surreal. The infirmary hadn't been so bad, but what would it be like to be in a cell? And how long would I be here?

My mind returned to less troubled times. My favorite memories to sink into were when Dixie and I had run untethered through Point De Concession. We'd spent lazy days drifting on the bayou, sipping colas and trying to acquire a skill for smoking cigarettes—which neither of us ever took to. In the evenings, we'd sniff out the closest cookout and manipulate our way into an invitation.

The realization of how I'd failed everyone washed over me again. What hurt most of all was knowing that Momma would have no one to turn to now but the judge.

The weeks stretched on in mind-numbing repetition. I was awakened each morning for breakfast and then spent the rest of the day sweeping, cleaning bathrooms, and doing laundry.

Finally, one day, a guard called my name. "Breaux, you've got a visitor."

A strange man sat across from me in the visit room. The guard stood a ways away from us, offering a small bit of privacy, but his eyes never left us. "No touching," he told me as I sat. "And no passing her anything," he warned the man.

The man was elderly and distinguished looking. He wore a suit that was slightly worn, but pressed and with crisp cuffs and collar. He sat against the back of the chair, legs crossed and arms draped across his lap. He made no effort to lean forward and didn't seem intimidated by the guards.

"Miss Breaux," he said in a low voice.

"Yes, sir?" I was still confused. Unsure of if I knew this man or if he was indeed, a stranger.

"You're to be tried tomorrow on charges of transporting illegal liquor in violation of the eighteenth amendment to the Constitution. And with resisting arrest."

I couldn't say anything. There was nothing to be said without offering up further proof against myself.

When he saw that I had nothing to say, he continued. "Miss Breaux, tomorrow the judge will ask you how you would like to plead. You will tell him that you are innocent of all charges."

"Innocent?" A laugh escaped my throat at the absurdity of the idea. "Mister, I was caught runnin' from a car that held at least twenty jugs of moonshine. I was shot when I didn't stop as commanded. Now, you want me to tell a judge that I didn't do none of that?"

"You will tell the judge that you are simply an innocent young girl, caught in the wrong place at the wrong time because of your misplaced affections for the wrong boy."

Ice filled my veins immediately and my jaw tensed in anger. "I don't know who sent you here, but you tell them they've got the story wrong."

He leaned his head forward, closer to me, and leveled his gaze. "You are to say that you fell in love with Remy Granger, and that your love caused you to cast a blind eye to his activities. You will say that you thought you were simply along for an afternoon drive when the dry agents surrounded you and that you panicked. You will further explain that Mr. Granger pulled you along as he ran from the authorities, and that you followed him out of fear for your own life because—as a good Christian girl, and an upstanding member of a founding family—you have no experience in the activities of criminals."

"I don't know who sent you," I hissed, "or what you're tryin' to pull, but I ain't blamin' anyone else for my actions. You should leave." I stood and pushed the chair back with my legs.

"Miss Breaux," he whispered, "I have been retained on your behalf by Mr. Granger, and he would very much like it if you would relay the story of the events leadin' up to your arrest as I have described them to you."

I sat heavily. "Remy?"

He nodded once.

"Why would I blame him? I could never!"

"It's the best way, Miss Breaux. You'll simply have to trust us."

THE FOLLOWING MORNING, I was awoken by a guard before the sun had even risen.

"Wake up, Breaux!" he barked. "You're goin' before the judge and you gotta be presentable for his court."

By "presentable" I found that he meant freshly showered—in frigid water—and dressed—in a highly starched jail-issued sheath. A pair of two-sizes-too-big white canvas sneakers completed my look.

Three guards marched me through a succession of doors. Each guard kept a hand on the gun at his hip and kept at last three paces between them and me. I wanted to laugh at their diligence in guardin' me. Me! I wasn't no violent criminal; I was a bootlegger.

It was all so absurd, but my nerves were still on edge. I was about to be sentenced for my crimes—how was that even possible—and, I realized, I might not see the outside of jail for a very long time.

I thought about the lawyer's plan. It was a ridiculous claim: that I'd simply been followin' a boy I was sweet on. No way would a judge believe that. Would he? I hated to admit it, but I still had hope. Hope that I would see Momma again, hope that I'd finish this day in Remy's arms.

As much as I hoped the plan would work, I struggled with it as well. Momma and Daddy had raised me to accept responsibility for my actions. I imagined myself walking into the courtroom and admitting my guilt. I would take my punishment and Remy wouldn't be implicated.

But then what would happen to Momma? She'd be left with no choice but to rely on the judge.

I had to do whatever would get me out of jail the quickest.

The ride to the Plaquemines Parish courthouse was a short one. As we pulled up in front of the brick building, I saw that the early hour of my trial hadn't discouraged the local lookey-loos from appearin'. It seemed like every reporter in Louisiana was set up on the courthouse steps as well.

"You're a celebrity," one of the guards said in a voice that made it clear he disapproved.

"I think the word is 'notorious'." The other guard chuckled.

I glared at them both before turning my attention to the window.

As the car approached, the courthouse reporters swarmed around it, calling out questions and yelling my name. The flash of camera bulbs caused spots to bloom in my vision and I could hardly see to walk.

The guards held my arms and led me through the crowd, up the steps, and into the courthouse. The silence inside was a welcome relief from the swarming, buzzing crowd outside the doors. The only sound in the hallways was the *clip-clop* of the guards' shoes and the soft shuffle of my own steps as we walked.

Inside the courtroom, my lawyer waited at a table near the front of the room. The courtroom seats were already near full and I heard the hiss of whispers as I was led past the crowd and to the table.

"Miss Breaux," my lawyer said and reached for my hand. His suit was of the finest quality; it was rare to see one like that in Plaquemines Parish—they were more suited to the big-time New Orleans lawyers.

"Umm," I stammered. "I'm sorry, I never did ask your name."

"Morton Lange," he said and shook my hand before indicating for me to sit down in the chair beside his.

"Why are there so many people?" I whispered to him.

"This was the biggest liquor bust in Southern Louisiana since the beginning of Prohibition," he said. "And because the Granger Gang got away. Again."

"The Granger Gang?" I wondered who'd seen fit to give us such a silly designation. We weren't no gang. Just a group of kids tryin' to help our families.

"The Grangers seem to have achieved nationwide notoriety," he said. "Most of the rumors are no more than tall tales. But I don't believe there's been this much fervor about a bandit —or group of bandits—since Billy the Kid."

"Ophelia." I heard Momma's whispered voice and turned to see her take a seat behind me.

Shame burned at my face. One tear rolled onto my cheek before I wiped it away and choked down the rest of them. I'd be damned before I'd cry in front of all these people. Or in from of the judge.

"It's gonna be all right, Ophelia," Momma said in a low voice.

I turned to look at her again.

Trust me, she mouthed.

Everyone stood as the judge entered into the courtroom. He cast a blistering glare directly at me. As he sat, his face assumed the neutral manner of a man in his profession.

The lawyers both talked, and each called on witnesses. I was especially interested to see the man who'd shot me and was surprised at how matter-of-fact he was in recounting his version of that day. He seemed to have no regret about having shot me, nor any pride in having been the one to bring me to justice.

When it was my turn to testify, I choked down the lump that had lodged itself in my throat and repeated the story the way Mr. Lange had coached me.

The truth danced about my tongue, daring to leap out, but in the end I stuck to the plan.

"I'm afraid I wasn't thinkin' right," I said in my most humble voice. "I was under the spell of Remy Granger. I loved him," I said and dissolved into sobs. "I thought he loved me too, but it's evident now that he was just lookin' for someone to take the fall for him."

I was fairly certain I saw the judge's eyes roll ever so slightly before he regained his composure.

The other attorney didn't buy my story one bit, but I stuck to it. I was careful that I neither implicated myself nor gave any further information about the Grangers' business.

"I swear I didn't know they was rumrunners...No, sir, this was the first time I'd gone anywhere with Remy Granger...No, I didn't know that..." On and on the questions went, for over an hour. I was exhausted when I was finally allowed to return to my seat.

The judge took forty-five minutes to reach a decision. I'd asked Mr. Lange to look for Momma while we waited.

"I'm sorry, Miss Breaux," he said when he returned a few minutes later. "I didn't see her anywhere."

Where could Momma be when I'm waitin' for a verdict? I wondered.

When it was time to return, the courtroom seemed even more crowded. Some of the reporters had made their way into the courthouse and milled about into the hallway. Momma slipped into the room quietly and took her seat behind me right as the bailiff announced the judge.

The judge's voice boomed and filled the room, reverberating through the tension in my body. "After considering the testimony of the witnesses and the defendant, I have been *persuaded*"—a strange, almost boastful sneer crossed his face— "to grant the mercy of the court of the State of Louisiana and Plaquemines Parish to the defendant."

A rush of euphoria coursed through me. *Did he just say that he's going to be merciful? And, what does that mean?*

"I have been convinced, by a preponderance of the evidence, that Miss Ophelia Beaumont Breaux was, indeed, an innocent and unknowing participant in the crimes being perpetuated by the group of individuals commonly referred to as the 'Granger Gang'."

I turned to see Momma's reaction. She was smiling, but I could see a sadness underneath the smile. She nodded at me, and then she mouthed, *I told you.*

"Miss Breaux," said the judge.

"Yes, sir," I said and stood as Mr. Lange did.

"Miss Breaux, while I am finding you innocent of the charges against you, I am going to offer some stipulations."

Stipulations? I found my optimism waning.

"It is expected by this court that you will keep yourself far away from all members of the Granger family and their associates—both known and unknown to this court. You are not to consort with, work for, or seek out any member of that family. Do you understand?"

No way would I agree to that. There isn't a chance in hell I'm going to stay away from Remy.

Mr. Lange subtly pinched my thigh.

"Yes, sir," I said in my most demure voice.

"Furthermore," he continued, "if you come across the Grangers, learn of their location, or any information related to their criminal activities, you are to inform the authorities immediately. Is that understood?"

Like hell. "Yes, sir," were the words I forced out of my mouth.

"The defendant has been found innocent of all charges and is to be released from custody," he said with finality.

The sharp crack of the gavel as it struck the block caused me to jump.

That was it. I was free. Free to go back to my life. I only had to decide which life that would be. "Ophelia Breaux, descendant of the great Breaux family" or "Ophelia Breaux, bootlegger"?

CHAPTER

TWELVE

The house felt quiet as I walked through the front door. Almost as if it was surprised to see me.

"How 'bout a sandwich?" Momma led me into the kitchen. Boxes were piled on the floor and countertops.

"What're these for?" I looked into one and saw Momma's mixing bowls and spice containers. "You're not sellin' these, are you?"

"Don't be silly," she said and pulled out a chair for me before busying herself with sandwich preparations.

I ignored the chair and walked through the kitchen, eyeing the boxes. Then I followed the hallway into the living room. More boxes. These contained Momma's record albums and pictures that had once hung on the walls.

In Momma's room were more boxes, these with some of her clothes and old bedding.

My room was as I'd left it. I peeked under the mattress and under the bed. The cigar box and envelopes I'd left were still in place.

Back in the kitchen, Momma placed a sandwich and glass of milk in front of me before sitting down to start on her own sandwich.

"Where you movin' to?"

She swallowed hard, clearing the bite she'd taken from her throat. Her face flushed. "Well, I don't know that I am moving anymore. Not right away, anyhow. And when I do, it might not be for a while now."

"Now that I'm out of jail?"

She nodded.

"Where?" I demanded.

She slowly finished chewing, wiped her mouth, and sat back into her chair with a sigh. "I'm gonna marry Charles," she said, her words barely loud enough to hear.

"You're gonna marry *the judge*?" I leapt up from the table, feeling more trapped than I ever had in my jail cell. This couldn't happen. Hadn't I just gone to jail because of the things I was doin' to keep her away from the judge? "How can you do that to me?" I asked. "To Daddy?"

I didn't know she'd jumped to her feet until after I felt the slap across my face. The sting of her blow caused my eyes to tear.

"Don't you try to shame me, Ophelia Breaux. We both know there's no way I would've agreed to marry that man on my own. It was bad enough that I had to use his feelin's for me to keep us in a house."

"Then why do it? Why marry the man who ran us all off from Point de Concession in the first place? You know how Daddy hated him."

She collapsed into her chair. "I know how much they all hated him: your daddy, Uncle Louis, your grand-mère and grand-père. But I wasn't left with much of a choice, Ophelia."

I couldn't figure what she was gettin' at. We had some

money. As long as we kept workin' like we was she wouldn't have to rely on the judge any more than she already did. And that was only until I could get the rest of the money to buy her house.

"Your daddy would never forgive me if I let you sit in jail. So I did what I had to do."

The words hung in the air. Momma had agreed to marry the judge in order to get me out of jail?

"No, Momma." I slid from my chair and knelt at her feet. "No, no, no. I had a lawyer. *He* got me out of jail."

Sadness pooled in her eyes and she cupped my face in her hands. "Oh, Ophelia. Did you really think that awful defense was what convinced the judge to set you free?"

It *was* a ridiculous defense and I'd known it the whole time. Hell, nobody'd been more surprised than me when it had worked.

"You *can't* marry him. Not when we're so close to gettin' our own house."

Fresh tears flowed from her eyes and she shook her head.

"Momma, we can do it. In only another month or two we'll have enough saved up to add to Daddy's money in the bank—"

"Daddy's...There's no insurance money, Ophelia. Hell, there ain't even a bank anymore. It shut down two weeks ago."

"How can there be no bank?"

"Same has been happenin' all over the country. I guess our luck finally ran out. It's gone, Ophelia. There's nothing that can be done. Believe me, I've tried."

The realization that all of Daddy's money—along with our hopes and dreams—was gone slammed into my chest and stole my breath. *All that money.* I sat back against the cupboards, my arms wrapped around my knees, and cried. *That was it. That was all we had to live for, and it's gone.*

"I'm so sorry, baby." Momma sat next to me and wrapped

her arms around me. "I had no idea they could just take the money and disappear."

"So, we have nothin'," I said.

"We have each other."

"And the judge has you. Like he always wanted."

"Yes." She didn't try to argue it. We were beyond that point now.

"I have to go," I said and stood up.

"What? Where are you going?"

"To find Remy."

She got up off the floor and tried to pull me back into the kitchen. "You cannot go see that boy. Judge Trudeau gave you strict orders."

"Momma, there's no way I'm lettin' you marry the judge. And even if you do, he ain't gonna want me in his house. One way or the other, Remy Granger is the only chance I have at gettin' us out of this."

I saw the realization that she wouldn't be able to change my mind pass across her face. She released my arm.

"We're in more trouble than I realized, ain't we?"

I nodded.

"I don't s'pose there's anythin' I can say to get you to change your mind?"

I shook my head.

"Just make sure we get out of this alive," she said.

I went to my room to put on fresh clothes and brush my hair. The walk to the store felt longer than it ever had before and, if it hadn't been for the unbearably thick humidity, I might have tried to run all the way.

The bells jangled as I walked into the store. Dixie's mouth hung open as she took me in. "In the back," she said, pointing to the back of the store.

I headed up the aisle and she called, "Remy!"

His face was like a beacon, drawing me safely into port. I ran full into him, wrapping my arms so firmly around his neck that there was a real possibility it could be crushed.

He buried his face in my neck and I could feel the moisture of tears, which caused my own to pour.

Neither of us pulled away for several minutes. He lifted me and carried me into the back room before he peeled away, but only far enough to kiss me.

I melted into him. It felt as if it had been years since I'd tasted the sweetness of Remy's kisses. I wound my fingers into his hair, trying desperately to pull him tighter into me, to absorb him entirely.

"I'm so sorry," he said when our kisses slowed.

"Sorry for what?" I asked.

"For leavin' you behind. For gettin' you shot," he said as though I was unaware of all that had happened to me since I'd last seen him. "And for gettin' you arrested." His fingers lingered over the mottled reminder my cheek still carried from the bullet. His brows knitted together in pain—or disgust.

"You got nothin' to be sorry for," I told him. I reached up and placed soft kisses along his bottom lip. "I knew what I was gettin' myself into, and I'd do it all over again."

I pulled his lip between my own then released it, but only so that I could move into a deep, hungry kiss.

He responded, pulling me into him, and his breaths became rapid. "I'll never put you in danger again," he said through his heavy breaths.

I pushed him back. "Excuse me?" I demanded. "Remy Granger, if you think you're cuttin' me out of the gang, you've got another thing comin'!"

He stepped back and held me at arm's length. "No," he said. "No way."

"Oh, yes," I answered. "I've got even more reason to keep

runnin' now. And not only that, I think we need to start makin' our own."

"Makin' our own what?"

"Shine," I said. I couldn't stop the smile. "I heard that people all over are fascinated by the Granger Gang—"

"The Granger what?"

"They're tellin' stories all over the country about the Granger Gang. All the way to California. Imagine how much they'd pay for authentic Granger Hooch."

"It's too dangerous, Ophelia," he said. "Look what already happened to you. I'll give you the rest of the money for the house, just don't do this anymore."

I shook my head. "You can't just give me the money anymore," I said and told him about the bank and Daddy's money. "And unless I start shining, Momma is gonna have to marry the judge. There won't be no reason for her not to."

Remy shook his head, resigned as always to helping me. "We should go talk to Eloi," he said.

"Fine, but when he starts goin' on about all the things that I'm gonna do wrong, I expect you to be on my side and remind him that I did my time in jail. I paid my dues."

We left through a hidden door that led out under the store. Remy explained that the revenuers had given up sittin' outside the store, waiting for the Grangers to show up, but they still dropped in several times a day.

"We ain't been home in a month," he said as he scanned the lot and surrounding trees for signs of law men in hiding.

Once he decided it was clear, we ran into the tree line and deep behind the shrubbery. We found an old pirogue stashed under some debris. Remy pulled it into the water and held it as I climbed in. He stepped in behind me and maneuvered the boat away from the bank, along the narrow channel and into the depths of the bayou.

Night fell fast and I was afraid of losing our way in the dark. The routes through the bayou were constantly changing as the water swelled and receded. I knew, though, that Remy had far more experience on the waterways than I ever did. I'd trust his ability to navigate through the bayou blindfolded.

We arrived at a fishing camp deep in the bayou. I didn't see any sign of people when we pulled up, but Remy whistled and moments later, Eloi, Sunshine, and Sirus emerged from the trees.

The smile that spread across Sirus's face threatened to over-take him. "Ophelia!" he called and reached out to help me from the boat.

"Careful," Remy warned him as Sirus wrapped me into his arms and spun me in a circle.

"How was jail?" Sirus asked with a smile, ignoring the warning from his older brother.

"Really fantastic," I told him. "I read some good books. They have a first-rate athletics program and the food was really quite divine. You should go sometime."

We both laughed as we headed from the dock toward the cabin.

"It ain't funny," Remy called as he tied off the boat.

Eloi nodded at me as we passed. *Wow,* I thought, *he's really warmed up to me.*

"You bring the rev'nuers with you?" he asked.

Nope. He still hates me.

Sunshine smiled and offered a bow as I passed. "A wounded warrior returning from battle," he said. "I knew you was strong enough to make it in there."

"Thank you," I said and bowed back at him.

We sat in the small room of the cabin and Remy explained my proposition.

"Ophelia has decided that we should start *brewing* the shine as well as runnin' it."

"That so?" The old Eloi was back, the one who wouldn't give any indication of what he was thinking. "And what does Ophelia know 'bout makin' shine?"

"Nothing," I admitted. "Yet."

Eloi lifted his brows as if he was humored, but not at all surprised, to hear that I had an elaborate plan and no idea how to bring that plan to fruition.

"I'll find out," I said. "This is Louisiana. There're people makin' shine everywhere. I just gotta find one person who'll teach me."

"You're just gonna go walkin' around, askin' people to show you how to make shine?" he asked. "You really did like jail, didn't you?"

"This is the only chance I have left to save my mom," I said. "I don't even know if I *can* save her, but I'm gonna do everything I can to try and I ain't lettin' you, or anyone else, stand in my way." I eyed Eloi.

He started. He wasn't scared, of course, just surprised at my sudden bravado. Sunshine, Remy, and Sirus all sat quiet and wide-eyed, watching our confrontation.

"All right," Eloi said.

"All right what?" I wanted a firm commitment from him. He had to say the words so he could be held to them.

"All right, you're gonna learn to make shine."

"*We're* going to learn to make shine," I corrected him and sat down hard on a chair.

I held his gaze and noticed the subtle rise in his brows and pucker of his lips before he said, "Well, here's the thing about that. We—me, Remy, Sirus, and Sunshine, here—*know* how to make shine."

Well, of course they do, I thought. *Who hadn't made bathtub gin at one point or another since Prohibition took effect?* "But I mean on a large scale, for sellin'. Why are we payin' someone to give us liquor to run when we could do it all ourselves?"

Eloi looked at Sirus and Sunshine. They both dropped their heads, their eyes focused on the floor.

Remy stood and walked over to sit right next to me. "The thing is," he stammered a bit, "we don't actually pay anyone to brew our shine."

"Yes, you do," I said. "You told me that you have someone who makes the shine and you do the runnin'."

"That's not entirely untrue," he said. He looked at Eloi, who sat as unwavering as ever.

"You?"

One quick nod was all I needed as confirmation. He turned his attention to a cigar, putting it in his mouth and lighting it.

"All this time the supplier has been you." The brilliance of their operation impressed me. The Grangers—who neither trusted, nor relied on anyone outside of their immediate circle—were solely responsible for every drop of liquor they dealt with, from start to finish.

There was no use asking why Remy hadn't told me, or any other question for that matter. The only question that really mattered was, "Are you gonna let me help?"

Eloi held my gaze for several beats before he nodded. "I don't s'pose I got any choice, do I?"

THAT NIGHT, we took the boats deep into the bayou and—deep in the overgrowth behind a row of old crop worker shacks—I was introduced to my first still site.

Remy led me through and explained every step in the process. "We have to let the corn, sugar, and yeast ferment in these barrels for two weeks," he said. "We have another site,

160

with more mash barrels so that we can move there when we've run this site out."

"Always on the move," Sunshine said, "and always brewing."

"With the Morets shut down, we started brewing more to cover their customers," Remy said.

Sunshine's voice was heavier than I'd ever heard it before. "'Course with Claude Moret bein' busted out of jail now, he's gonna want his customers back."

"Moret is out of jail?" I turned to Remy. My life as a criminal was still in its infancy, but I recognized the danger in Claude Moret finding out that it was the Grangers who'd taken over his customers.

Remy ignored my question and turned, instead, to a lesson on the copper still and how it worked. Within the hour, I'd figured out all the intricacies of the thump keg, the worm—a coil of pipe within a smaller barrel—and how to seal the seams of the still.

"Ready for your first run?" Remy's smile reflected the excitement I was sure he saw in mine.

I nodded and he handed me the matches so that I could light the fire for my maiden batch of moonshine.

The orange glow of the fire danced along the underside of the copper still. I strained to hear beyond the popping and crackling of burning wood, wanting to hear the boiling that would indicate the liquid gold I needed to look after Momma was close to becoming a reality.

"It's beautiful," I whispered. The warm glow of the fire against the black of the night was my promised land.

"It's just liquor," Eloi grumbled from behind me.

Sunshine handed me a bucket. "We gotta get cold water for the worm," he said and indicated I was to follow him to the water.

"Why?" I wanted to know the reason behind every single thing that was done. I wanted to understand, as well as master, everything about this new life I was living.

"Cools the vapors and turns the alcohol back into liquid," he said.

"Oh," I said. I followed Sunshine and filled the bucket with cold water from the stream. Before we turned back to the still site I said—as quiet as possible, so as to not be overheard by Eloi, "Vapors?"

Sunshine smiled and proceeded to give me a quick lesson on what was happening *inside* the still while we heated, sealed, and cooled the outside of it.

"Thank you," I told him.

"Any time," he said. "It ain't everybody was raised brewin' shine."

Back at the still, my anticipation grew as we waited for the first drops of crystal liquid to make their appearance.

Remy handed me an empty jar. "You should do the honors."

I sat on an upturned bucket in front of the spout and set the jar underneath it. Minutes later the first drops of liquor began to trickle out. When the jar was near full Remy handed me an empty jug. I placed it under the spout and lifted the full jar to smell my first batch.

"Don't drink that!" Remy, Eloi, and Sunshine all yelled at once.

"I was just smellin' it!" I said. "Why so jumpy?"

"The first jar is too strong," Remy explained. "It's poison. We gotta throw it out."

We passed the second jug around once it was topped off. Each of us took a sip. The liquor bit at my tongue and warmed my throat.

"S'good." I coughed.

The jug came around again and we each gave it a second

tasting. And then a third. I don't remember when we all decided to sit down, or when everything became so damned funny. Sunshine and Sirus were rolled against each other, tears in their eyes, recounting a story about a local boy, a bicycle, and an amorous goat. Even Eloi had a smile on his face.

The sky was beginning to lighten as we capped the last jug of liquor and put out the fire.

"What do we do now?" I asked. "When do we make more?"

"Calm down." Remy laughed. "I appreciate your eagerness, but this site is run out. We'll come back tonight and move the still to the next site."

"How long until we can make more?" Every day we weren't making shine was a day that Momma might be convinced to give in and marry the judge after all.

"We're already mashed in," he said. "We can brew in two days."

Two days seemed too long. *I'm at the mercy of the Granger Gang*. I realized. *I can't do any of this without them*.

We were halfway back to the fish camp when I realized something else: I wasn't at the mercy of the Granger Gang; I was a *member* of the Granger Gang.

CHAPTER
THIRTEEN

JULY 31, 1930

I n two weeks we brewed three new batches of whiskey.
Each time I made sure I was involved in every step in the
process. I couldn't shake the desire to prove my worth to
Eloi, to show him that takin' me on wasn't a mistake.

We heard rumors that Claude Moret was threatening to find
whoever had taken over his customers.

"We keep on with what we're doing," Eloi said. "We ain't
never gonna get the chance to do this much business again. We
earn what we can while we have the chance."

"Ain't you worried he'll keep his word and come after us?" I
asked him.

"Are you more worried about Claude Moret or gettin' your
momma that house?" he snapped at me.

I didn't let the Moret Gang occupy another thought.
Momma's house was well within my grasp. A few more runs
and she'd be free from the judge forever.

In order to increase our production, Sirus and I took to

starting the mash while the others brewed, scouted new locations, and moved the still from site to site.

I was surprised late one night when Remy led Sirus and me to an abandoned barn. All the other sites were deep in the bayou or remote overgrown land.

"Indoors?" I asked him. "What have I done to deserve such luxury?"

He wrapped me in his arms and kissed me before pushing the door open.

The mash barrels, as well as sacks of corn, sugar, and the yeast had all been delivered earlier in the day while I was working at Vieux Piersall's.

"I brought a table for you," Remy said. "And there's a lamp. Eloi borrowed two stills." He indicated the obvious new additions that were also in the barn. "We'll be back when we finish the run to Metairie."

"Be safe," I said and pulled him in for a lingering kiss. I knew that every kiss tested his resolve to hold out against my advances. I found a deep satisfaction in tormenting him with the passion that flurried within me every time we were together.

He groaned as he pushed me away. "I have to go," he said and pulled the door closed behind him.

Sirus and I surveyed our surroundings and decided on a plan for the night.

"I'll start the mash," I told him. "You take watch. I'm too tired to just sit up there. I'm afraid I'd fall asleep."

"All right." He reached for the shotgun and a canteen of water. "You let me know if you need help."

"It's just the mash, Sirus." I laughed at his concern. "You Grangers are gonna have to trust that I've been well trained at some point."

"Trained by the best," he said with a wink and stepped onto the path, into the dark overhang of the trees.

The swamp songs filled the night air. Despite the late hour, it was still hot and the stifling July air hung thick all around me. I swatted at the mosquitoes that landed on my arm. They seemed to become affixed to my skin with the sticky sweat that seeped from my pores.

The sacks of corn were heavy. I strained to stand one of them upright, giving it a heavy bump as I set it down so that all the grain would be forced to the bottom of the bag to create a wider base, preventing it from tipping over. I pulled out the serrated blade that Remy had left for me and cut through a sack of corn. The teeth of the blade grabbed at the sack, cutting and shredding strings loose. When the opening was big enough, I heaved the sack up into my arms, using my legs to help give a good shot of power so that I could get the bulk of the corn high enough to pour into the vats. The water drops mingled with the beads of sweat that rolled down my forehead and dripped into my eyes.

The bags were heavy and my muscles fatigued quickly. My arms and legs shook from the effort of lifting them and the muscles in my abdomen and back were rigid and overworked already. But I continued to work. In the back of my mind, I worried that if I didn't carry my own weight, Eloi would make sure I was cut loose. I couldn't risk exhaustion, even now, without anyone there to watch me.

The sacks of sugar were smaller—had it not been from the exhaustion of lifting so many bags of corn, they would have been much easier to pour. When all , the ingredients were in the barrels I stirred them. I was careful to thoroughly mix it all. Sunshine had stressed—several times—the importance of the sugar and yeast being evenly absorbed into the mixture.

I lifted the lids back onto each of the vats, ensuring that they were sealed as best as they could be.

My legs shook, threatening to collapse, and heat radiated along my back as I set about to picking up the empty sacks that littered the floor of the old barn. I scooped up an armload of trash, trying to hurry the job.

"Ow!" I felt the sharp sting of metal cut into my finger. I dropped the sacks and shook my hand. Blood trickled down my palm as I held my hand up to find the source of the injury. Besides the dark path of my blood, I couldn't see anything else in the dark corner of the barn. I wrapped my other hand around the sight of the stinging and crossed the barn to where the oil lamp burned on a table.

I wiped the blood on my skirt and held my hand up to the glow of the flame. A ragged slice of skin was missing from the side of my third finger. I reached for the canteen and poured a small bit of water over the wound. A sharp, lightning bolt of pain shot up the length of my arm and made my insides seize and then shiver as I tried to shake off the pain. I bit my lip to hold back any noise that might escape my throat and breathed with a soft whimper.

The blood began to flow again. I retrieved an empty corn bag and searched for the blade. I was determined to cut up loose strips to use as bandages. It wasn't on the table, nor was it on any of the lids of the mash vats.

Where the hell is that damn knife? My irritation increased. I couldn't risk being found by Sunshine or one of the Grangers with a self-inflicted wound actively bleeding.

I scanned the entire barn, trying to remember where I'd last used the knife. I was opening the sacks, I knew that. It had to be near the barrels somewhere. I kicked the empty bags aside and then it dawned on me. Carefully, I moved the bags aside, one at a time. There, hung up by the loose and ragged strings of a sack, was the blade. My own carelessness and been the cause of my injury.

"Damn your carelessness," I chastised myself in a whisper.

I pulled the blade free from the strings and carried the sack along with it back to the table. I sat on a stool and carefully cut a thick strip from the sack, then folded it to make it thinner and after another excruciating rinse of my finger I began to bind the wound with the strip of the ratty sackcloth.

I wrapped my finger several times, assuring that it had enough pressure to staunch the flow of blood. Then, seeing the size of my wrapping and realizing how it would impede my work to have the lump bumping against the other fingers, I proceeded to wrap the pinky finger as well. And then the middle. I left enough of the strip of cloth to wrap around my palm and wrist, securing the bandage in place.

I cursed myself again before setting the blade on the table, right next to the lamp, and returned to my task.

As I collected the bags, I was still lost in my own thoughts. Each time my finger moved in an attempt to work together with its neighboring digits, sharp pains shot through my hand. The pain distracted me so much that I didn't initially register the sound of whistling. It was soft at first, similar to a bird's call. Then again, a bit louder.

The third time it sounded I lifted my head and cocked my ears to listen, trying to work out the sound. It was vaguely familiar.

"Raid!" I heard Sirus's voice yelling from his watch point.

My heart dropped. Fear flooded through me, propelling my legs as they pushed me around the empty ghosts of the stills, to the back of the barn.

Lights suddenly flooded through the thin spaces between the wooden barn slats.

I stopped running immediately, my legs pushing back

against further forward momentum. The hay on the floor caused my feet to slide out from underneath me. I landed firmly on my hip and fought to smother the cry of pain that threatened to find its way out.

Shadows moved across the invading light as bodies circled the barn and moved into position near the doors.

I scrambled on the floor, desperate to find some hiding spot I hadn't noticed before. There was nowhere.

The doors swung open and light flooded in, illuminating me where I sat on the floor, my bandaged hand shielding my eyes from the glaring lights of automobiles that had pulled right up to the doors.

"Cut the lights." I heard the deep, commanding voice of the judge.

What is he doing on a dry raid? I wondered.

"Go find the rest of 'em," he ordered and the shadowed forms of the revenuers in the dark night turned the other direction. I heard the snapping of branches and the crinkle of leaves as they headed into the trees looking for others.

Wherever you are, Sirus, stay there, I prayed silently.

The judge retrieved the stool from beside the table and set it near where I still lay on the floor.

I was terrified to move. The realization that I was certainly headed back to jail fell heavy in my gut. More than that, though, I'd failed again and the judge would have the pleasure of telling Momma—and being the one to console her.

As he sat, he pulled a cigar from his pocket, bit off the end, and lit it. "You wanna tell me what you're up to here, Miss Breaux?"

"No, sir," I said.

He took a deep pull of the cigar, studying the dancing undulations as they rose from the orange embers. He blew the smoke from his mouth into the path of the slow, rising smoke that emanated from the tip of the cigar. The two streams danced together, mixing and melding into one trail that rose to the height of the barn.

"If I recall, Miss Breaux..." His steely cold eyes turned to me again. They seemed rheumy and the icy blue color around his pupils lacked any sort of humanity. "Haven't I already offered you a significant bit of leniency in lieu of your criminal endeavors?"

"I was innocent of the bootleggin' charge, Judge. I swear, I got mixed up with the wrong boy, like I said before. I was in the wrong place."

"And it seems you've found yourself in the wrong place again, now haven't you, Ophelia?"

I didn't answer. I didn't want to implicate myself, but how could I explain my being here? I'd just been found in a barn full of barrels filled with mash. And I was the only person here.

"I came lookin' for him." The lie suddenly rolled smoothly off my tongue. "I been torn up 'bout tellin' his name when I came to court. I wanted to apologize. To tell him that I didn't mean him no harm."

He leaned back on the stool, lifting one foot to the support brace and resting the arm that held the cigar across it. His other fist was held to his hip and he surveyed me. I knew he didn't believe me—not fully, in any case.

"And how did you know to come here?"

I couldn't admit that I knew Remy or anyone else had ever actually been here before—that'd be as good as admitting that each and every one of us knew about, or participated in the moonshining part of the business. "I heard rumor in town," I said. "I was sittin' in the park and overheard some men talking 'bout how the law was after the Grangers and if they wanted to find them they should come out here." I gave him my most innocent look. "So I did. And then I heard the commotion outside and the lights and I got scared, but I fell when I ran for the door."

He dragged on the cigar again, but he kept his eyes on me as he played with the smoke, pushing it from his opened mouth in burst after burst. His chin bobbed just before each puff escaped, as if his jaw was forcing the smoke out.

"Why you mixed up with Remy Granger?" he asked. "That's one thing I could never figure out. With your momma, and your family, why would you go scatting around after the likes of a Granger?"

Fury and indignation swelled in my chest, but I refrained from letting him see it on my face or in my posture. "I don't know, Judge." My voice was forlorn and full of regret. "I guess the heart wants what it wants. We can't make no sense of it and we certainly can't turn love away when our souls tell us it's right. Can we?" I turned the question to him, appealing to the love I knew he had desperately clung to for so many years.

"No," he said. "I don't suppose we can." He was silent for a moment, as if lost in his own thoughts. Then he stubbed out the cigar and stood from the stool. He walked the two steps to me and held out a hand.

I was hesitant but reached up, allowing him to help me to my feet.

"What happened to your hand?"

Damn! "I cut it when I tried to get the door open, sir. It wouldn't budge."

"I see you had time to tend to it," he said, holding my hand higher to inspect my bandage. I could see the gears turning in his mind, processing everything I said, every move I made.

"Yes'sir," I said, deciding that this part of my story would be completely honest. "I used some strips from some old sacks I found on the floor and bound it up. That's what I was doin' right before your men showed up."

He didn't let go of my hand and his gaze found my own. I thought his grip tightened just enough so that if I tried to pull away, he could stop me.

I swallowed.

"And did you get the chance to apologize to your beau? I'd be interested to know if he was the forgiving sort."

"No, sir," I said. "Remy wasn't here when I got here. None of them are. Maybe they knew you was coming?"

"You've put yourself in quite a bit of trouble for that boy," he said. "Again."

"Yes, sir, I s'pose I have."

"All for love." His voice was soft, almost tender.

"Yes, sir." My nerves lit with electricity, like they were warning me that this shift in the judge's demeanor was dangerous.

The judge reached a hand up.

I flinched and then felt the cool skin of the back of his fingers as they touched and then stroked down the length of my cheek. "You're so much like her," he said in a breathy voice. "So full of passion and love. No one place—or person—is big enough to hold it all."

I tried to not shrivel away from his touch. The judge was in love with Momma. I may have reminded him of her, but certainly he knew that I *wasn't* her. *Doesn't he?*

"So beautiful," he whispered and stroked my face again.

I stayed motionless. My breath began to shake in anticipation of the danger I felt growing.

His hand trailed from my cheek, along my neck, and then down the length of my arm.

The muscles on the opposite side of my body contracted in an effort to pull away from his touch. I didn't dare look up at him for fear he would misinterpret that as a sign of acquiescence. My gaze found the floor.

"Just like her all those years ago." Out of the corner of my eye, I saw his tongue flick to moisten his lips. "But even more beautiful, if that's possible."

He held my bandaged hand and reached his other to my other shoulder. His touch drifted down my body, slowing to appreciate the contours of my curves.

I realized he'd closed the gap between us. There was barely a hair's width between us now. He towered over me. His hot breath, stale with the stench of cigar smoke, wafted over the top of my head and down across my brow.

"Please, Judge," I said in an effort to break his trance.

"Yes," he breathed, misinterpreting my words and crouching down to press his mouth to my own. His tongue, wet and snake-like, slipped between my teeth and stroked my own tongue.

I pushed against him, gagging and grunting in an attempt to refuse his advance. I rolled my head to the side, breaking the assault of his kiss.

His arms stiffened around me, his hands cupping my backside and pulling me into the swelling of his excitement. The moist path of his tongue and lips traveled from my jaw to my ear and then down my neck.

"No." I pushed at him, begging. "Stop, please, Judge. *Please.*"

"Yes," he breathed and his fingers grasped at my hair. I pulled back until I was staring at the decaying barn wood ceiling. "*Please, Judge,*" he said, either mistakenly or intentionally misunderstanding my use of those two words. "Ask me again."

"No," I cried. I tried to push at his shoulders, but his enormous size prevented me from having any impact against his advances. I lifted one foot, trying to wedge it against his thigh to help push myself away from him.

In a single second, both of his hands slid from my buttocks and grasped the back of my thighs, causing my knees to bend.

He lifted me, my feet leaving the ground, and sat me on one of the barrels of mash—positioning himself firmly between my legs. With one hand in my hair, he pulled my head back and turned the attention of his mouth to the low neckline of my dress.

I pushed at his head, crying now, begging him to stop.

The touch of bare skin high under my dress fueled my panic further. His fingertips trailed the edge of my undergarments, trying to make their way under the thin cotton.

The reality of what was about to happen dawned fully and my tears flowed with renewed intensity. Screams, high-pitched and panic-fueled, erupted in the barn. *Was that me?* Based on the burning in my throat I knew that it was. But my screams did nothing to interrupt his attentions, and I couldn't do nothin' more than prepare for the inevitable trespass on my body.

I closed my eyes to block it all out—the barn, the judge, my own screams.

I heard the judge grunt and his body landed hard against me. He was heavy, his weight fully on me.

I tensed in anticipation of what would come next.

And then I felt him slide to his knees.

His weight now removed from my body, I took desperate and deep breaths to fill my lungs, though I didn't dare open my eyes.

"What the hell—" the judge slurred. He wobbled against my leg, his weight wavering and unsure.

"Ophelia!" someone called my name.

I opened my eyes.

The judge held a hand to the back of his head and pushed himself to his feet unsteadily. His stance was wide and clumsy as he spun around.

Behind him, with a shovel held high over his shoulder,

stood Sirus, prepared to take what I knew would be a second swipe at the judge.

"You little sum'bitch," the judge growled as he tried to pull himself up to his full height. "Little Granger bastard."

"Ophelia." Sirus's voice was firm. "Run, now. Go."

I pushed myself from the barrel. My legs wobbled as they hit the ground. My knees slid forward, one of them scraping against the floor of the barn as I tried to get the other firmly underneath me. Using my hands to help propel me, I made my way to Sirus, putting him between the judge and me.

"Go on," Sirus said again. "Get out of here."

"I can't leave you here," I said.

The judge finally managed to pull himself up to his full height. He was still rubbin' the back of his head. I saw the flaw of blood red on the collar of his shirt and knew that the presence of blood would exponentially increase the trouble that Sirus would face when he appeared in court.

The judge pulled his hand away and took note of the blood for the first time. Rather than seeming alarmed, or angry, he smiled. His chest heaved with the short burst of a chuckle. He lifted his eyes to Sirus and said to me, "Yes, you'd better go on now, Miss Breaux."

I shook my head and then saw the small pistol as the judge withdrew it from his pocket, pulled the hammer down, and pointed the gun at Sirus.

"No." A wave of fear crashed over me, knocking me back a step. "Please don't." I held my hands in front of me, trying to maintain a calm presence. "I'll do whatever you want. I'll let *you* do whatever you want. Please just don't hurt him."

Sirus held his hands up, palms open at the level of his shoulders. He reminded me so much of Eloi in that moment. He appeared neither angry, nor afraid. He held the judge's steady gaze with an unwavering bravery that belied his fourteen years. There was an unreadable expression on his face, one of a man who was prepared for anything that might lie ahead.

I heard footsteps outside as people came up the old trail. *The other agents!* Relief flooded me. The judge couldn't hurt Sirus with the other agents present, could he?

"Get over here," the judge commanded me, swinging the gun toward me. He indicated for me to stand in front of him.

"Don't, Ophelia," Sirus said in a quiet voice.

The judge took three large steps toward Sirus and stopped with the gun aimed straight at his head.

Indecision froze me in place.

The judge's finger slipped onto the trigger. "Or I could just shoot him right now."

"No!" I said, and before I could register my own actions I had stepped between Sirus and the judge. I placed myself so that the barrel of the gun rested firmly on my own temple. I lifted and bent my arms, hands out so that the judge knew I had no intent to try anything foolish.

"Put the shovel down," the judge ordered.

Sirus complied with a regretful shake of his head.

"Now get down on your knees and stay right there," the judge told him.

When Sirus was on both knees, I felt the gun thrust into the back of my head and the judge grabbed my shoulder, pushing me toward the door. "You stay quiet," he said as he positioned me behind the door. He opened it as his men approached, but he used his large frame to block the door while his arm remained behind it, gun digging into my ribs.

"They ain't out there, sir. They must be long gone by now."

"You all head back to town," the judge ordered. "Check the side roads, anywhere they might have pulled off. I'm goin' to wait and see if they come back here."

"Yes, sir," the agent said. "I can have Boone and Rohan wait with you."

"Son, do I look like a man who needs the protection of a couple of scrawny kids?"

"No, sir," the agent answered quickly.

"Do as I said. Let me know if you find any sign of the Grangers."

The agent yelled the order to the others, and hope plunged into the dark recess of my soul as the car doors slammed and engines whirred to life.

The judge closed the door and slid a board into the braces on either side of it. Nobody else would be entering that door unexpectedly. My hands trembled and my breath assumed a staccato rhythm. My eyes swept the room, looking for any escape, any sign of hope. But all I could see was the solitary figure kneeling in the center of the barn, his gaze steady and unyielding.

Stop, Sirus, my thoughts screamed—though I didn't dare utter a word. *Stop challenging him.* I lifted my brows in a silent plea to Sirus. He didn't waver in his bravery. The trembling in my hands began to consume my entire body.

As the engine sounds faded, the ballad of the bayou filled the night air once again.

The judge led me to the other door. I looked over my shoulder where Sirus remained kneeling on the ground. A dark energy had settled low in the barn, choking out any optimism or hope. One or both of us was going to die here.

I was filled with the urge to turn on the judge, or run—I would rather force his hand and make him kill me now than allow him to have his way with me before I died.

Sirus seemed to read my thoughts. He shook his head ever so slightly.

When we reached the door, the judge ordered me to stop.

He shifted the gun; the barrel dug into my waist, pointing up toward the ribs.

He stepped in right behind me, his hips brushing against me. He leaned down, resting his head alongside mine, and whispered in my ear, "Now, you go on home, and you stay there. If I hear a word about any of this, you *will* be in jail, and I will make sure that your momma is mine forever."

He reached for the door and my neck wrenched as he shoved me through the opening and into the dark night.

I fell to my knees, tiny rocks digging into my skin as I skidded across the dirt.

The door slammed behind me and I heard the lock slide into place.

I heard the judge's voice as he said to Sirus, "Now boy, about my head."

There was no way I could leave Sirus. I knew within the very core of my being that the punishment would far outweigh the crime and that there was no court of law that would hear about this offense, or the justice that had been meted out for it.

The door was locked, but I tried the other on the off chance that it wasn't effectively blocked.

I heard the *"oomph"* of Sirus sustaining what I assumed was the first of many blows.

I put an eye against the outer walls of the barn, straining to see through the spaces in the slats. Sirus lay on the ground and the judge stood over him, yelling and throwing an occasional blow.

I ran around the barn, reaching my fingertips between the wooden slats, trying to find one loose enough to pull. I became more frantic as I heard Sirus absorbing the blows. He never yelled out, but I knew it must be taking every bit of control he had to stay silent as the judge beat him.

I was becoming desperate. The judge was so much bigger

than Sirus; I knew Sirus couldn't withstand that kind of beating for long. Even a Granger had to have a breaking point, though I'd never seen it.

Finally a board slipped as I pulled. The bottom of it was loose, so I set my feet wide apart and braced myself as I pulled up quickly, trying to pry it open further. The weathered slat cracked in my hands, throwing me back and off my feet.

"No, no, no," I whispered anxiously to myself. Rather than giving way as I'd expected, the board had simply cracked—only a narrow splinter of it had actually pulled free.

I scooted to the wall, bracing my feet on either side of the board, and pulled with all the strength I could muster. Loose splinters of wood drove into my hands as I lifted up on the board over and over, until the wood finally cracked and the board gave. I repeated my efforts on the next one until that one cracked and gave way as well.

There was a small opening now, barely big enough for me to slip through. But I pulled myself through nonetheless, and shards of wood caught on my dress, tearing at the material.

I stood, rounding one of the stills just in time to see the judge pull Sirus to a standing position. His hands were locked around Sirus's throat and, although the boy thrashed about, his size and strength were useless against his opponent. The judge slammed Sirus onto the table, his grip holding firm as he leaned over the smaller boy, who struggled to get free.

"Let him go!" I yelled and grabbed at the judge's shirt and arms, trying to pull him off Sirus.

Sirus's eyes had swelled, his lips had grown purple, and his face was dusky under the golden glow of the oil lamp.

I reached over the judge's head, hooked my fingers into his eye sockets, and pulled backward, as I'd seen Remy to do that boy in the old barn at Miller's Point that first night. The judge's head jerked slightly back and then I felt his elbow connect with my ribcage, knocking me to the ground, driving the breath from my body.

He looked at me as if I were a minor annoyance to be dealt with later and redoubled his efforts on Sirus's throat.

The fight left Sirus's body as I looked on. He pulled at the judge's arms, but his effort had faded.

I had only seconds to do something. Even as the air fought its way back into my body, I struggled to my feet. A glint of metal shone from behind the Judge's foot. I lunged for the blade and drove it into the back of his leg.

"Arrgh!" he yelled, kicking back at me. His pant leg was rapidly seeping red, but he still didn't release Sirus. "You bitch!" he yelled and kicked at me again while pushing Sirus even harder against the tabletop.

I rolled from his kick and leapt, running like a wild animal. I jumped onto his back, the blade tight in my fist. As I leapt onto his back, I used my free arm to grab him about the throat and wrapped my legs to prevent him from throwing me easily to the ground. I raised my right hand and, as I landed on his back, dropped it into his chest, burying the dagger deep in his body. My wrist turned and I nearly lost my grip as the blade passed and careened off the judge's sternum.

Don't lose the knife, my most primal brain warned me, *don't let him get it.*

The judge screamed. He stood and tried to shake me from him, grasping where the knife had entered his chest.

I held tight and yanked the knife from him, bringing it down again, this time catching him just below the collarbone.

He thrust forward while reaching behind him, trying to shake me loose. I locked my legs tight around his waist and cinched my arm tighter across his shoulders.

His hand dug under my leg, reaching for something.

The gun, I realized. I immediately knew where it was—I could feel the hammer digging into my leg.

I pulled the knife from his chest and sliced it across his arm, rendering it useless.

I had only a split second to act. I let loose the hold of my legs the moment I'd cut his arm. As I dropped, I grasped for the gun, pulling it from his belt. The judge pitched forward and to the right, causing me to be thrown over his shoulder. I landed hard again, but this time, my arms were in front of me, stabilizing the judge's pistol.

Confusion and then realization colored his eyes.

The blast filled the barn; my ears began to ring immediately. Smoke erupted from the gun and the smell of gunpowder assailed my nose. My teeth were numb from the shock of the shot moving through the gun and the power that traveled through my body.

I scrambled to my feet, holding the gun at the ready.

The judge was on the floor. He didn't move.

I pushed at him with a foot then jumped back out of his reach.

Still, he didn't move.

"Sirus?" Tears flowed from my eyes. "Sirus, answer me. Please," I begged. I was too scared to take the gun from its aim at the judge. I wasn't convinced that he wouldn't still stand up and come after me. My body continued to shake with terror.

A cough sounded from Sirus. He rolled onto his side and I heard him wheeze as he tried to breathe.

"Sirus, oh God, you're okay." I cried. I stepped around the judge, keeping the gun aimed at him. As I reached Sirus I used one arm to help him sit up and pulled him to the far side of the table, opposite of where the judge lay on the floor. "Relax," I told Sirus. "Just try to breathe the best you can."

He nodded at me. His eyes were wide in confusion, his

hands wrapped around his own throat, feeling for injury or tracing the areas of pain. He looked into my eyes and then his gaze followed the trail to my shoulder, along my arm, which held the gun, and to where I still had it pointed, to the figure on the floor. He looked back at me, his question apparent.

"I think so," I said. "I ain't checked, but he hasn't moved."

Sirus coughed and, on weak and shaking legs, stood and walked over to the heap of man on the floor.

"Be careful," I warned, reaching the gun further toward the judge, determined to not be caught unaware.

Sirus reached down, grabbed the judge by the shoulder, and pushed him over.

The judge rolled, eyes open and mouth agape in seeming surprise. Blood had pooled on the floor beneath him and I saw the perfect round hole the bullet had made just over his sternum. He lay on his back, legs contorted beneath him, staring up to the heaven that—I had no doubt—would reject his very presence if it hadn't already.

Sirus lifted the judge's shirt and looked underneath. "What's those?" he croaked the words and winced immediately at the pain they must have caused him.

He was looking at the other wounds, I realized.

"I stabbed him," I said matter-of-factly. I felt no remorse. The judge had been a horrible person and his evil deeds were done. I wouldn't allow myself to feel a bit of sorrow for removing him from God's green earth. "He would've killed you."

Sirus looked at the judge again. He nodded his head and let the shirt fall back into place.

He walked over to me. His hands were soft as they snaked around my hand and wrist, to relieve me of the gun.

My body was still shaking. Sirus stepped in and wrapped

his arms around me. He kissed the top of my head. "You saved my life," he whispered.

"And you saved mine," I said.

We stood that way for several minutes, me crying and both of us holding firmly to the other.

Finally Sirus pulled away. "Let's get out of here."

We walked down the road to the place we'd hidden the old truck. Sirus held the door open for me and I climbed in.

"Where do we go?" I asked him as he started the truck.

"I'll take you home," he said. "If anyone asks I was teachin' you to drive out at Miller's Point. Remy didn't want you to learn to drive so we was sneakin' and didn't tell him."

"I can't go home," I argued. "They'll be lookin' for us."

"Ain't nobody lookin' for us," he said. "The judge told them we wasn't there."

Our first stop was at the old well to wash the judge's blood off ourselves. Sirus's hands were easy to wash, but the thick blood had congealed on my hands and arms, making them sticky and resistant to cleaning. When all the blood was finally washed from my hands I looked down at my dress and then at Sirus. He turned his back to allow me some privacy so that I could remove it and try to scrub the stains from the material. I rinsed it out the best I could then dropped the wet dress back over my head.

"That's the best it's gonna get," I said.

Sirus turned as a shiver moved up my spine.

"Take this." He unbuttoned his shirt and wrapped it around me, leaving him in only his undershirt.

"You'll get cold," I protested and started to take it off.

"Nah," he said. "I'm a Granger, and in case you ain't heard, we've run naked through the bayou since birth." He smiled and winked at me then led me back to the truck. He kept an arm around me for warmth until he'd helped me into the truck and closed the door.

We rode in silence. I snuck several glances at him, trying to figure out what exactly he was thinkin'. Did he know how close he'd come to dying tonight?

"You ever wish you hadn't gotten involved in everything, Sirus?"

He pulled in front of my house and turned off the engine. "Sometimes I wish we had a different business. Maybe that we was just runnin' the store." He turned in the seat to face me. "But I'd never give up the chance to be with Eloi and Remy. No matter what it is, we're in it together. That's all that matters in this life."

I smiled at him and reached a hand to his cheek. "Did anyone ever tell you how lucky your brothers are to have you?"

"Nah." He smiled back. "One of these days they'll know, though. And maybe they'll even be answerin' to me."

"Maybe they should've been all along."

I looked at the house. Momma was peering out the front window.

"You're a good fella, Sirus Granger," I said and leaned over to kiss his cheek. "Don't ever let anyone tell you otherwise."

I got out of the truck and took the steps slowly, tryin' to decide what, if anything, I'd tell Momma. Things had gone too far. I decided. I couldn't keep the truth from her any longer.

CHAPTER

FOURTEEN

Momma stood at the door as I came in.

"What is goin' on, Ophelia Breaux? And don't tell me another story 'bout bein' in the wrong place at the wrong time."

"No, Momma," I told her. "I won't." Then I made the first of many confessions. "I been up to no good and I'm in a lot of trouble, Momma."

My tears were swift and fierce. As resigned as I'd been to doing whatever it took to help Momma, my brave face was just a charade. Months of guilt and lies poured out of me, and I collapsed on the floor in tears. Momma wrapped me in her arms and let me purge the guilt I'd been carrying.

When I caught my breath, I told Momma that I really *had* been bootlegging with the Grangers when I was arrested, and that now we were brewing our own hooch.

"I'm not stupid, Ophelia," she said. "I knew you were just as guilty as any of those boys. Why do you think I begged the judge to be lenient on you?"

I sat back and held her at arm's length. "You knew?"

She nodded and was about to say something else when a

crash out front of our house caught our attention. Lights flashed in through the front window and continued to shine, illuminating the darkness of every corner on the front side of the house.

"Emmaline Beaumont Breaux, you get out here this instant!" The voice was loud, female, and angry. I recognized it at once. *Marie Granger.*

"You stay in this house, hear me?" Momma demanded.

"Now, Emma!" The razz of the car horn sounded over and over, shattering what had been a quiet night.

"You hear me?" Momma asked again.

"Yes'm," I said, nodding. But I went to the window to look out at Marie Granger. Her car was pulled halfway onto the grass in front of our house. One arm reached through the driver's window, pushing the horn over and over.

Momma wrapped a shawl around her shoulders before she went outside. Although she made sure to push the screen door closed behind her, she'd neglected to pull the door firmly enough to stick. The door swung open slowly, beckoning me closer, so that I could better see what was happenin'.

The grinding of the car horn stopped as soon as Momma stepped onto the porch, but Marie Granger was obviously not ready to quell her fury.

"You promised me, Emmaline!" she yelled across the yard.

People up and down the street had begun to come out onto their own porches to see what the commotion was about.

"Marie." Momma's voice was calm and just loud enough to carry over to where Marie stood. "Come sit on the porch and let's talk about this."

"No, Emma." Marie took two steps toward our steps but went no farther. She leaned forward, and I worried that if Momma were any closer, Marie Granger might just attack her.

Despite the word I'd given to Momma, I pushed the screen

door open just enough to slip out behind her. My skin prickled as much from the cool night air as from concern for Momma and Marie both.

"You promised me," she yelled again, and I could hear that she'd begun to cry. "You promised that if I helped you back then, the law would never again show up on my doorstep on account of you or one of yours."

"Marie, please." Momma's voice took on a pleading tone. "I didn't know—"

"You lied!" Marie screamed.

Momma took two steps down closer to Marie. "I didn't know what they was doin', Marie. I just thought they was sweet on each other. And Ophelia wouldn't never mean to get nobody hurt."

"No," Marie said, her voice suddenly filled with a quiet resignation. "Just like you never did, ain't that right, Emma? Men just fall in love with you and eventually someone ends up dead."

"That ain't fair, Marie. And you can't blame Ophelia."

"I ain't blamin' your girl," she said. "This is still all 'bout you, ain't it, Emma? One more boy dead in town, and it all goes back to protectin' Emmaline Beaumont."

A dead boy?

Momma pulled her shawl tight around her throat but said nothing.

"Who's dead, Miss Marie?" I was down the stairs in two heartbeats, despite Momma reaching for me as I ran past. My heart thumped, threatenin' to burst through my ribs.

Marie Granger's stance wavered. Her knees buckled, and I reached to grab her as she grasped for the front of the car. Tears poured from her eyes, and I could tell from the discolored trails that streaked across her pale skin and the red swollen end of her nose that she'd been crying for some time.

Grief threatened to rise up in my own throat. Had Remy been nabbed after Sirus left me at home? Had the revenuers caught up to them after all? I kneeled down next to her, reaching for her hands, trying to get her to tell me what'd gone wrong and wanting more than anything to know that Remy was alive. As long as Remy was safe, I could withstand anything else.

"Please, Miss Marie, who's dead?"

She reached a hand up and cupped my cheek. Her brows were pulled tightly together in the center of her forehead and she unleashed a fresh flood of tears. "My baby," she cried. "They killed my Sirus."

An explosion erupted in my chest. "No!" I cried and the pain I felt caused me to double over. Spasms of grief wracked my body.

How could Sirus be dead? It's barely been two hours since he's left me. He'd been fine. He'd been young, brave, and full of life. How could he be dead?

"What happened, Miss Marie?" I held her arms, trying to get her to focus on my question, but grief overtook her and she collapsed against me. She heaved under the weight of her sobs.

Marie clung to me, and we cried together.

From behind, I felt Momma wrap her arms around me. "Shh," she whispered in my ear and rocked me the same as she'd done when Daddy had died. Momma drew Marie into her embrace as well.

Sirus's warm, friendly face took up residence behind my closed lids. I held them shut, refusing to open my eyes to a world in which Sirus Granger wasn't there to bring joy to each and every minute of the days ahead.

We sat like that, a huddled mass of grief, for nearly half an hour before Marie quietly extracted herself from our arms, got in her car, and drove away.

Momma pulled me to my feet and led me into the house. She sat me at the kitchen table, wrapped a quilt around my shoulders, and set about starting a kettle of tea.

"Momma, why did Miss Marie call you a liar?"

"She was upset, Ophelia." Momma stood from the table and poured the hot water into a couple of mugs.

"No," I said. "It was more than that. She said you'd promised her that the law wouldn't ever show up at her front door again on account of you or one of yours. She said *again*," I emphasized.

Momma set my tea in front of me then sat down, blowing on her own. She raised her eyes, looking at me over the mug. She let a deep breath out then set the cup down. "It all has to do with the feud and why we left," she said. "You know that story. Judge Trudeau was tryin' to start trouble for your daddy and his family."

"Because he was in love with you."

"Yes," she said and picked up her tea, as if that was all there were to the story.

"And Nunkie Louis died," I said. I'd never tried to piece together the bits of information I knew about this puzzle before. Honestly, I'd never even seen it as a puzzle. I'd always accepted that what I knew was all there was to the story of the great Breaux-Trudeau feud.

"Yes, your uncle died, and that's when we all decided to move on."

"Nunkie was shot," I said. "By the sheriff?"

"No," she said. "By the judge."

I set my tea cup down hard; the saucer cracked.

"It's a long story, Ophelia."

"Maybe it's time I heard it."

"Fine," she said, "but keep in mind, this ain't something I

ever wanted you to know. And you ain't gonna think highly of me after you know it."

"Tell me. I want to know." My voice betrayed me, coming out as only a whisper.

"Fine. I met your uncle Louis first. He was handsome and charming and the kindest boy I'd ever met in my life. I wasn't allowed to spend time alone with boys, so we'd meet behind the school and sneak behind trees for kisses. I even sneaked out of my bedroom to go lie under the stars with Louis all night, sneakin' back into my room just before the sun came up."

I was filled with an immediate sense of betrayal as she told her story. Momma had loved Nunkie Louis? My thoughts turned to my poor daddy, and I hated her for betraying him that way.

"Did Daddy know?"

"Yes," she said. "Louis introduced me to his brother one day at school. Your daddy had been out sick for several weeks. His first day back, Louis introduced us, and I immediately felt like I'd never be able to stay away from Phillipe Breaux. It was like there was some invisible lure that had reached out, hooked me in the chest, and was pullin' me toward him. But I couldn't do anything because I was already Louis's girl."

Momma spent the next hour tellin' me how she'd been pulled between the two Breaux brothers before finally finding her way to my daddy for good.

"Louis was so sweet, though," she said. "Even though I'd picked Phillipe, he didn't harbor no bad blood. He said he'd always love me, and if I ever decided I was really meant to be with him after all, he'd take me back." Her eyes glistened.

"And he loved me right up until the end," she said. "He threw himself in front of that bullet so that your daddy could get away. So that he could come home to us."

I didn't dare make a noise, or even breathe loud for fear of interrupting the trance she seemed to be in as she revealed secrets of the past that I'd never known.

"I held Louis as he died," she said. "I told him I'd never stopped lovin' him. I kissed him as he took his last breath." She looked at me quickly. "Not that I didn't love your daddy. I did. I was bound to him fully and eternally, but I'd never stopped loving Louis. How could I?"

"Why'd the judge shoot at Daddy?"

"There was a brief time when I couldn't choose between Louis and Phillipe. I decided that I wouldn't be with either of them in that case. I tried to distance myself from them. It was excruciating, and I tried to dull the pain by dating another boy."

"CheeChee Trudeau," I said in confirmation of what I already knew. The judge.

"Yes. CheeChee was sweet and attentive, and he loved me like I'd never been loved. He once beat up a boy just for cursing in my presence. But I couldn't get away from the Breauxes," she said. "I didn't mean to, but I broke CheeChee's heart. He was filled with rage and jealousy toward your daddy and Louis from that point on. He'd beg me to come back to him ev'ry time I saw him. Even after I'd had you, he swore he'd be a good husband to me and a daddy to you—if I'd only come back to him."

I was appalled. The judge had tried to kill my daddy, had killed my uncle, and she was still defending him? She was actually sleeping with the man who murdered my uncle.

I stood from the table so quickly the back of my knees knocked into the chair, sending it toppling into the enamel sink with a jarring *clang*. "The judge murdered Nunkie Louis. He drove our family out of town because of his jealousy. And you let him into your bed?"

Her eyes flashed with anger and then I saw sadness replace it. "Charles didn't kill your uncle because of jealousy. He may have been quicker to pull the trigger because of his feelin's for me, but he did what he did because he had to. It was his job."

"His job?" I slammed my palms onto the table and leaned toward her. Fury drove me to be daringly disrespectful. "Since when does a judge have a reason to shoot an unarmed man?"

"He wasn't a judge at the time," Momma said, her voice growing quiet again.

I sensed another piece of the puzzle was about to slide into place. "What was he then?"

"A revenuer," she said, watching as I processed that information.

A revenuer? Why would a revenuer be after Daddy and Nunkie Louis? It took two beats for me to slide that puzzle piece into place. "Daddy and Nunkie were runnin' shine?"

She nodded.

I felt weak. I bent and picked up the chair, turnin' it upright and easin' myself into it.

"Neither of them was workin' at the store," she said. "They didn't want Breaux's General to be their life. We was havin' some hard times. We was gonna lose the house. I loved that house. Eventually they started runnin' shine for a man here who was brewing his own." Her eyes cut to mine quickly like she was gauging if I knew who she was talking about.

"Vieux Piersall." So he wasn't just an old-time bootlegger, he was a moonshiner. I wasn't as surprised as I might've been before.

"The revenuers caught up with Phillipe and Louis one night. I was with them. CheeChee drew a gun on your daddy. He was angry, yellin' about how stupid your daddy was to risk his life when he had everything already—he had me. Your daddy was afraid that CheeChee would shoot him just cuz of me, and he made the mistake to reach for a shovel. CheeChee pulled the trigger. Louis musta known what was about to happen; he jumped right in front of your daddy." Fresh tears rolled down her cheeks.

I was numb. I'd never known my uncle's final moments or the facts that had led up to them.

"I screamed for your daddy to run. Told him I'd be okay. Later, I went to the only people I knew who might be able to hide him until we could get out of town."

The Grangers.

"They didn't have no reason to want to help us. I promised Marie and August that if they'd help us, they'd never get caught up in anything on our account ever again. Then, tonight, the judge sent the revenuers to chase after you."

"And they went lookin' at the Grangers'," I finished for her.

She nodded. Her shoulders had slumped and her arms lay limp in her lap. The shawl dipped below her shoulder.

She took a resigned breath then looked into my eyes again. "And it all comes back to me. Again."

I felt for her. It was a heavy burden that hung from her shoulders. For all the love in Momma, I realized she was a flawed woman. She had let men love her so much that it had brought about their destruction. Something about her wasn't able to turn a man's affections away. She let them linger, and hope, until it did them in.

I stood up. "I have to go find Remy."

She didn't move. Only looked up at me as if she knew she could do no more than say the words. "Ophelia, no. Stay here."

"I have to find Remy," I said. "And Eloi and Dixie. And Sunshine. We have to leave town, Momma."

"Why'd you even get messed up with them?"

"I told you already. I wanted to get you the money for a house of your own. So that you'd be free of the judge." There wasn't any emotion or desperation anymore—Momma wasn't my concern anymore. I'd done all I could for her. I had to get to Remy.

She wiped away a tear that rolled over her lashes and stood as though she were gonna embrace me.

"No, Momma." I stood behind the chair so it was between us. I couldn't risk allowing her the opportunity to weaken my resolve. "I'm going. I have to, before someone else dies—this time on account of me."

"Ophelia, Sirus wasn't your fault."

"He was." I realized then that I'd brought death upon the doorstep of the men who'd loved me and the ones who'd stood by me. I was no different than Momma.

I walked to the door and paused with my hand on the screen. "There's a bunch of envelopes under my mattress. You be sure and take it all—hide it before anyone comes lookin' for it. They *will* come lookin', Momma."

What I was sayin—the fact that I wouldn't be back—seemed to dawn on her slowly. She shook her head and leaned against the sink, crying silent sobs.

I took a breath, forcing myself to do what I knew had to be done. I pushed the screen open and stepped onto the porch.

I stopped and turned to her. She looked small and weary from a lifetime of grief and unrealized optimism.

"You don't have to worry 'bout the judge anymore, Momma. You're free of him. We both are."

"What do you mean, Ophelia?"

"I killed him," I said and walked out of her life.

CHAPTER

FIFTEEN

AUGUST 1, 1930

A heavy darkness had settled over Point de Concession. It was as evident in the lack of light as it was in the weight of the air that pushed down on my shoulders as I crept through town in the early morning hours. I wasn't sure if anyone was looking for me or not, but I certainly didn't want to make myself an easy pick for a passing lawman.

Plenty of time had passed since I'd killed the judge. There was a chance that he'd been found. If that were the case, the revenuers who'd been with him would know I'd been there. They'd come looking for me. It was only a matter of time.

I was desperate to find Remy, but had no idea where he could be. He was certainly in hiding, but where?

I followed the darkened route behind several houses to the far end of town. From under a weathered porch, I was able to watch both Breaux's General and Piersall's Garage. There was no movement, nor any light, from either place. The cool soil under me grew warm as I waited and watched. My eyes burned from straining against the dark, searching for any sign of movement in the surrounding area.

Dogs barked in the distance, calling out to one another over the songs of bullfrogs and crickets.

The fear and desperation that coursed through my body couldn't be quelled—even in the absence of an obvious threat.

You've got to do something, I admonished myself. *You can't lie in the dirt all night.*

I blew out the breath I'd been holding, along with my indecision, and crawled into the open night.

My steps were swift and my senses acute as I walked toward Piersall's Garage. I approached from the back, maintaining a close proximity to the tree line. Reluctant to leave the cover of the trees, I bent and ran my hand across the ground, retrieving several small stones. Slowly, I tossed them—one at a time—at the window I assumed to be Vieux Piersall's bedroom. After only four stones, I saw movement behind the widow. Several seconds later, the back door opened. Vieux Piersall pushed the screen open and stepped out, shotgun in hand.

"Mr. Roland," I whispered as loud as I dared.

"*Qui c'est q'ca?*" he demanded. *Who is that?*

I stepped from the trees. "*C'est moi,* Mr. Roland."

"Pheli? What you doin' out there?"

"I need help. I'm, I'm in—" I searched my brain for the Cajun words to let him know I was in a bad situation. "*Mal pris.*"

He opened the screen door. "Get inside," he said and scanned the area for anyone who may have followed me, or who might be lurking. He closed the door, slid a chair under the handle, and then led me into the living area.

"You hurt?" He lit a candle and held it up so that he could better see me.

"No, sir," I answered. The tears began to flow from my eyes. "But I hurt someone. And Sirus Granger is dead."

Vieux Piersall's shoulders fell and his head followed, shaking back and forth as if to deny my words. Or maybe in resignation that what he'd expected all along had finally come to fruition.

"Who kill't da boy?"

"The revenuers, I think." I realized Miss Marie had left without telling me what happened. "All I know is the law showed up at her house and..." I couldn't finish he sentence.

"N'who *you* hurt?" he asked.

My stomach roiled at the thought of making this admission yet again. "I killed the judge," I said. I was surprised that I still felt no emotion at having taken his life.

Vieux Piersall stared at me. His mouth fell open and disbelief widened his previously sleepy, heavy-lidded eyes. "Jesus *Christ*! Why you do dat, Pheli?"

"He attacked me," I said simply. I couldn't go into detail about the humiliation and fear I'd experienced at the hands of the judge. "And then he tried to kill Sirus. I didn't have a choice."

Anger lit a spark in his eyes and his face flushed. "*Bon rien*!" He nearly spat the words, calling the judge *good for nothing*. "I a'ways knew dat boy wa' more trouble'n he let on."

"Will you help me, Mr. Roland? I got nobody else to ask. I need to find Remy."

He looked at me then nodded his head. "Daylight's nearly here. We cain't risk movin' ya now. You'll have ta stay 'ere, out of sight till dark."

I didn't know how I could endure the wait until the sun went down again, but I also knew I had no choice. If I wanted to stay out of jail long enough to find Remy, I'd have to be patient. And Vieux Piersall was the only person in town I trusted to help.

The day was as excruciatingly long as I'd feared it would be. I stayed in the living area with the curtains drawn while Vieux Piersall went on about his work in the garage.

I tried to sleep, but each time a car drove past I'd jump and peak out, certain I'd find that Sheriff Alberti and his men had come to collect me.

Dusk finally settled over town and the sun gave up its hold on the sky.

A car pulled into the gas station and I watched through the sliver of space between the curtains as Vieux Piersall consulted with its driver. A moment later the car pulled away, to the far side and behind the garage.

I heard the sound of Vieux Piersall locking the front doors and then he called to me. "Come'n out, Pheli. 'S time ta go."

As eager as I was to get out of town, I was nervous about leaving the safety I'd found with him. "Where am I goin'?"

He led me through the garage and out back where the car sat idling. "Ophelia, dis here's George Allemond."

I recognized Sunshine's beaming smile in the man instantly and knew this had to be his father.

Vieux Piersall opened the door to the rear of the sedan. "When George tells ya, get out da car. Walk straight in da trees. You'll find a boat by da water. Take it t'da first dock n'git out."

"Then what?" The thought of walking into the bayou alone terrified me as much as the thought of returning to jail. Maybe more so.

"You'll know'n you git there." He handed me a sack. It was heavy, but in the dark I couldn't see what it held. He ushered me into the car and indicated I should lie down. "You be safe, Pheli," he said as he covered me with a blanket and shut the door.

I felt the car accelerate. Mr. Allemond didn't make a noise and the silence engulfed me. Loneliness flooded through me, diluting the fear that had propelled me this far. There wasn't a time in my life that I hadn't been with someone else. Someone I could rely on to guide and protect me. Momma and Daddy, and then Remy.

The fact that I'd navigated this far on my own, and under such horrible circumstances, surprised me. But I didn't want to be alone. A deep ache burned in my chest. It yearned to be comforted, to feel the warm blanket of safety. And love.

I pulled the blanket from my eyes so that I could watch the tops of the trees as we passed underneath. It was a strange sensation to be in the care of someone I didn't know, going to a place I didn't know. I wasn't even sure what I'd find when I got there.

It has to be Remy, I told myself. *I have to be going to Remy.*

The sway of the car as it traveled the road lulled me into a more relaxed state. I pulled the blanket back over my head and tried to relax my burning eyes. There was no use in tryin' to see outside now.

"You need to get out here." Mr. Allemond's voice sounded like it was echoing through a cavern. "Miss Breaux," he said with some degree of urgency in his voice, "get out."

I crawled from the car, pulling the sack that Vieux Piersall had given me along with me. The instant I'd shut the door behind me, the car pulled away, leaving me engulfed in the darkness of the night.

I strained my eyes, trying to make out any details that would give me a clue as to where I'd been left. Nothing looked familiar. Trees loomed overhead on both sides of the road. I listened carefully, tuning in beyond the calls of the swamp creatures for the sound of water.

The slushing of water moving along the bank was faint, but I followed it, walking carefully into the overgrowth. The water's edge was closer than I'd expected. As my eyes adjusted to the dark, I was able to make out the pirogue I'd been promised I'd find. I struggled to turn it over, then placed the sack inside it and eased it into the stream. I felt along the bottom of the boat and found a long reed to push myself away from the shore.

Please let it be a straight shot, I prayed. I knew there was no way I could navigate around an angry gator. The current was slow, and I kept my eyes trained downstream, watching for the dock.

Relief flooded my veins when I found that the dock was directly in front of me. I was able to navigate alongside it easily. I tied off and grabbed the sack, then followed the dock into the dark overgrowth of trees.

I stood, listening for clues as to what to do next. My heart lurched when I heard a bird call. *Or was that a whistle?*

Another followed the call, within moments. The pattern was familiar; I'd heard it before.

"Remy!" I yelled, knowing without a doubt that he was there.

He stepped through the bushes, and I ran to him.

Remy pulled me in tight to him and we stood, engulfed in each other's comfort.

"I'm so sorry," I cried after several minutes. "Sirus—" I couldn't find any words to verbalize the pain I felt, knowing he'd lost his brother.

Remy only squeezed me tighter.

When we finally pulled apart, Remy took the sack from me and led me into the dark. "Come on," he said. "Everyone's waitin'."

He led me to a row of abandoned crop workers' houses and up the porch stairs. Sunshine was inside, sitting by an oil lamp. He smiled when I entered, but his eyes had the haunted look of someone who had seen too much sadness for one lifetime.

Remy handed the sack to Sunshine and they both descended on the food items that poured from it.

"Where's Eloi?" I asked.

Sunshine looked at Remy but didn't say anything. Remy returned his gaze for several seconds and then looked back at me. "In the next cabin. With Dixie."

"Dixie's here?" I couldn't imagine why Eloi would let Dixie get mixed up in this mess. We were now officially on the run from the law, and Eloi had brought Dixie along? I fumed. *Wasn't he supposed to protect her?*

"Ophelia," Remy started to speak.

I felt the knot of apprehension growing in my gut. It was the same feeling I'd had on the day I was shot. As bad as things had been since last night, I sensed the thick, dark cloud that had descended over us was doomed to become darker yet.

"Why is Dixie here?"

Remy tried to pull me into his arms. I braced myself, arms out to prevent his attempt to redirect me. I stepped back when he advanced again.

"Remy, why is Dixie here? She shouldn't be with us, it isn't safe." If Dixie were found with us, she'd be just as guilty as the rest of us. I had enough guilt on my conscience; I wasn't about to let Dixie's life be ruined too.

Remy approached me again, his face soft, trying to hold my gaze. His voice was low and calm as he said, "The only place Dixie is safe right now is *with* Eloi."

I couldn't imagine how he thought having Dixie on the run with Eloi was the same as keeping her safe.

"Ophelia," he continued, "something happened last night."

I pushed him aside and ran through the door and onto the porch. "*Dixie*," I hissed. I looked at the row of houses, trying to determine which one she and Eloi were in. A soft yellow glow penetrated the dust-covered window of the cabin immediately to the left.

I ran down the steps and called Dixie's name again as I neared the cabin, demanding that she respond.

Instead, Eloi stepped through the door and onto the porch. His bulk prevented me from trying to slip past him and through the door.

"I want to talk to her," I told him.

He stood in the doorway like a statue: solid and unmoving. I tried to push past him, but his stance didn't waver at all.

In frustration, I hit him in the chest with both of my fists. "Let me see her!" My voice cracked. I didn't know why he was so resistant to let me in to see Dixie, but I sensed that something was wrong.

"Eloi," Dixie's voice came from behind him. It was soft and raw, but unmistakably hers. "Let her in."

Eloi's stance softened and he took a reluctant step aside, sweeping his arm toward the door to allow me to pass.

Dixie walked farther into the cabin and I followed her, closing the door behind me.

She stood at the window, looking out through the soiled glass.

"What're you doin' here?" I hissed at her. "You have no idea how much trouble we're in."

"Oh, I think I do," she said with an ironic snicker. She turned toward me and stepped into the glow of the candlelight.

The sight of her knocked me back a full two steps. I clasped my hand over my mouth to contain the gasp as tears flooded my cheeks.

Dixie's beautiful, cherubic face was swollen. Her left eye was hidden and the surrounding tissue engorged with purple fluid. Her right eye was a blue iris swimming in a pool of red. The cupid's bow lipstick was smeared clear up to her cheek and her lips split in several places. Congealed blood seemed to be the only thing holding her lip together.

Dixie's pale white skin was mottled with swirling patterns of purple, red, and yellow. Her jaw was swollen on the right side and I saw the discoloration from her face had traveled down her neck. Bruises were evident on her collarbone.

"Who did this?" I reached for her, careful to avoid any area of injury that I may not have seen.

She stepped into my embrace and her tears immediately dampened my shoulder. I felt her knees give and I eased myself to the floor with her still in my arms.

Eloi came through the door the moment she'd cried out and I looked at him for some kind of support. In that moment I saw that Eloi Granger felt as helpless and lost as I did. Dixie may have carried the bruises, but Eloi suffered her pain as well.

I sat with Dixie until her cries slowed and her breathing grew heavy. Exhaustion had overtaken her. I laid her head on a bedroll and stepped away, pulling Eloi onto the porch with me, where Remy and Sunshine were waiting.

"Who did that to her?" I demanded.

Eloi's voice was hard. "Moret."

"I'm gonna kill that son of a bitch," I said with the full conviction that I would accomplish just that. Fury took hold of my body, and I paced across the porch, feeling like a wild animal in a confined space.

Remy stepped in front of me and eased his hands around my waist to stop me. "There's more."

"More what?"

"It was Moret who killed Sirus," he said. "His men dressed like revenuers and went to our house lookin' for us. Sirus came home, saw revenuers, and tried to run. But they shot him."

I was too numb to cry again, and my body held too much rage to contain any more. I could only stand and listen as

Remy told me how they'd come up the bayou by boat and heard the yelling as Moret's gang saw, and then shot Sirus—seven times.

"We got to the store too late," Remy said. "Dixie was lyin' out back. She was unconscious when we found her."

Eloi's face pinched and he took the steps two at a time and disappeared around the corner of the cabin.

Eloi was right about me, I thought as the sour taste of bile crawled up my throat. *He said I was gonna be the reason someone died.* Sirus was dead and now Dixie was hurt. Momma was free of the judge and I didn't need nothin' else in my life but Remy—it was time I put my mind to gettin' us both out of this mess. Gettin' all of us out of it.

"We need to get out of Plaquemines Parish," I said to Remy and Sunshine. "Before someone else gets killed."

"We've got business with Claude Moret before we go anywhere." Eloi's voice cut through the dark.

"Are you crazy?" I leaned over the railing. "Sirus is dead. Dixie could have died. Are you really gonna risk Dixie's life again just to get revenge? Are you gonna risk Remy and Sunshine?"

He considered what I'd said, then answered, "You take Dixie. All of ya'. Get out of town. I'll meet up with you when I've seen to Moret." He walked back onto the porch, past us, and opened the door.

"What if you *don't* meet up with us?" Remy asked.

"Then I don't." Eloi stepped through the doorway and closed the door behind him.

Remy led me back to the other cabin.

"I'll take first watch," Sunshine said and sat on the stoop with the shotgun.

My skin tingled in exhaustion, both physical and emotional. I couldn't block the image of my beautiful friend's swollen and battered body or the thought of sweet Sirus being gunned down in the Grangers' front yard.

I lay beside Remy and molded my body as tightly to his as I could. The numbness I'd felt earlier had grown and threatened to consume my entire body. I needed to *feel*.

I reached up and pulled Remy's mouth toward mine. His soft, sweet kisses turned hungry.

I wrapped my arms around him, pulling him harder into me. Heat flowed through my belly and my breath came more rapidly. My body craved the feeling of Remy's heat against my skin. I pushed myself up and swung one leg over him. Sitting across his hips, I was able to free him from his shirt and I pulled my hands across the surface of his chest. His skin was hot and smooth and the muscles in his abdomen quivered as my fingers traced along the top of his pants.

I leaned over him, desperate to taste him again. My lips collided with his and our tongues met with equal intensity.

Remy grasped behind one of my knees and sat up, flipping me onto my back and rolling on top of me. His weight held me in place and I felt grounded for the first time in days. I pulled him tighter to me, reaching through his arms to wrap my own arms around his back.

I craved the heat that emanated from Remy—it consumed me. Before I could think of how, I'd shed my dress. Every inch of my body electrified as it made contact with Remy's.

I was desperate for him, yet afraid he would pull away like he had so many times before.

"Please don't stop." I gasped.

"I won't, chèr," he breathed in my ear. "Not this time."

And he didn't.

We pulled at each other, our hands trailing the contours of each other's bodies.

The pressure of Remy's weight on top of me wasn't enough.

I grasped greedily, pulling further into him. I wrapped myself around him, creating a cocoon of fervent energy.

Heat radiated from us and seemed to meld us together. My craving for him continued to grow until fulfillment exploded throughout my body.

Remy fell beside me, his body damp, breath rapid.

My muscles wouldn't respond. A sense of peace washed over me. I couldn't worry about Momma or bootleggin'. I could only focus on the thundering of my heart and the satisfied heat that had begun to spread through my entire body.

I rolled into Remy's arms and lay my cheek against his warm chest. His breath had grown heavy with sleep.

"I love you, Remy Granger," I whispered.

SIXTEEN

AUGUST 2, 1930

I woke up the next morning alone under the blanket. As I sat up, I saw that Sunshine was lying discreetly against the farthest wall, facing it as he slept.

My dress was in a wrinkled heap, but I pulled it on and stepped onto the porch to look for Remy.

He was sitting on the top step, shotgun lying beside him.

"Good mornin', chèr," he said and wrapped his arms around me as I sat in front of him.

The world seemed peaceful in that instant. The white glow of sunshine rose over the trees and illuminated the earth. Birds chirped their welcome to the new day.

"We have to leave," I said in a soft voice.

"I know," Remy answered.

We sat for nearly an hour, looking out at the last bit of peace we'd seen in days.

"All right." Eloi came up beside us. "We'll leave."

I was surprised. Only hours ago, Eloi had been determined

to go after Moret, even if it meant his own death. I could only guess that Dixie was behind Eloi's change of heart.

Remy nodded. "We leave."

Sunshine stepped through the door. "We gonna need money," he said. "Can't go home for sure."

"I got forty gallons stashed," Remy said, "and a buyer in West Pointe à la Hache."

"That's too risky," I told him. "We need to go now."

"We ain't goin' anywhere far without money," Eloi said.

I told them about the money I had under the bed in Momma's house.

Eloi shook his head. "Too dangerous. If the Moret gang was waitin' on Dixie, they certainly know about you, too. Remy's gonna have to do that run."

My heart plunged into my stomach; I knew that Eloi was right—we needed the money to get out of Plaquemines Parish for good. I couldn't risk attracting gangsters to Momma's house. Doin' one more run was the only way to get the money we'd need to flee. It was Remy's buyer; he couldn't send anyone in his place. Eloi was the only one I'd trust to get Dixie safely away, so he couldn't help with the run.

"I'm goin' with you," I announced to Remy. I interrupted him before the words could pass his lips. "And don't think you're goin' to change my mind."

"Me, too." Sunshine clapped a hand on Remy's back and sat next to him on the step. "Another set of eyes and ears to make sure everything's as it should be."

"All right then," Remy said. "It's settled." The words were far more confident than the voice that carried them.

Eloi listened as Remy told him how to get a message to the buyer, then he helped Dixie into the truck.

"You take care of her," I warned him. "I *will* be comin' along to make sure she's safe."

He nodded once, climbed in the driver's seat, and drove away.

We stood shoulder to shoulder for several minutes, watching the dust kicked up by the tires slowly engulf the truck as it grew smaller in the distance.

A hollow feeling engulfed me as I realized this would be my last day in Plaquemines Parish. Deep in my heart, the door to the Cavern of Things Past swung open and I remembered the day I'd stood watchin' as Momma and my grandparents loaded our belongings into their cars. At the time, I was too young to know what it meant to flee the only place I'd ever wanted to call home. Now, I had a better appreciation for what Momma must have been feeling that day: a frantic desire to save the man she loved.

"Let's go," Remy said. He reached for my hand and led me back through the trees to the old dock.

The boat was where I'd tied it off the night before. The three of us climbed into it without a word. Remy navigated through the maze of waterways. I was relieved when I finally recognized the camps just south of the store.

"We'll get out here and walk," Remy said. "That way we can hunker down and watch the area for a while. If we see anything suspicious, we head back to the boat."

The going was painfully slow. We walked with deliberate steps to minimize any noise we might make walking on dried leaves and twigs. When we were close enough to see the store and the area around it, we lay on our bellies under the brush and watched for an hour before deciding it was safe.

It was nearly dusk again when Remy finally said, "Let's go."

We crept from the bushes and ran directly to the shed. Sunshine and I held the doors open as Remy drove out. He slowed the car just enough so that we could jump in without being dragged along.

"The liquor's stashed in a barn up by Belle Chaise," Remy said. "It'll take us twenty minutes to get there and get it loaded."

"Remy, if we get caught—"

"Don't," Remy interrupted me with a look of warning.

I nodded and let the words die away.

Silence engulfed the car as we drove. Each of us was preoccupied with our own thoughts and fears.

Last shot, I thought. *Just one last run. Please, Lord, see us through this.*

The last bits of daylight were just passing as we pulled up to a barn. It wasn't what I'd expected.

Every other barn I'd encountered since I began runnin' shine had been run-down and abandoned. This bright red structure was teeming with life. Cows meandered along one side and horses brayed from interior stalls. An ornery goat followed us inside, biting at my hem and Sunshine's shirttail.

"It's under the hay bales." Remy pointed to a stack and we set to work pulling aside the heavy bales.

Deep under the stack was a wooden box filled with forty jugs of moonshine.

We moved as quickly as possible and filled our arms with as many jugs as we could each carry. We hauled them to the car, sometimes while pulling that stubborn, clothes-biting goat along with us.

Sweat-drenched and fatigued, we got back in the car for the drive to West Pointe à la Hache. With the back seat filled with shine, Sunshine sat in front with Remy and me. Remy rested his arm across my shoulders and I scooted firmly into his side and laid my head on his shoulder.

"We're here," I heard Remy say as he slowed the car.

I must have nodded off during the drive.

"I don't see nothin'," Sunshine said as he studied the darkness outside his window.

The car crept along the road and gravel popped under the tires as we drove.

"There." I pointed to a truck that was pulled over along a crossroad.

Remy stopped the car. "You stay here," he said. "Take this."

I felt the cold weight of a gun as he pressed it against my thigh.

I wrapped my hand around the weapon and noticed that Sunshine had propped the shotgun between us. He had a pistol of his own tucked under his thigh.

Remy got out of the car and approached the man in the truck. They talked for several minutes.

I pulled the hammer back on the gun. The click as it locked in place reverberated in the silence of the car.

"Careful," Sunshine murmured.

I blew the air from my lungs, willing the tension to go with it.

Remy returned to the car, leaning toward Sunshine's window. "Let's go," he said. "Ophelia, you stay in the car."

Sunshine slid his pistol toward me before he opened the door and stepped out to help Remy with the shine.

I sat in the dark of the car, my hands wrapped around the gun, thumb tracing the contour of the grip. I felt the firm presence of Sunshine's pistol under my thigh.

Remy placed the last jug in the back of the man's truck.

I tensed as the man returned to the cab of the truck and reached under the seat.

Remy hadn't noticed the man move—he's been too busy securing the whiskey bottles. Sunshine was halfway back to our car, his back to Remy.

Just as I was about to yell a warning to Remy, the man said something to him and Remy turned.

I nearly cried out in relief as I realized that the man was handing Remy payment for the liquor.

Sunshine reached the car and leaned against it. He watched as Remy thanked the man and they shook hands and parted ways.

The man climbed into his truck and I heard the grating sound as the engine started.

Remy stood back as the truck rolled onto the main road. As he passed our car, the truck slowed. The man leaned an arm out the window. He smiled and nodded at me.

I returned his smile, grateful to finally be done with this run.

"Claude Moret sends his regards," the man yelled. He accelerated his truck quickly and sped past.

My heart dropped into a pit of terror. "Remy!" As I yelled his name, I slid into the driver's seat and cranked the engine to life.

An explosion erupted around us. Bursts of light invaded the darkness, assailing my eyes. I tucked to the side, lay on the seat, and covered my head with my arms. The continuous explosion of gunfire filled my ears, not quite drowning out my screams.

Part of the front window shattered, showering me with shards of glass.

Finally, my rational brain took over. *Do something, Ophelia!*

I started the car again and yelled, "Remy! Sunshine!"

The gunfire finally slowed and I was able to determine where the shooters were. There were several of them hiding behind the tall growth of grasses and the trees on the opposite side of the road.

I peeked over the dash, just long enough to see Remy lying prone at the side of the road. Sunshine crawled toward him.

I held the pistol out the window with one hand and I shifted into gear with my other. My shots were slow, deliberate. I only hoped Moret's men would take shelter for just a few moments so that I could get to Remy and Sunshine.

A sharp pain coursed through my left shoulder as I released the clutch and pulled ahead slowly, using the car to shield Sunshine. I recognized the burn of a bullet, but knew that I couldn't give in to the pain.

Once I was parallel to Remy and Sunshine I stopped the car and reached across to throw the passenger door open.

"Remy!" Relief washed over me as he lifted his head.

Sunshine reached him and together, they scrambled toward the car. Their bodies had no more than touched the seat when I let the clutch pop free from under my toes and stomped my other foot on the accelerator.

The tail end of the car pulled to the side and the tires danced across the gravel, looking for traction.

The night exploded in another hail of gunfire. Searing pain bit into my thigh and I cried out as the tires finally caught and we escaped the assault.

The steering wheel jerked in my hands and I tightened my grip in an effort to control the car. Each bend in the road felt tighter than the one before and I adjusted my speed at the turns to try to get the car's fishtailing under control.

"Are you hurt?" Sunshine asked.

"Nah," Remy said. "I'll be fine."

"You?" Sunshine had turned to me.

Pain and terror had taken over my body. I couldn't speak. Every bit of control I had was occupied with a primal urge to flee from danger. I nodded. *Yes, I'm hurt.*

Sunshine must have mistaken my silent assent to mean *I'll be fine.*

We drove in silence. Sunshine murmured something to Remy, who offered a quiet response.

"Where do we go?" I asked.

"Turn right up ahead," Sunshine said.

He led me through several more turns until I saw the familiar sign hanging across a drive: Fortunate Farms.

I turned onto the road and followed it through the abandoned, overgrown orchards toward the old storage sheds that were set far back into the land.

"Go on in, chèr," Remy said. "I got somethin' to talk to Sunshine 'bout."

I started to protest.

"Go on, now." His voice was firm.

"We'll be right in," Sunshine said in a soft voice. "It'll just be a minute."

The pain in my left shoulder had reached near intolerable levels. I used my right hand to open the door and retrieved the pistol from where it'd fallen on the floor of the car. I whimpered as I stepped onto my left leg and the muscle screamed in protest.

I ignored the pain and focused instead on my anger at Remy and Sunshine. I slammed the door. *Didn't I just save both your lives? But for some reason I can't be trusted with whatever you got to say.*

The shed had obviously been cleared out years ago. Moonlight invaded the small room through the weather-rotted slats. There was nothing there but a stack of empty grain sacks and the broken handle from some long ago stolen implement.

I retrieved the sacks and folded them, creating a cushion to sit on. I sat, crossing my arms and legs, determined for Remy to walk in and see exactly how furious I was at having been dismissed.

I inspected my wounds as I sat. A bullet had torn through my shoulder, but it had exited the muscle only an inch from the place it had entered. The wound on my thigh was a simple grazing across the top of the muscle. I'd need to clean them and watch for infection, but I was lucky. We *were lucky*, I corrected myself.

After only a few moments, the door creaked open and Sunshine stepped through. Remy was right beside him, his arm slung across Sunshine's shoulders. I realized that Remy was leaning against Sunshine.

"What's the matter?" I jumped from the floor and helped Sunshine ease Remy to the folded sacks.

As my hand pulled away from Remy's waist I felt the slippery fluid that extended from his waist to his hip.

"Is that blood?" Though I couldn't see the color, my hand was covered in dark fluid. "Oh, no!" My hands shook as I ran them along Remy's body, feeling for any other injuries.

"Just let me lie down, chèr," he said. "I'll be okay."

My gaze met Sunshine's. I knew he didn't believe Remy any more than I did.

"I'm goin' to find us some food and water. And some bandages," he said.

Remy leaned up on one arm and groaned. "No," he said, "it's too dangerous. We just need to sleep." He rolled onto his back and his breathing grew heavy.

"Remy?" I whispered. "Can you hear me?"

He didn't respond.

I grasped Sunshine by his arm. "We have to get something to clean the wounds. You go, or I will, but if we don't get supplies he'll die for sure."

Sunshine nodded. "I'll go."

"Promise me you'll come back?"

We both knew he couldn't make that promise—not really—but he nodded anyway.

As the car pulled away, I lay next to Remy, holding pressure to the seeping wound and whispering in his ear, "You stay with me, Remy Granger. You can't leave me like this." I sniffed back the tears. "You can't leave."

SEVENTEEN

AUGUST 3 TO AUGUST 4, 1930

S unshine returned just before the sun began to lighten the sky.

"All I could get was some whisky to clean the wound, some bandages, and a salve from a traiteur I know on Bayou Concession."

It didn't seem like enough, but our options were limited and I knew that the folk medicines often worked better than any doctors'.

"She wouldn't come?" More than anything, I didn't want to be the one person solely responsible for Remy's survival.

Sunshine shook his head and looked at where Remy lay on the floor. Pain and regret pinched Sunshine's face. "She's got a new momma who just started laboring. Could be all night the rate she's goin'. Nanny'll come when she can, though."

If Remy makes it that long, I thought.

Sunshine returned to the car as I opened the whiskey bottle and pulled out a clean bandage. He returned with water, food, and an oil lamp.

"Remy." I shook him gently. "I need to clean your wound."

He was slow to awaken and his tongue seemed thick as he said, "I'll be fine, chèr, I just need to sleep it off."

"Let me look," I coaxed, pushing his hands back when he tried to brush mine away.

I undid the lower buttons of his shirt and folded the fabric aside. Blood pulsed from the wound. The edges were blackened from the heat of the bullet. *The bullet is in there,* I realized. I had no idea how to retrieve a bullet even under the best circumstances, much less in a run-down shed on an abandoned orchard. All I could do was to try and stanch the flow of blood and keep the wound as clean as possible.

"This is gonna sting," I warned before I poured the liquor over his right flank.

A primal scream erupted from Remy and he tensed in an effort to roll away from the pain.

Sunshine pushed him back flat.

"I am so sorry," I cried.

"Again," Sunshine instructed me. "Right into the hole."

My hands were shaking and Remy fought against the pressure Sunshine exerted on his shoulders.

I blinked away the tears and lowered the mouth of the bottle to the wound. With one hand, I used my fingers to apply pressure on two sides of the wound until it yawed open. Then I poured the whiskey again, assuring the stream was delivered directly into the wound.

Remy's scream reverberated through my body. I pressed a clean bandage to the wound just as he lost consciousness.

"Let's bandage him up quick," Sunshine said. "Before he wakes up again."

We took the opportunity to rinse out the wound again then applied the salve, a bandage, and wrapped cloth strips around Remy's waist to hold pressure on the wound.

Sunshine helped clean my own wounds. I nearly screamed when the whiskey burned its way into my tissue—I couldn't imagine the pain Remy must have felt.

"We have to get him to town," I told Sunshine. "He needs a doctor."

Sunshine shook his head and reached into his pocket. He withdrew a folded paper and handed it to me.

It had been torn from the newspaper. I saw right away that it was the front page of the *Times-Picayune*. The words were thick and dangerous: *GRANGER GANG AND MORET GANG AT WAR. JUDGE KILLED IN THE CROSSFIRE.*

Below the headline was a picture of Remy and one of Claude Moret.

"There's a bounty," Sunshine said. "On Remy and on Eloi."

So there would be no doctor. Doctors led to questions and questions led to the authorities. I knew Remy would never walk willingly into the arms of the law.

I woke Remy hourly and assured that he had a drink, but he refused to eat anything.

"I'll just throw it back up, chèr."

My efforts to convince him to let me take him to a doctor were in vain.

"I ain't never goin' to jail, Ophelia. I cain't."

We cleaned his wound and changed the bandages every two hours. The faint light from the oil lamp cast a sickly glow across his face. By midnight, Remy had grown feverish.

"We can just take him," I said to Sunshine. Our voices had assumed a whisper so as to not disturb Remy. "He isn't in any position to fight us."

Sunshine shook his head. "You don't know what jail did to his père. We decided early on that ain't none of us goin' to jail. Ever."

There was no room for discussion.

"We promised each other," he added.

I thought about my own père and how his death had torn Momma's life apart. Mine as well.

"I can't lose him, Sunshine." The desperation hung thick in my words. "I can't go through somethin' like that again."

"It ain't been that long since your père passed, has it?" He leaned back against the wall on the other side of Remy.

I shook my head, unable to put voice to words, and dunked a cloth in water. I wrung the cooling water from it and wiped Remy's forehead. His dark curls glistened in the yellow light. The more I busied myself with the task of tending to Remy, the less my mind fretted about how useless my actions might actually be.

"What happened with him?" Sunshine asked.

I was taken aback. Nobody'd ever come out and asked me about Daddy. Most were content in whispering behind my back.

"Daddy joined the military after we moved to Charlotte. One night he was guardin' an outpost where he was stationed in Nicaragua. There'd been warnings that the post was gonna be attacked. A group of people ran from the village in the middle of the night. They were yellin', but he couldn't understand them. The crowd started to run right at him. He got scared and started shooting."

The memory of hearing what Daddy had done washed over me. I'd been devastated for him. Everything he'd ever done in his life up to that point had been out of love. Even with him halfway across the world, I'd felt his pain.

"The villagers had been fleeing from a local mobster. They'd been runnin' for their lives when Daddy shot them."

Sunshine blew a deep breath from his chest and his head shook in disbelief at the horrible events.

"Daddy couldn't bear the guilt," I continued. "For the

villagers as well as for every decision he'd made that had led him to that moment." The pain poured freely from my eyes and warmed a path down my cheeks.

"He took his own life?" Sunshine asked in a hushed voice.

I nodded.

Sunshine stood and retrieved a clean bandage. He handed it to me and squeezed my shoulder before returning to his place on the floor.

I wiped my eyes. The door to The Cavern of Things Past cracked open and I let myself peek inside for a moment, just to catch a glimpse of a few of the happy memories I'd stowed there.

"I never did understand why you wanted to be a bootlegger," Sunshine finally said. "I knew you had problems with the judge, but runnin' shine seemed a strange choice."

"I guess it got to the point that every day in my life was filled with darkness. Then I saw a glimmer of light shine through, and I ran toward it and put all my hope on it." Remy had been my light, but now the dark was so dense that the light didn't seem bright enough to chase it away.

"Maybe you was too focused on the dark to see the other sources of light," he offered.

"You're probably right," I conceded. It was true: I'd had Momma, Dixie, and my freedom. I'd had everything a girl could need, and I'd lost everything.

Remy moaned.

Exhaustion settled in and I curled next to him on the hard ground.

"I'd do it all again, Remy Granger," I whispered and stroked his cheek.

His head rolled toward me, and he placed a kiss on my forehead.

I snuggled in closer to him.

There was a soft rustling as Sunshine dimmed the lamp and lay down to sleep.

At some point in the middle of the night I heard Remy's voice. "I love you, chèr."

I reached up and placed a kiss on his lips. "Do you need anything?" I whispered.

"Nah," he said. "I'm just fine."

Bird songs filled my dreams. I couldn't recall the last time the birds had begun to sing before I was awake.

"Ophelia."

A gentle pressure encircled my upper arm.

"Wake up."

Sunshine leaned over me. His face was gaunt. He jerked his head to Remy.

I lifted my head and sat up to my knees.

Remy's mouth was open. His breaths were short and gasping.

"What's happening to him? What do I do?" I shook Remy, trying to get him to open his eyes.

Sunshine knelt behind me and put his hand on my shoulder. "He's dyin', Ophelia," he said softly. "There's nothin' we can do."

"No!" I swatted Sunshine's hand away, turned, and shoved him away from me. "Remy, wake up," I begged. "Please wake up."

Sunshine and I were both engulfed in tears as we kneeled beside Remy.

His breaths slowed, but the gasping continued.

Sunshine placed a hand on Remy and bowed his head.

"It might be for the best, Ophelia. Remy'll always be a wanted man now. The only freedom he's gonna find is in death."

"No. He'll make it." I refused to believe that death was the best option for him. Despite how close he already appeared I couldn't imagine life in a world that didn't include Remy Granger.

I leaned over, a hand on each side of his face, and absorbed every detail of him, searing him into my memory—just in case.

Sunshine placed a hand on my back. The warmth of his touch was comforting and replaced the chill that had taken up residence deep in my body. "No matter how it comes about, Ophelia, Remy Granger can never return to Point De Concession. You have to be prepared for that."

The sound of a car approaching the shed sent my heart racing.

"They found us," I hissed at Sunshine as I scrambled across the shed for the pistol I'd left on the ground the night before.

I rolled into a seated position, my back braced against the wall, gun balanced on my knees and at the ready.

Sunshine scrambled into place next to me. He held the shotgun steady, his sight squarely focused on the door.

The crunching sound of footsteps cautiously approaching the shed were barely audible over the thundering of my heart. My finger twitched at every step I heard, eager to pull the trigger and be rid of our latest threat.

"Easy," Sunshine whispered.

I steadied my breath.

A soft knock rapped against the door. *"C'est moi, Sunshine. C'est Nanny."*

Sunshine lowered the shotgun as the door crept open and the small room flooded with the yellow glow of daylight.

A small Cajun lady—she didn't have to stoop to pass through the low doorway—stepped into the small space. She held her hands in front of her to show that she posed no threat.

Sunshine laid his gun on the floor as he stood to great her.

His voice was full of relief as he pointed to Remy. "You made it. He's real bad off."

She glanced at Remy before looking at me. Her dark eyes were kind, but questioning. I realized I still had the pistol pointed at her. I released the hammer and slid the gun into my pocket.

I knelt next to her as she inspected Remy's wound.

"Can you help him?"

Her face was pinched as if she, herself, doubted she possessed the ability to provide the kind of healing Remy needed. She pulled a small bottle from her pocket and poured it over Remy's wound and then a small bit into his mouth. "I'll do what I can, child."

She mumbled words I couldn't understand as her hands hovered over Remy. When she was done she snapped her fingers and four men came into the shed. Before I knew it they'd carried Remy out and placed him in the back of a truck.

I tried to climb in beside him, determined to go wherever Remy was heading. Sunshine held me back. "We can't go," he said.

I pulled against him, but he held me tight as he turned to the diminutive traiteur.

"We have an agreement?"

Nanny nodded at Sunshine without a word and then climbed into truck.

"No! You can't let them take him," I yelled and fought against Sunshine as the truck—and Remy—drove away.

Sunshine's arms wrapped tighter around me as I fought against him.

"You have to trust me on this, Ophelia," he said calmly in my ear when I finally collapsed in exhaustion. "And if you don't trust me, you have to trust that Remy knew what had to be done."

. . .

SUNSHINE and I returned to Plaquemines Parish with the news that Remy Granger had died of a gunshot wound to the belly. We explained that Sunshine and I had been forced to leave him behind when we'd fled. The revenuers never did find Remy's body.

"Gator's prob'ly got it," Sunshine explained to them when they'd questioned us again.

Before Remy's headstone could be placed next to Sirus's, Sunshine and I were arrested.

"How do you plead, Miss Breaux?" Judge Campbell asked.

I looked at Mr. Lange for confirmation before I answered, "Not guilty, your honor."

EIGHTEEN

MAY 26, 1934

The crunch of gravel and whine of brakes told me that a car had pulled up in front of the garage.

"You stay here," I told Sunshine. "I'll take care of them. See if you can't jimmy that bolt loose for me." I handed him the wrench and grabbed a rag on my way through the garage, wiping the grease from my hands.

The sign swung in the breeze over the gas pumps: *Piersall's Garage*. I'd had no desire to change the sign, and it still brought in business.

It was obvious that the man didn't belong in Plaquemines Parish. By the looks of him, he'd never stepped foot in Louisiana before. He removed his suit coat and slung it over his shoulder as he assessed the building and surrounding neighborhood. As he turned to survey Breaux's General, I noticed how the thick material of his shirt hung heavy with perspiration. From his collar to his belt, it was damp.

How far north you come from, stranger? I guessed New York.

Maybe Chicago. Somewhere that was still cool now. He certainly wasn't prepared for bayou weather.

I leaned back into the garage. "Hey," I said in a quiet voice to get Sunshine's attention. "Keep an eye out back. Make sure they don't come walking in while this fella's here."

Sunshine nodded and walked through the back screen door. He eased it closed without noise and I went back to watching the stranger. He wasn't with the Morets. He was definitely from north, but he didn't have the look of a government man. The U.S. Marshals hadn't been around in over a year. I was convinced they'd finally given up hope of finding Remy alive.

The man turned his attention back to the garage.

I took a deep breath, squared my shoulders, and stepped out through the door.

"Can I help you, mister?"

He smiled and the kindness of that smile reached his eyes.

I relaxed a little. He didn't seem to be a threat, and he definitely didn't have the look of the law.

"Yes, ma'am." He took the hat from his head and held it in his hands. "I was hoping to talk to Mr. Piersall."

"What about?"

"Well, ma'am, in all honesty, I'm a reporter for the Chicago Daily Tribune. I'm doing a story on the Granger Gang. It's been almost four years since Remy Granger went missing."

"You mean since he was killed."

"Well, yes, ma'am. Either way, it's quite a story—the stuff legends are made of. Anyway, I heard that Remy Granger used to work for Mr. Piersall."

I swallowed against the grief that rushed back to claim its place in my throat. It was a grief that still stifled my breaths and made it impossible to swallow the tears that were its constant traveling companion.

"Vieux Piersall ain't been here in two years."

His shoulders fell, as if the direction of his life had been entirely dependent on this one meeting. I saw the question form as he thought it and lifted his eyes back in my direction. The glare of the sun caused him to squint and shield his eyes with a flattened palm.

"There ain't no forwardin' address," I said, interrupting his optimism. "He died."

His head bobbed to the right, following the drop of his shoulders. "I thank you for your time, ma'am," he said and turned back toward his car.

It'd been so long since I'd heard someone say Remy's name. Nobody in town spoke it anymore—not out loud anyway, only in whispered voices that ceased when I entered the room.

The good people of Point De Concession remained grateful to the Grangers. They'd refused to cooperate with the authorities so long as the effects of the Depression didn't set foot on their doorstep. Despite what was happening across the country, every family in town still had a roof over their heads and food on the table.

Claude Moret had officially been declared as the man who killed Judge Trudeau, but the rumors would never subside about the Grangers.

Eloi and Dixie were focused on raising their kids on the right side of the law. Eloi wouldn't risk losing the store—or his family—by ruminating over his lost brothers. Especially when there were lingering question as to exactly how Claude Moret had been killed—beaten to death, as it happened.

The ache in my soul was constant. The guilt I carried about the past was a lonely burden to bear. So many lives had been destroyed—and lost—on my account.

"What do you want to know 'bout Remy Granger?" I called after him.

He turned around, wringing his hat brim in his hands as if

he were strangling one last bit of hope from it. "Well, ma'am, if you knew anything about him, I'd like to talk to you. As I said, I'm writing an article. Maybe even a book. I want to be sure that the whole story is told."

The whole story.

I'd read the papers.

I'd heard the gossip told in town.

Nobody had ever bothered to tell the whole story.

I'd never heard one person talk about how Remy Granger was a beautiful and caring person. How he'd risked his life to save a very confused and troubled girl.

The reporter took a few steps toward me. "Did you know him, ma'am?"

"I knew him." My voice was barely audible, even to me. I nodded in case he hadn't heard me.

"Would you be willing to tell me about him?"

I nodded. Stories of Remy Granger had been trapped in my mind for a long while; the promise of them being set free was too much to turn away from. The Cavern of Things Past burst open and memories catapulted in my chest, each clamoring for attention.

"Come on, have a seat." I indicated the table on the porch. "Would you like a Coca-Cola?"

"If you wouldn't mind," he said.

I retrieved a soda for each of us and joined him at the table.

"So," I started, bursting to begin but unsure of what it was this man wanted to know. "Where should I start?"

"Just start at the beginning," he said. "Whatever you think is important for my readers to know about Remy Granger."

I inhaled slowly. The air filled all the spaces in my lungs in preparation for the story I was about to tell. The story I had never said out loud before.

"I didn't go lookin' for Remy Granger that night," I said,

smiling at the memory. "I was tryin' to avoid the man in my momma's bedroom the same as she was tryin' to ignore the fact that I knew he was in there with her."

It was dusk before I'd finished talking.

The man—Marshall was his name—had scribbled furiously for hours. He'd interrupted me only a few times to ask questions or clarify some bit of information.

"I appreciate your time," he said as he gathered his notes. "If you think of anything else, please call me. Any time."

He handed me a business card. His name was centered and in bold type: *Marshall R. Porter*.

"Thank you. If I think of anything, I'll call." I wouldn't, though. I'd purged myself of our story. I'd set it free and wouldn't revisit it again. There was too much good in my life now. Looking back at the dark origins of it served no purpose.

I climbed the steps and leaned against the porch railing to watch as he drove away. The car disappeared into the indigo night that crept in from the bayou.

The screen door creaked behind me and strong arms wrapped around my waist. I leaned back into the warm curves of Jacob's body.

"I'm sorry that took so long."

"Sunshine found us at the dock," he said. "Si was tired, so Sunshine took him to Dixie. She fed him and put him to bed."

"We should go get him." I couldn't stand to be away from my son. He had the same infectious joy his uncle Sirus had possessed. Every day with him was bliss.

"He's fine. He loves to be with his cousins," he said. "I snuck in the back door and listened while you were talking to that reporter." There was no judgement in his voice. No panic or fear. We were well beyond that now.

I turned and pressed against him. "I'm sorry. It was just nice to hear your name again. To *say* it out loud." Four years later the name *Jacob* still wasn't natural and was never the first name to my mind.

"It's a dangerous habit," he whispered and nuzzled against my neck. His lips grazed the tender skin and moved along my jaw line.

I wrapped my arms around his neck and met his kisses.

"One more night?" My voice was whispered, but the plea was as crystal clear as the liquor that led us to this point.

"Okay," he acquiesced, as he always did. "Just once more."

"I love you, Remy Granger," I said as he picked me up and carried me inside, kicking the door closed behind us.

AFTERWORD

Dear readers,

First, I'd like to thank you for reading *A Shine That Defies the Dark*. I realize how lucky I am each time someone makes the choice to read my books.

When I finished writing *A Shine That Defies the Dark*, I honestly thought the story was finished with Ophelia and Jacob (aka- Remy) walking into that cabin. But my mind never really left southern Louisiana—or 1930. As more people asked me about "the next book," I realized there was so much more happening in that region, stories that—while Ophelia and Remy may have been unaware of them—had directly impacted their story.

One of the greatest contributing factors in the Grangers' sphere has been the Moret Gang. I thought about what life was like for the Grangers' rivals. What was happening when Ophelia interrupted that Moret deal? What caused the Moret Gang to make an attempt on the Grangers' lives after so many years? Was it simply rivalry, or had the Morets devolved within their own organization to the point of desperation? I wondered what—or who—would have brought them to that point.

It wasn't long before Deirdre Cassidy "spoke" to me and let me know what an absolute bastard Claude Moret was. And this young Irish immigrant, alone in the world and hell-bent on avenging her family, became the force that cast a light on the dark deeds of the Moret family.

Although *The Light at Finnigan's End* is about the Moret Gang, their storyline closely parallels and converges with that of the Grangers. While reading book 2, you'll recognize keys scenes from *A Shine That Defies the Dark*, and the Grangers (Remy, Eloi, Sunshine, and, yes, Sirus!) even make appearances in *The Light at Finnigan's End*.

ABOUT THE AUTHOR

Jodi is a YA & NA writer, black belt, registered nurse and case manager for a busy home health agency. She lives with her husband, three sons and an evolving herd of undisciplined animals in Colorado. She has a well-earned fear of bears, but tolerates the Teddy and Gummy variety. She has been obsessed with books, both reading and writing them, for most of her life and prefers the written word to having actual conversations.

www.jodigallegos.com

Acknowledgements

To my husband & my boys who've always believed in me, supported my dream, and understand that NaNoWriMo, loosely translated, means "no cooking, cleaning, or expectations for 30 days".

To the rest of my family for supporting, believing in—and bragging about—me.

To The Sinner's Club (Clint & Dana Eddy and Nick & Mandy Nelson). I realize I represent the group and I'm glad to do my part for enduring mischief, mayhem and camping.

To Sherry Ficklin for letting me be clingy and patiently answering all my writing and publishing related questions (for YEARS!!!), And for being a champion for this novel from early on.

To Elaine, Robin and Amy, who endured the earliest (and ugliest!) versions of this novel.

To Dea Poirier and Kate Angelella, who saw the potential of this story early on and helped it shine a little brighter.

And to everyone at CTP (Courtney, Rebecca, Marya, Sherry, and Ethan) for giving this novel a home.
Thank you, thank you, thank you, thank you, thank you...(really, I could go on forever!)

AFTERWORD

Dear readers,

First, I'd like to thank you for reading *A Shine That Defies the Dark*. I realize how lucky I am each time someone makes the choice to read my books.

When I finished writing *A Shine That Defies the Dark*, I honestly thought the story was finished with Ophelia and Jacob (aka- Remy) walking into that cabin. But my mind never really left southern Louisiana—or 1930. As more people asked me about "the next book," I realized there was so much more happening in that region, stories that—while Ophelia and Remy may have been unaware of them—had directly impacted their story.

One of the greatest contributing factors in the Grangers' sphere has been the Moret Gang. I thought about what life was like for the Grangers' rivals. What was happening when Ophelia interrupted that Moret deal? What caused the Moret Gang to make an attempt on the Grangers' lives after so many years? Was it simply rivalry, or had the Morets devolved within their own organization to the point of desperation? I wondered what—or who—would have brought them to that point.

It wasn't long before Deirdre Cassidy "spoke" to me and let me know what an absolute bastard Claude Moret was. And this young Irish immigrant, alone in the world and hell-bent on avenging her family, became the force that cast a light on the dark deeds of the Moret family.

Although *The Light at Finnigan's End* is about the Moret Gang, their storyline closely parallels and converges with that of the Grangers. While reading book 2, you'll recognize keys scenes from *A Shine That Defies the Dark*, and the Grangers (Remy, Eloi, Sunshine, and, yes, Sirus!) even make appearances in *The Light at Finnigan's End*.

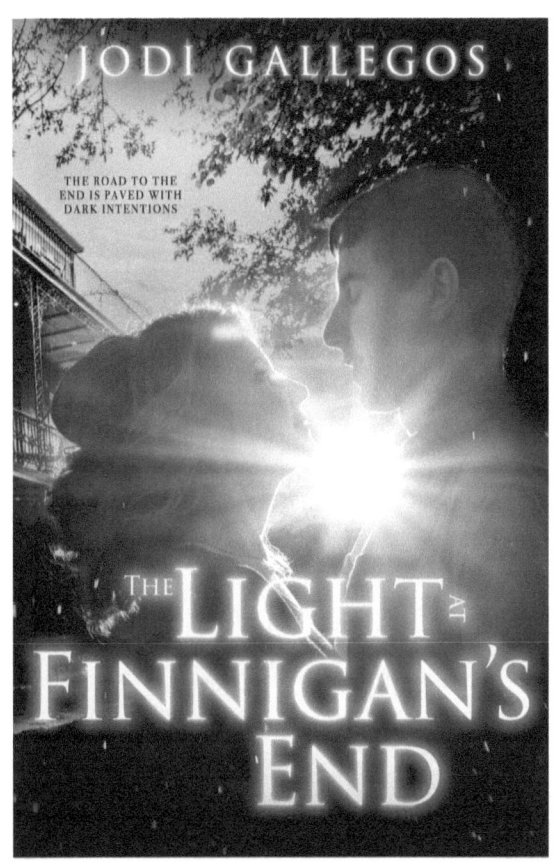

Cleric's Cove is home to the most brutal gang of bootleggers in Louisiana, the Moret family. Desperate to find her missing brother Finn, Deirdre Cassidy is determined to infiltrate them. But the one thing she never counted on is Mo Moret—danger-ous, yet magnetic. But Mo may never set aside family loyalty for love. Even if he did, Deirdre has vowed to see the end of the Morets—whatever the cost.

Get your copy today!

ALSO BY JODI GALLEGOS

RUM RUNNERS SERIES

A Shine that Defies the Dark, book 1

The Light at Finnigan's End, book 2

THE HIGH CROWN CHRONICLES

The High Crown Chronicles, book 1

Queen of the Ruins, book 2

The War Of Myths And Mortals, book 3

www.ingramcontent.com/pod-product-compliance
Lightning Source LLC
Chambersburg PA
CBHW021028130626
46552CB00005B/1736